D1233745

AMERICAN DESERT

AMERICAN DESERT

A Novel

Percival Everett

HYPERION

NEW YORK

Library of Congress Cataloging-in-Publication Data

Everett, Percival L.
    American desert : a novel / Percival Everett.—1st ed.
      p. cm.
    ISBN 0-7868-6917-8
    1. College teachers—Fiction. 2. Funeral rites and ceremonies—Fiction. 3. Traffic accident victims—Fiction. 4. Regeneration (Biology)—Fiction. 5. Suicidal behavior—Fiction. I. Title.

PS3555.V 34M9 2004
813'.54—dc22

                                                    2003056757

Hyperion books are available for special promotions and premiums. For details contact Michael Rentas, Manager, Inventory and Premium Sales, Hyperion, 77 West 66th Street, 11th Floor, New York, New York 10023, or call 212-456-0133.

FIRST EDITION

10 9 8 7 6 5 4 3 2 1

TO CHARLES ROWELL

Then to this earthen Bowl did I adjourn
My Lip the secret Well of Life to learn:
And Lip to Lip it murmur'd—"While you live
Drink!—For once dead you never shall return."

—RUBAIYAT OF OMAR KHAYYAM

AMERICAN DESERT

BOOK ONE

CHAPTER ONE

THAT THEODORE STREET WAS dead was not a matter open to debate. The irony of his accidental death went unobserved as no one knew that Theodore was on his way to commit suicide when he was, shall we say, interrupted. Now the irony is lost amid the confusion created by Ted's death, departure, demise, dissolution and further by the fact that Ted chooses to relate his own story in third person, an unusual (the occasional politician and athlete aside), but acceptable device, given that, in a most profound way, he stood—or stands even—outside himself, not so much on the parapet of consciousness but of life itself, it being perhaps the case that neither entails, necessarily, the other. But regardless of where Ted stood, or stands, he was on his way to the beach where he had every intention of marching into the ocean until it was over his head and taking a deep, lung-filling breath of water which, according to his limited knowledge of human physiology, would result in a termination of his life, barring the interference of some lifeguard or Boy Scout or Girl Scout, though he had never found Girl Scouts to be terribly overzealous or meddlesome. He was driving at a respectable clip along Ocean Boulevard when a fat man chased his nails-painted poodle out into the street before a UPS truck, causing the driver of the huge, brown block to swerve and slide into a lane of oncoming traffic, the oncoming traffic in this case being Ted Street in his 1978 Lancia coupe. The truck and the Lancia met violently and whereas his vehicle halted quite abruptly, Ted did not, but continued in the same direction he had been traveling through the already cracked windscreen. Remarkably, Ted's face suffered not a single scratch and neither did his body break about the ribs, clavicles, arms or legs, but his head did become rather cleanly detached from the rest of him. It was a jagged but complete wound around his neck that left one seasoned police officer vomiting by the accordioned front fender of the Lancia while the young rookie on patrol with him stood, mouth agape, staring at the head lying on the asphalt. Unlike the stories of beheaded Frenchmen stealing one last, pitiful look at their cast-off bodies, Ted had no such perception. He died instantly and, in a manner of speaking, completely. The UPS man was beside himself, so much so that he would later attend Ted Street's funeral and subsequently take a civil service examination in order to change his profession. The coroner's wagon came with a representative of the coroner, not the coroner himself, and the young man observed Ted's head from his wagon door and was satisfied that he was dead, making the requisite marks on his clipboard, but having to call his office to ask whether head and body should be placed in the same or separate bags. Ted's head was placed under his left arm, the fingers of his hand falling over his mouth which was frozen partly open, and the cool vinyl bag was zipped from bottom to top. The ride in the coroner's wagon to the morgue was protracted, the medical examiner's assistant stopping at a fast-food restaurant, his mother's house, a comic-book store and a remote parking lot where he charged gang thugs a dollar each to "see the stiff."

* * *

At the morgue, which turned out not to be deep in the bowels of some hospital but on a second floor of the sixties-vintage medical examiner's offices with lots of windows that didn't open and a unisex restroom, Ted's wife, Gloria, viewed his head on a video monitor as it sat in a metal bowl. She let out a short but reasonably justified scream. She then fell into the arms of her sister, Hannah, who "had never liked Ted anyway," and wept convincingly and no doubt sincerely, the image of the head on the screen etching itself into her forever-memory. The image blurred just a bit, there on the screen, but finally looked exactly like the head she had slept with for so many years. The matter, however, rang with an air of incompleteness, as it was the case that the *body* was never identified, only the head and isn't that what is always required? That the *body* be identified? "We want you to come down and identify the body," the cop always says. Never, "Is that his head?" So, Gloria signed papers and said that Ted had never mentioned that he wanted his organs donated to medicine, science, or the needy and that such a decision should have been his and that he, all of him, should be sent to the Iverson, Ash, Graves and Shroud Mortuary over in Garden Grove and so he was. Sent over there.

In the embalming room, Ash and Graves agreed that Ted had lost enough blood that there would be poor draw on the fluid and that no one would notice the difference anyway if they didn't fill him with formaldehyde and methyl alcohol and certainly they were not going to waste humectants and anticoagulants on him. Besides, as Ash pointed out to Graves, poor draw could create embarrassing results, as when Pope John Paul I began to swell up and make sounds during the live broadcast of his funeral ceremony. "Don't you remember how that poor altar boy had to keep wiping the purge away from the pontiff's mouth?" Ash said. Ash sewed Ted's head back onto his body, his stitches sloppy but tight, using blue thirty-weight fishing line, and instead of sewing the mouth shut by passing the thread through the nose, Ash simply put eight stitches between the lips.

Iverson and Shroud were trying to talk Gloria into buying a gaudy bronze coffin with eagle- or some other bird-of-prey–sculpted handles, her sister balking the while, the children, Emily and Perry, twelve and seven, sitting some feet away, their little faces blank with confusion, but knowing enough to be terrified of the place—the drapes, the maroon flock and foil wallpaper, the dark corridors, the ashen-faced men smiling those ashen smiles which were not quite smiles.

"Mommy," Perry said, "I want to go home."

"As soon as we find Daddy a nice casket, dear," Gloria said. "Come over here and look at the book with Mommy."

Perry and Emily walked from the floral print sofa—irises—across the dark carpet to the desk, where they stood on either side of their mother and looked at the catalogue of final resting containers.

"He won't be able to turn over in there," Perry said.

"Daddy's dead, stupid," Emily said. "He won't be turning over." Then, having said it, the girl understood and began to feel her grief, a contagious condition that reduced both children to tears.

This left Gloria at the mercy of the tall, chilly-handed morticians and she ended up buying the most expensive box, the lining of which even she at the time recognized as something appropriate for a brothel, however "cloudlike." "Come along, children," she said and they escaped, went to a fun place to eat.

* * *

The funeral was held three days after Ted's decapitation, at a church that Ted never attended when alive. In fact, Ted had never attended any church, but where else does one hold a funeral service; this was what Gloria thought and so with her sister's help, Hannah no doubt thinking it a fitting final insult to Ted to have his last earthly function held within the walls of a place he would never have entered alive, she found the Sacred Blood First Christ Church of the Everlasting Spirit over in Long Beach.

* * *

During his life, Ted had been a college professor, teaching Old English and various survey courses at the University of Southern California. He had taken ten years to obtain his doctorate and had put off his tenure review by taking leaves of absence, but the time had come to be considered for tenure and the pressure was on. His book had not been accepted by any publisher, though Cornell University Press had kept it for a long time, finally rejecting it, writing "It is too much like books we published last year." He had for the past two semesters felt as if his colleagues were staring at him, avoiding him, treating him like some terminally ill patient. "Good teaching evaluations just aren't enough," said Horace Shiply, an Early Americanist with a Melville beard and a mole that stuck out of it. When his department hired a new person in his field, a young woman who had not only already published a book on *Beowulf*, but was on the cutting edge of digital imaging of manuscripts, Ted saw the writing on the wall.

* * *

Now, the cast were all crammed into the roasting-hothouse of God, the department chair, the insufferably pompous dean of the college, and the *Beowulf* woman included, to watch Ted being sent off to wherever, stretched out in his expensive box with a bit of the blue fishing line showing just over his starched white collar. He was casketed in the standard position, his right shoulder slightly lower than his left, so as not to have him appear as what he was, a dead body flat on its back. As well, he was slightly elevated in order to diminish the prominence of the coffin. Gloria and the children were in the front row, just feet away from the casket, their backs straight against the tired wood of the pew. So was Gloria's sister, wearing a khaki dress and white sandals. There was a choir dressed in powder blue robes singing some songs that Ted would never have recognized about their God coming back to earth and pastures and sheep and they swayed the while. A maroon-robed minister, a big man named Larville Staige, stood and cleared his throat, made a brief comment about the heat, fanned himself using a fan bearing the image of Martin Luther King, Jr., on one side and advertising a funeral home on the other, and said that he didn't want to keep everyone too long,

"But we must send our brother off to his final resting place with the proper blessing and the love of Christ, our Lord. Poor, poor Theodore Street met a violent and senseless death on the streets of our sin-ridden city. His blood spilled into the same gutters that carry away our daily filth and urine. Yes! Brothers and Sisters, Theodore Street is nothing less than a neon marker in the road of life, having looked both ways before crossing perhaps, but like so many of us, having failed to look up. He is a marker telling us that at any second—any second!—everything earthly can end. One minute, you're driving along and the next, your head is over there and your body is over there!" A yelp escaped one of Ted's children and then both buried their faces in their mother's sides. Staige spread his sausage fingers wide and wrapped them over the edge of the lectern in front of him. "Theodore Street was a teacher and he is teaching us even now. He is teaching us that life is temporary and that we had better have our affairs straight. The Book of Isaiah, chapter thirty-eight, verse one, says, 'Set thine house in order: for thou shalt die, and not live.' Never were truer words spoke. Just ask Theodore Street. But finally, I must admit that I did not know Mr. Street. But Jesus knew him!"

An "amen" shot out from the choir.

"Thank you, Sister! Yes, Our Lord knew Mr. Street and He knows him even better now, though we have no idea if he got to the house of God in one piece. Maybe his head got there first and had to wait for the rest of him, but it is no matter, because both parts have moved on. But to speak about the living Theodore Street, let me introduce the head—pardon me, the chairman of the department in which the deceased taught, Professor Orville Orson."

Orville Orson was a fat pig of a man, a Joyce scholar who despised Joyce with a passion and had devoted his career to exposing the great author as a mediocre writer who happened to be very, very smart. Orson wore suspenders, which he called "braces," and seersucker suits no matter how cool the weather turned. He was wearing a heat-crumpled seersucker when he rose and walked from the third row to the altar. His sweaty, meaty palm pressed into Staige's sweaty, meaty palm and the lectern was turned over. Orson was perspiring about the neck and forehead, but he was used to that and so his constant wiping with his handkerchief did not make him appear nervous or uncomfortable. "I first met Ted nine years ago," he said, the point of it significant to everyone save Larville Staige and the members of the Sacred Blood First Christ Church of the Everlasting Spirit. "He came into my office, having just finished his degree at Duke, with bright eyes and enormous energy. He immediately became a cherished colleague to all of us in the department and the college as well. Though he never published anything or, to my knowledge, wrote anything, he was a dedicated teacher." Then in his usual, forgetful manner, he paused, then said, "I'm sorry, Ted did write something. He wrote a book, though I have no idea what it could have been about. I know only that no one wanted to publish it. Anyway, Ted's students admired him greatly. He was, in fact, twice voted by the students as Outstanding Teacher of the Year. His classes were for years oversubscribed." He paused again, then, as if thinking while talking, he said, "Until his tenure review loomed rather largely on his horizon and his attention span

apparently dwindled to a few seconds and he stopped preparing
his lectures. But you know how that goes. The important thing to
remember today is that Ted Street was a good man, a devoted husband and a loving father. One doesn't have to be a good scholar to
be those things and what's more important? Ted was what he was
right up to the very end. It's a shame that such a gruesome death
befell him, but from all reports, he died suddenly and suffered little
if at all." Orson tugged at his collar. "So, we bid Ted a final farewell.
Perhaps in that university system in the sky, Ted will, after all, get to
publish his book. Goodbye, Ted."

The choir sang a song called "This Is the Road to Our Savior
Lord Our Christ" while the attendants stood with hymnals open
before them, mouthing the words and flashing to each other bewildered looks. Then, as the choir ended its final *amen* with a harmo-
nious hum, Theodore Street sat up in his coffin. A hush filled the
church, as one might expect, but it was not long-lived. Emily Street
screamed and tried to crawl up her mother's side while Perry Street's
mouth formed the word *Daddy* over and over. Gloria Street fainted
but remained frozen upright with wide-open eyes. Gloria's sister
made a break for the door, her large feet tripping her near the end of
the aisle's red carpet, causing her to roll to a stop at a blind man's
feet with her dress over her head. Orville Orson farted and farted
again. The dean prayed, loudly. The *Beowulf* woman reached into
her bag and readied the pepper spray her fiancé had bought for her.
Larville Staige raised his hands and shouted to the ceiling of the
Sacred Blood First Christ Church of the Everlasting Spirit, "Lord
Jesus God! Jesus Lord, my God! Hallelujah! A miracle in my church!
In my little house of God! Jesus! Jesus! Jesus!"

Then the choir joined in with him, chanting, "Jesus! Jesus! Jesus!"

Amid the chanting and screaming and farting, Ted Street climbed out of his box and faced them all. As it turned out, his trousers had been just Mr. Ash's size and so he was naked from the waist down, his tallywacker hanging rather handsomely out in front of him. Ted Street looked at all the faces, studying them one by one and remembering their voices and their turns to and away from him. The *Beowulf* woman might have been the most frightened of the lot.

* * *

Rachel Ruddy visited the campus for the first time just after the Modern Languages Association meeting. It was January and it had been raining for six days straight, flooding the canyons and washing away expensive homes and making the freeways frightening sheets of water and oil. Ted Street had been conspicuously left out of her itinerary, but was included in the forty-five-minute lunch preceding her lecture. Leonard Foreman escorted Rachel Ruddy to the faculty club and they were to be joined by Henrietta Blues, but Henrietta Blues's Irish setter began to have seizures and so she couldn't make it. Then Leonard Foreman's wife called to say that she was stuck on the 405 and asked if Leonard would pick up their daughter and so Ted was left alone with Rachel Ruddy, both apparently all too aware of their impending career changes.

"I read a very positive review of your book," Ted said.

Rachel Ruddy poked at her salad. "I heard you give a paper two years ago in Kalamazoo," she said. "I remember it was quite good."

Ted nodded, but for the life of him he could not recall the paper in question. "Your *cv* shows a new book out soon."

"Yes, Cambridge is publishing it," she said and then, as if she was sorry she had said anything, added, "They asked for so many changes that I thought it would never be finished."

Ted watched her eat and decided that he liked her. He felt sad that she had to be so painfully aware of her coming to replace him and that circumstances had stuck her across the table now. He said, "You don't have to feel bad. You're not to blame for anything going awry in my career. I've enjoyed teaching here, but you're a hot property. You have to accept that fact. I do. So, why don't we relax."

Rachel Ruddy smiled. "You're a very nice man," she said.

Ted nodded. "You seem nice too. So, what do you want to know about this place?" But he didn't believe then that he was a nice man. He was saying these things to her so that he, not she, would feel more comfortable.

"You'll give it to me straight?" she asked.

"You bet."

* * *

Ted's staring at Rachel Ruddy had bad consequences in the hot and crowded church, as she raised her pepper spray and began to blast away wildly, blinding those who were seeking the door, causing, as if that were possible, louder and more intensified screaming. Orville Orson fell back into the pew, his hand on his chest.

. . .

Orville Orson was not the chair who had hired Ted Street some "nine years" earlier and rumor had it that Orson had been against his appointment in the first place, but the fat man was generally cordial.

"Come on into my office," Orson said as he spied Ted in the hallway one day. "Have a seat."

"New lamp?" Ted asked.

"Yes, my wife bought it for me," Orson said. He closed the door and kicked a rolled-up towel across the bottom of it. "Would you like a cigar, Ted?"

"No, thank you," Ted said.

Orson stuck a fat stogie in his face and sat behind his desk, lit up and then rested his hands on his big belly. "You know you've got to come up for tenure next semester."

Ted nodded.

"How's the book coming?" Orson asked.

"Cornell kept it for six months, but didn't take it."

Orson looked out the window and drew on his cigar. "Your teaching evaluations are superior. You know that. Ted, do you think you're going to get this book published? Don't bother answering. Ted, Ted, Ted. Do you have any other prospects?"

"Are you telling me that I don't have a chance at tenure?" Ted asked.

"You've published two articles in eight years."

"I know how much I've published," Ted said.

"And haven't published," Orson shot back. "Listen, Ted, I'm not against you, but a lot goes into preparing a tenure file. There have to be meetings and class visitations sometimes and outside letters and then the chair has to write a long letter explaining why the department is recommending what it's recommending and on and on and do you really think you're going to publish this book?"

"Are you saying that I don't have a chance at tenure if I don't publish a book?" Ted asked.

"Basically."

"But I'm a fine teacher," Ted said.

"Well, you get good evaluations, anyway."

Ted looked out the window at the parking lot and the street beyond it. "What's that supposed to mean?"

But Orson didn't answer. Instead he looked at the cigar between his fingers with a befuddled expression, then began to turn red about the face and neck, throwing back his head and straightening his enormous legs in front of him.

"What is it?" Ted asked. Orson fell out of his chair and Ted ran around the table to kneel beside him. "Orville, Orville," he said. Then he yelled out for help, grabbed the phone and dialed 911 and asked for an ambulance. He called out again, then realized that Orson was blue and that he was not breathing.

Ted bent over him and began CPR, placing his lips over the cigar-reeking mouth and blew, wondering if one had to blow harder to inflate a fat man. Between each breath into Orson, Ted shouted out for help until finally Leonard Foreman came in with one of the department secretaries. They watched while Ted saved Orson's life.

As he was being wheeled away by the paramedics, Orson pointed a fat finger at Ted and said, "You get that book published. You hear me? You get that book published!"

. . .

It was clear that Orson was having a massive heart attack right there in the pew on the lap of the dean who, by similar appearance, could have been judged to be engaged in a coronary fit of his own. Ted wanted to call out to the people in the church, tell them to calm down and take their seats or, at least, leave in an orderly fashion, but his mouth was sewn shut and so he could only say, "Mumm, mmmmm, mmum."

Ted's son was standing now, walking blank-faced toward his father as if hypnotized.

But matters of the family will be revealed in due course. To say the least, Ted's resurrection caused a stir, a terrible riot which spread from the church and into the streets, resulting later in the arrest of seventeen gang members who saw the shocked, *enlightened* mass as prime targets for robbery and their general entertainment. On that day, Orville Orson and the dean died from heart attacks right on the floor of the Sacred Blood First Christ Church of the Everlasting Spirit. Gloria's sister Hannah suffered a broken arm. Rachel Ruddy pepper-sprayed herself out of the church and to her car where she was able to drive to the freeway and then a few exits away where she stopped at a Carrow's or Denny's and called her boyfriend in San Francisco who first thought she was joking, then decided she had lost her mind and hung up on her. The UPS man who had been seated in the last row, having taken time out from his rounds and so was still wearing his UPS browns, slipped quietly out at the first sign of movement from the coffin. Mr. Graves, from the funeral parlor, had been sitting off to the side and remained there throughout the confusion, studying over and over again his clipboard, on which was fastened the medical examiner's vital statistics form, otherwise known as the death certificate.

"Mummmm, mmmmm," Ted said. He went and stood in front of Mr. Graves. "Mmmmumf."

Mr. Graves took out his Swiss Army pocketknife and with trembling hands slit all but three of the stitches of Ted Street's mouth before fainting.

"Ehvabuzy cam zoun," Ted said. "Wuwax."

By now Gloria had regained at least a few of her senses and could see that her husband was not dead, but alive in front of her. She and the children ran to him and he lowered himself to hug them all, becoming suddenly ashamed of his nakedness. He took his wife's mantilla and draped it around his middle. The four of them looked at the mess in the church, at the choir praying and sweating under the direction of Reverend Staige, whose hands were reaching ever higher for the heavens, at the final, pitiful twitches of Orson and the dean, at Hannah holding her injured arm close to her chest and whimpering on the floor by the double doors. Ted and Gloria and the children walked from the altar, down a narrow and dark corridor and out the back into the alley. They would not have known that there was a riot going on except for the screaming and blowing of horns which seemed so far away.

"Daddy, how can you be alive?" Emily asked.

"Ahn dn nnoh."

Gloria reached into her bag and came back with a fingernail-trimming scissors and cut the remaining sutures from Ted's lips.

Emily, Perry and Gloria recoiled at the thought, the sound and the sight of the snipping. Ted spat away the debris.

"Thank you, honey," Ted said. "That's much better."

Emily began to cry.

Ted looked at her, sad about her fear and confusion, but he was confused too, trying to piece together what had happened, remembering only the rapidly approaching UPS truck and the sensation of splashing water. He realized, from the scene in which he had come into—or back into—consciousness, that he had been perceived as dead. But he couldn't quite wrap his thinking around the fact that he had just come from his own funeral. He touched around his neck and felt the sloppy sewing job that was holding his head in place, the line itself slick, the bumps of the sutures bothering his fingertips.

"Was my head—" He stopped.

Gloria nodded. "Completely severed."

"Ouch," Ted said.

Gloria's and the children's faces showed concern.

"Just the idea of it," Ted said.

"I had to identify your head at the morgue," Gloria said, the recent memory of it beginning to overwhelm her. She started to cry again, but spoke through her tears. "You were in a metal bowl and I had to look at you on a TV and your eyes were closed, but your mouth was open like you were trying to say something and and and—"

Ted embraced Gloria. "I'm okay now. I don't know how, but I'm okay." He looked at the children, touched their heads, perhaps to see if they were securely fastened.

"Daddy?" Emily cried.

"I don't know, sweetie. All I know is that I'm alive. Well, I'm not dead, anyway." He looked at the sky, at the leaves of a nearby eucalyptus tree, at the clouds. It all seemed so beautiful.

Perry squeezed his father's waist. Ted hugged him and the boy reached out to touch the stitches.

"Does it look awful?" Ted asked. He was looking at Perry, but he was asking all of them.

"It looks terrible," Gloria said.

"Does it hurt?" Perry asked.

Ted shook his head. "No, I can't even feel it." Ted shook his head again, but not in response to any question, but to clear his brain. He wanted to remember the time he was supposedly dead, being in the bowl as his wife described, having his head sewn on or his mouth sewn shut. But all he could recall was that splashing sensation. Not a bright light. Not an authoritative voice beckoning him seductively toward it. He wanted to know if he had been close to knowing any secrets, or simply knowing more.

Emily was trembling now. Her eyes were saucers. "Are you a ghost, Daddy?"

Ted considered the question and wanted to say no, but the fact of the matter was that he didn't know. During his silence, Perry became anxious and began to chant, "Daddy's a ghost, Daddy's a ghost."

Ted touched Emily's hair and marveled at the softness of it, feeling that he was taking forever to admire its texture but knowing that only a fraction of a second had slipped by, and said, "No, I don't think I'm a ghost, honey."

The noise of the riot came to them again, like the crash of a wave at the beach and they huddled closer. "Come on, let's get home."

Clouds gathered to the west, over the ocean.

They walked several blocks, trying to hurry but not moving very fast. They came to a pay phone outside a defunct garden shop. Ted stood in the booth and called a taxi while Gloria tried to calm the children. It was a hot day, but Ted didn't feel it.

CHAPTER TWO

THE TAXI RIDE HOME took Ted and his family along a street just blocks from the riot. At the intersections Ted saw police with face shields and big black batons held high, and fire trucks with water cannons and slope-backed German Shepherds on the ends of taut leads. The shouts, screams, crashes and reverberations found them through the open windows of the car. Perry huddled tight against his father in the backseat, but Emily kept her distance. The driver of the taxi tossed numerous jittery glances into the back using his mirror.

"Something must really be going on," the driver said. He was a Pakistani man, his head all done up in a white turban. "This city is crazy." He made circles with his index finger by his right ear. "You people are lucky you did not get caught in that mess." Then he was attending to Ted.

"I noticed when you got in that you are not wearing any pants," he said. "Why are you not wearing pants?"

"They got wet," Ted said. "I spilled gasoline on them and had to take them off."

"Gasoline is very dangerous. It burns very quickly. What is wrong with your neck?" the man asked.

Ted reached to his throat and moved his numb fingers along the bumpy stitches. "Nothing," he said.

But the man kept staring, nearly wrecking the car for his distraction. "Sure there is," he said. There was fear in his voice. He had no doubt observed the family's strange behavior and was sensing that somehow they were involved with the rioting, the way they watched and didn't watch as the ruckus became available to view at the intersections. "Your throat has been cut," the Indian driver said. "Someone has slashed your throat. That is bad, very bad."

Ted was not put off by the man's interest and didn't, as he no doubt would have in the past, find the man's attention frightening or intimidating. "Actually," Ted said, "my head was completely severed from my body and I was presumed dead until I sat up in my coffin at my own funeral and so began the riot, which you can witness by looking to your left."

The driver listened and then sat silently for a few seconds taking it all in. "Ha! Ha!" he laughed. "You are a very funny fellow. I see your joke. Very funny. So, your head was cut off. Ha! Ha! I must tell that one to my cousin. He is in dental school."

Emily whimpered a little, on the edge of crying, but was too stunned to actually shed tears. Ted looked at Gloria's face and saw how frightened she was. Of course she was frightened. Anyone, save a religious nut anticipating the rising of the Messiah, would have been terrified. She closed her eyes and let her head fall back against the cloth seat. Ted looked forward at the back of the turban and felt his sutures once more. He felt oddly alive, though he couldn't feel his heart thumping in his chest as he had at other times in the past when he thought he was feeling acutely alive, like the time he had

been chased by a bear when camping in the Sierras. Now, he wondered if his heart was beating at all. He put his hand flat against his
chest and searched, but found no pulse. He felt strangely that without the sound of his heart, his ears were even more open to the
sounds around him. He could hear the driver's molars pull from
then sink again into the gum he was chewing, every crackle of the
taxi's radio, the miss of a bad lifter in the engine, gravel crunching
under the weight of the driver's heel as he shifted between accelera-
tor and brake pedals, the barking of a young dog away from the
direction of the rioting. From the riot he could make out words in
the screaming and shouting—*dead, God, devil, communists, taxes,*
among others—names, curses. His ability to locate the sources of
sound seemed enhanced. And it was not only his hearing that was
whetted, but all of his senses. The distraction of his heart's noise
removed, he was a live wire of sensation. He was able to smell the
spearmint of the driver's gum, the not-so-tightly sealed vial of cheap
cologne stashed away in the closed glove compartment, the small
fart which he knew had been let by his son, who was always letting
small farts. And no smell got in the way of any other, but remained
distinct and constantly present to his senses. As all of his senses
were so acutely awake to the world, the absence of any stimuli ema-
nating from himself became notable. There was no heartbeat, of
course, but neither was there a gurgling from his stomach or a rumbling from any region below, and no breath scratching through dry
sinuses or cracking joints. He searched but could not find any smell
of death about him. But the stitches of his neck disturbed his fingertips greatly, the slickness of the fishing line, the lumpiness of the
folded flesh, the uneven spaces between the sutures. He counted

them, starting at his Adam's apple, and found that there were 360 separate entries, one for each degree, 360 exits. Like the hem job on a pair of trousers, a continuous thread—360 little bumps.

The whole business of coming back to life was nearly made worthwhile by the dropped jaw of Ted's neighbor, the ugly Mr. Willis, with whom he'd had ongoing difficulties concerning the maintenance of the hedge. Willis was standing in his front yard, pruning the rather garish platoon of hybrid tea rosebushes of which he was so proud, when Ted and his family fell out of the taxi. "Willis." Ted nodded as if it were any other day, as they walked across their yard to the front door. The sponge-handled shears fell from Willis's hand and he might have fainted, but Ted did not see, as soon they were inside the house, the door locked, the blinds of the windows pulled down and turned shut.

Ted took in his home. The foyer was as it always had been, the small, three-legged table just inside the door, beside it the unattractive metal umbrella stand which Emily had had a fit to buy at an antiques mall in Chapman, and the Navajo area rug which had been sent to them by Gloria's mother while she was visiting New Mexico, the summer the woman died. Now, as Ted looked down at the rug, he wondered if she was in fact alive somewhere, as he was now, and he was sorry for any bad things he had said about her. Gloria was marching through the house switching on every ceiling light and lamp, muttering that the house was "too dark, too dark, too dark," that she needed to be able to see. Emily was standing at the open pocket doors that led to the dining room. She was staring at her father, staring with frightened, angry and confused eyes.

"You're a freak," she snapped. "How can you be alive?" Then she started to shake all over and call for her mother. "Mommy! Mommy!"

Gloria ran to the child and hugged her tightly. "It's okay, honey. It's okay, really it is. Okay, okay, okay. Isn't it wonderful that we didn't lose Daddy?"

"I'm glad you're not dead, Daddy," Perry said.

"Thanks, sport," Ted said.

Ted looked at his daughter, her eyes shut tightly as she buried herself into her mother. She had asked a good question and he had no answer for her. Was he alive? Was he dead? Had his head actually been separated from his body or was it one of those exaggerations that gets started when things are bad enough, like when people say the whole block burned down when in reality only three of seven buildings had been partially damaged, or like those reports of towns being washed away by floods when actually it was only a couple of houses, though every house was in fact filled with mud? Ted realized that in addition to having no pulse, he could stop breathing entirely if he chose and there would be no change in his condition. He did have to inhale and exhale to speak and, in a way, he expected to feel his breath as this icy blast passing up through his sloppily reassembled esophagus, but he felt nothing of the sort, though he could, with his intensified hearing, locate a catch in his throat when making the *ah* and *oh* sounds.

The house felt more comfortable than ever, a place Ted wanted to be, warm and welcoming, unlike the cold tomb it had seemed to him in the months before his accident. Perhaps it was simply relief at not being dead, a reliable indicator that either he would have been unable to carry out his suicide plan or that he would have regretted it. He even found pleasure in viewing the flowered wallpaper of the dining room as he went in and sat at the table. Perry tagged along and sat opposite him. Gloria and Emily were elsewhere in the house, Gloria no doubt attempting to convince her daughter and herself that Ted's resurrection was indeed a good and welcome thing.

Perry stared at his father.

"What is it, son?" Ted asked.

"Are we in trouble?" the boy asked.

"Why do you ask that?"

"Because of what happened in the church and all that fighting." Perry looked at his knuckles on the table. "Were they fighting because of us?"

Ted loved Perry for using *us* in his characterization of the situation. How easy it would have been for him to pass it all over to one person, namely to Ted, but that would have been an adult move. For Perry, he was part of his father; whatever happened to his father happened to him. And suddenly, Ted was overcome with contrition and sadness as he considered that he had been about the business of killing himself when he had been killed. How could he have done that to his son, to little Perry, who was so delicate and trusting, who still insisted on believing in the tooth fairy and the Easter bunny? "They were fighting because of us," Ted told the child. "They were fighting because something unexpected happened, because they couldn't explain it and understand it."

"Do we understand it?" Perry asked.

Ted shook his head. "No, we don't, but in a way it's easier for us because it's happening to us." Ted reached across the table and touched Perry's little fingers, then, noticing the yellowness of his own nails, pulled his hands back into his lap. "Do you remember when you got that cut above your eye?" He watched the boy nod. "Well, you said it didn't hurt that much, but you recall how your mother reacted."

"She went crazy," Perry said.

"That's right. She was worried about you and she couldn't feel what you were feeling, namely that it didn't hurt that much. She was just worried about you."

"Those people are worried about us?" the boy asked.

"You could say that," Ted said.

"Ted!" Gloria called from the living room. "Ted, you'd better come see this."

Ted and Perry hurried into the living room, where Gloria and Emily sat on the sofa and stared at the television. On the set, a woman from Channel 5, dressed in a trench coat and holding a large microphone, described the mayhem that had by now spread through most of Long Beach. She spoke to the anchor in the studio. "Bill, what we have been able to piece together is that a man who was presumed dead, and was being funeralized at the church you see burning behind me, sat up in his coffin and walked out. Details are terribly sketchy, as you might imagine." She and the camera crew ducked some flying debris. "You can see that things are pretty wild and woolly out here."

"Tracy, what can you tell us about the dead man?" Bill asked from the studio. "Or rather the alleged dead man, since obviously he wasn't dead really."

"Well, Bill," Tracy said, "that's one of the things we and everyone else are trying to figure out. It seems this man's head was completely cut off from his body in a traffic accident just three days ago."

"Tracy," Bill said, "we actually have some footage of that accident scene. We're rolling it now. There, there's the head behind that policeman's foot. Can you roll that back? Yes, right there." On the film it was difficult to make out the object behind the foot as a head at all, much less that it was Ted's head in particular.

Tracy said, "There have been two deaths reportedly caused by this riot, both heart attacks." Someone handed Tracy a note. "Bill, this we just learned. The risen man is believed to be one Theodore Street. He was an English professor at the University of Southern California, but that's really all we have right now."

Ted reached down and picked up the remote control from the coffee table and turned off the set.

"What's going to happen?" Gloria asked.

Ted rubbed a hand over his hair. He felt dirty, sticky. "First, I'm going to take a bath and then I suggest we all get some sleep."

"It's only four o'clock," Emily said.

"It's been a busy day," Ted said, considering privately that resurrection was no small feat. "We'll try to take naps now. Then we'll eat. How does that sound?"

Gloria clapped her hands, an act which all of them recognized as her way of seeking the strength to go on, as well as to hold them all together. "It sounds like a plan to me," she said. "After a little rest, I'll make brownies."

* * *

Ted sat in the bathroom on the edge of the tub and watched it fill. He was still wearing the scarf around his middle. His pecker lay harmless beneath the black lace and he wondered if it was dead too. He listened to his family outside making bedtime sounds in spite of the early hour. Emily was complaining that she had more homework to complete and Gloria was telling her not to worry, that she probably wouldn't be going to school the next day anyway. Ted took off his tie and shirt, but made a point of avoiding his reflection in the mirror. He wasn't yet ready to see himself. He loosened his tie and pulled it off, then removed his shirt. Steam rose from the water that lapped at the overflow drain and he turned off the faucet. He plunged his hand into the water and as he suspected, he felt no burning. His hand was not so much numb to the heat of the water as it was acutely sensitive to the exact temperature of it, while simultaneously immune to its bad effect. The water would have scalded anyone else, being nearly 140 degrees Fahrenheit. He lowered himself into the tub and sat there, not leaning back, but erect, like an invalid waiting for someone to bathe him. And then Ted Street did something he had not done since he was eight; he cried.

Ted was still sitting there when Gloria came into the bathroom and sat on the toilet next to him. She looked at his face—made a point of looking at his face, and no doubt the rest of him, especially his neck—and she was frightened. Ted was aware of her new fear of him and understanding it, he said, "It's okay, Gloria. I'm a little afraid of me too."

"What has happened?" she asked.

Ted lathered soap on his arms, smelling the sandalwood deep in his nostrils. "I don't know, but I'm sorry," he said.

"Honey, I'm so glad you're alive," Gloria said. "You *are* alive, aren't you?"

Ted shrugged. He wondered now not whether he was alive, but if being alive was something he wanted. Not that he wanted to be dead the way he intended when on his way to his suicide, but like he was now, if now he was indeed dead. Being alive had never felt the way he was feeling and so what must he have been then? Hyper-alive? Meta-alive? Sub- or super-alive? The fact was that he was not exactly alive and so, he assumed, he was indeed dead, but not gone. Poor Ted was not *dead and gone*; Ted was *dead and still here.* "Does my skin look a different color to you?" he asked.

Gloria looked at the hand he held up and shook her head. "Your skin looks like it always did."

"Gloria, what do we really know about being dead?" Ted asked.

"Apparently, nothing," she said. Gloria looked up at the light. "Did you see anything or hear any voices or anything like that?"

"No, nothing. I saw the UPS truck and then I was in the church. Though I have to admit that I knew immediately what was going on. That was a little surprising. Maybe I was aware of what was happening and simply wasn't aware of my awareness." Ted shook his head. "Listen to me. I sound like a nut."

"Your head was off your body," Gloria said, each word sounded distinctly. "A person can't live once that happens. Maybe this is a dream. Am I dreaming?"

"You're not dreaming," Ted said.

"How do you know? You don't even know if you're alive," she said.

"Point taken." Ted studied his wife's weak, tired eyes. "How are the kids?"

"I don't know. Confused, of course."

Ted nodded. "I suppose tomorrow I should go see a doctor. Rather, have one see me." Then he laughed. "I don't know why. What's a doctor going to tell me?"

"Maybe he'll tell you if you're alive," Gloria said.

"As if it makes any difference." Ted put the soap in the dish and slid down to dunk his head. "Can I tell you what this is like?" He didn't wait for an answer. "I feel as if there is not a stimulus around me that I can't sense completely. Like right now, I not only can smell the soap in the dish, but I can smell the potpourri in the linen closet. I can smell your perfume over there by the sink. I can smell that sour smell deep in the drain that we used to notice only once in a while. I can hear the cat purring outside somewhere and your heart beating and Emily snoring. My senses are crazy."

Gloria stared at him.

"Maybe there'll be all sorts of dead jokes now," Ted said. "Like, how many dead guys does it take to screw in a lightbulb? None?" He noticed that Gloria was not amused. "Anyway, I'll let the doctors look at me. At least maybe I can get these stitches out of my neck."

Gloria began to cry.

Ted just watched his hands splash around in the water like caught fish. Then he grabbed the soap, raised up his body and lathered his testicles. "I'm really sorry," he said.

"Please stop apologizing, honey." Gloria looked at him with a sympathy in her face that he had long forgotten she could express. She gazed at him as if she appreciated how frightening it all must have been for him. "You've been through an awful lot." Then, as if actually hearing her words after the fact, she laughed.

Ted smiled.

"We're together," he said. "That's what matters." Ted swallowed hard and held his hand over his middle. He recalled his infidelities and his periods of self-indulgent retreat and withdrawal and felt the guilt and pain that had had him driving to his date with suicide in the first place. Having survived death hadn't erased his painful assessment of himself as a person and as he sat there, his head sewn back onto his body with monofilament, he did not so much believe that he had been given a second chance as think that perhaps he wasn't quite done with his first one. He looked at Gloria's tear-streaked face and remembered the last time they had sat in the bathroom like this, only that time she had been the one in the tub, naked, while he told her that he had been sleeping with a graduate student. He'd realized even then that telling her something like that while she was naked and trapped in a bowl of tepid water was mean and the act of a coward. He was able to admit to himself now that telling her at all—though at the time he'd convinced himself that he was acting bravely—was a pantywaist thing to do, since his confession was prompted by his burning fear that the young woman was going to spill the beans to Gloria anyway.

* * *

The woman, whose name is immaterial—though her name was in fact Inga—had been a student in Ted's History of the Language seminar. It was somewhere around the discussion of voiced fricatives that Ted found the woman in his office with her back plastered to the side of his file cabinet and his front plastered up against her. She seemed to have an abnormally long tongue that reached far into his mouth and caused him to think that she had touched him differently than had any other woman. This might well have been the case, physically, but Ted was using the thought as an excuse, a rationalization for his desire to do something bad, something wild, something stupid. His dick had gotten really hard and he was saddened by the realization that he was surprised by it.

"Are you all right?" Inga had asked him. She was not Swedish, didn't look at all Swedish with her red hair and freckles.

"I'm married," Ted said.

"I know," she said. "I don't mind. If you don't mind, I don't mind. I don't want anything from you."

Ted looked at her stupidly.

"Are you all right?" she asked again. "I could leave right now."

His hand was on her narrow waist and he really didn't want her to leave. He liked the way she felt. "I'm okay," he said.

Then she plumbed his throat once more with that serpent of hers and made him dizzy. She grabbed his hand and put it between her legs and he discovered that under her flowered sundress she was wearing no underwear. Her hair was soft and damp and his penis was so very hard and her tongue was so very long and her sighs were so very soft in his ears. He kissed her with his eyes closed and realized that it had been ages since he had kissed like that. She grabbed his dick suddenly and he made a high-pitched noise which embarrassed him slightly. But he did not back away. The door was locked and a woman named Inga was licking his brain. His life, his boring life, his wife and kids and concern about publishing and tenure and paying off the car were all outside. He got his pants undone and put himself inside her, trying to drive as deeply into her as she was driving into him. The noises she made drove him crazy, as she stopped kissing him and threw back her head, smiling and moaning and he *shhhhh*'d her and she laughed softly and stared at him, looked straight into his eyes, and whispered, "I'm having an orgasm right now," and with a shudder, she was softer than ever and limp in his arms. He wanted to hold her that way forever, but after twelve seconds, panic set in and he was pulling up his pants.

"Are you all right?" she asked.

"I'm fine," Ted said. "It's just that I'm late and I really need to get going."

Inga smoothed down her skirt. "Thank you," she said.

Ted looked at her mouth and wondered how it could look so normal and yet house such a tongue. "Well, I hope I've helped you with the assignment," he made a stab at humor.

Inga laughed politely. She walked to his desk and he watched the way she walked, one foot finding the floor directly in front of the other. She grabbed a pen and wrote on his notepad. "Here's my number," she said. "Use it if you liked it." And with that, she walked out.

The sessions with Inga became regular, having relocated from his office to her apartment that he entered each time with great trepidation, fearing that someone he knew might see him and say, "Are you sleeping with that woman with the twelve-inch tongue?" He felt like her student in bed and knew as she did it the first time that fellatio with her would remain etched in his mind as a kind of religious experience. It felt like, though it could not have possibly been the case, her tongue was able to slip down out of her mouth, which encased his penis, under and around his testicles, and actually tickle his anus. His eyes fluttered and he felt so lost that he felt stupid, which in fact he was.

Afterward, sitting at the little table in her little kitchen which looked out over the little courtyard of her apartment complex, they drank tea. Ted's head was still swimming and he couldn't seem to erase the feeling of a smile from his face. He did not know if he was indeed smiling, but he certainly felt like he was smiling.

"Are you all right?"

"Oh, yes," Ted said.

"I've really enjoyed our time together," Inga said.

The words sounded rehearsed and Ted just looked at her.

Inga reached across the table and grabbed his hand, stroked the top of his thumb with hers. "Ted, I think we're something special."

"Of course we are," he said. At that second his mind was swamped with questions of how he could be there and what in the world did he have in common with this young woman and what outside of sex could either offer the other.

Inga, steely Inga, cool Inga, eyebrow-licking Inga, shed a single tear which appeared at once as the most controlled emission Ted had ever seen from a human body and as a flood of terrifying un-controlled emotion. "I've fallen in love with you, Ted," she said.

Ted sat firm in his chair, but in his mind he had sprinted through the door and left shattered wood and a human cutout.

Inga walked over and sat on his lap, kissed him sweetly on the lips and said again, "I love you."

Somehow Ted managed to get his clothes on without having sex again and got out of there. He went home and sat at the dining-room table, ate tuna casserole and watched Emily and Perry argue about something silly. Then, Gloria startled him nearly to death by asking,

"Are you all right?"

"What?"

"Where were you?" Gloria asked.

"What?"

"Just now? What were you thinking about?"

"Oh, nothing. I guess I was thinking about my book. Cornell has had it for a couple of months now."

"Well, these things take time," she said. "Did I tell you that Rachel is leaving? Yep, she told Tyler to stuff it and walked out. The rumor is she's going to start her own agency."

Ted dipped his head. He found he hated hearing about Gloria's work at the travel agency, was in fact embarrassed by it, though he didn't know why. He had never been to her office or met the people she worked with. Her boss, Tyler, played golf and was always asking if he was in on that *tenure deal.* "Her own agency, eh?" Ted said.

"Yes," Gloria said and fell still and silent, no doubt picking up on his boredom.

"You know what?" Ted said. "We should drop everything tomorrow and drive the kids out to Palm Springs. You know, take that tram up the mountain."

"Yeah," Perry said.

"I've got soccer," Emily said.

"You can miss it this once," Ted said.

"I don't want to miss it," the girl said.

"Just this once," Ted said.

"That sounds lovely," Gloria said.

That night, the phone rang while Ted was reading to Perry from

The Phantom Tollbooth. Gloria picked up downstairs and called to him. "Ted-DY!" she sang, a holdover from their *cute* days, "Phone!" Ted picked up, said, "I've got it," heard the click and then felt a tongue slip through the receiver and clean out his ear.

"Inga," he whisper-barked.

"Are you all right?" she asked.

"No, no, I'm not all right, not now." He looked down the hall at the top of the stairs, listened for steps. "What are you doing?"

"I just needed to hear your voice," Inga said. "Are you mad at me? It's just that when you left, things felt different, funny between us, you know what I mean?"

"I can't talk now."

"Can you come over tomorrow?"

"No, I'll be gone," Ted said.

"Just for a minute?"

"No." He hung up and stood there, staring at the phone, which seemed so dangerous at that moment, like a bomb or a snake, and he wanted to unplug it, but there were three of them in the house and he couldn't leave the receiver off the hook because it would make that god-awful sound designed to tell a wife that a husband has left the phone off the hook.

In the time between his hanging up and being consumed in dread, Gloria was able to creep up the stairs and completely around him. "Are you all right?"

He wanted to scream, but nodded instead.

"Who was that?" Gloria asked.

"No one." He felt a noose tightening around his neck and other parts. "A student who didn't understand the assignment."

"Calling you at home?"

"Some nerve, eh?" Ted swallowed hard.

"I'll say," Gloria said. "She used your first name."

"Boy." Ted shook his head. "Can you imagine either of us doing that with our professors?" He watched as Gloria tossed him a side-long glance as she walked into the bedroom.

Later, while Emily snored down the hall and Gloria snored beside him, his usual peaceful sleep was interrupted by waking and bad dreams alternately. He nearly jumped out of his skin when the alarm rang the next morning, thinking immediately that it was Saturday and how could the alarm be on since they didn't need the alarm and so it must be the phone and if it's the phone then it must be Inga calling from a phone booth down the street. Gloria was just sitting up, rubbing her eyes.

"Why was the alarm set?" he asked.

"I thought I'd make us a nice picnic and we don't want to get too late a start," Gloria said reasonably.

* * *

Gloria did make a lunch of cold cuts, tuna and jelly sandwiches and stowed it all nicely in their big wicker basket that was very difficult to carry, especially when packed. In the car, Emily listened to her radio with the headphones and Perry listened to one of his tapes on the car stereo, a tape with songs about elephants and firemen and cowboys. Gloria sang along, to the delight of the boy, and though Ted did not much care for the sound of his wife's singing voice, it, along with the unfurling highway, served to relax him.

At the tram ticket office, Ted began to feel antsy, nervous and he attributed it to his long-standing fear of heights, as they were about to be suspended high in the air on a thin cable. The kids even tried to tease him about the last time they had gone up, telling him that the jagged rocks were really a lot closer than they looked, assuring him the cars hardly ever fell. The passes purchased, they sat on a bench to wait, like an awful Rockwell, Ted thought, for the tram car to arrive. Emily still wore her headphones, though, judging by her conversation with Gloria concerning the length of a nearby woman's shorts, she didn't appear to be listening to music. Ted studied her face framed in that halo of black plastic and pronounced his daughter plain, not a pretty girl, not ugly by any stretch, but plain and destined to remain plain and he hoped that being plain would not become a problem for her later in life. He felt some guilt for his observation, but also a sense of superiority, having been able to see through his parent's haze to the truth, however ugly or, rather, plain. He looked from Emily to the floor to a pair of shoes which seemed vaguely familiar.

"Oh, hello, Professor Street."

The Streets looked up as one unit.

It was Inga and if there was one thing Ted was not at that moment, it was *all right*.

Inga's hand was already pushed forward to greet Gloria. "You must be Mrs. Street," she said. "I'm Inga Malloy. I'm in your husband's Tuesday-night seminar." After shaking Gloria's hand, she knelt in front of the children.

Gloria looked at Ted and Ted shrugged.

"And who do we have here?" Inga asked.

Ted cleared his throat. "These are our children, Emily and Perry," he said. "Kids, this is Inga."

"What are you listening to?" Inga asked Emily.

"Dead Papa Rock," Emily said.

"Awesome," Inga said. "I saw them in concert last year."

"You did?"

"So," Ted said, "what are you doing here?"

"Oh, I got tired of studying and was just looking for a diversion and here I am." She looked at his eyes long enough to make him uncomfortable. "Imagine, running into you way out here."

"You're in Daddy's class?" Perry asked.

Inga nodded.

"Is he funny in class?"

"He's very funny. All the students just love him."

The people awaiting the tram began to move and shuffle. "Well, here we go, I guess," Ted said.

"Well, it was nice to meet you," Inga said, looking at Gloria, then at the kids. She looked at Ted. "I guess I'll see you Tuesday night."

"See you in class," Ted said.

"You're here alone?" Gloria asked.

Ted saw it coming, wanted to leap over the children and shut up his wife, but couldn't, wanted to close his eyes and ears and make the scene go away, but couldn't. It was coming.

"Yes," Inga said.

"Why don't you hang out with us?" Gloria said. "We have plenty of food and, well, it would be nice."

"Oh, I couldn't," Inga said.

"That's too bad," Ted said and tried to move his family along.

"Oh, pish-posh," Gloria said. "You're going to stay with us for a while. After lunch, you'll no doubt be sick of us, but until then, you're our guest. Right, Ted?"

"Of course."

The tram car was crowded, people cheek by jowl, reaching over one another to find the center poles and the rails along the walls. The day was clear and the sight outside might even have appeared beautiful to Ted if Inga had not been standing next to him, her back against his side, while she faced and talked to Gloria. He refused to turn around and participate in the idle chatter, but looked out the window with Perry. Inga was pushing into him and he felt pathetic as he discovered he liked it, the firmness of her ass, the softness of her shoulder. He stole peeks at the back of her head and neck and felt his dick growing hard in his pants, only to have panic come over him and shrink it again.

It was a miserable lunch, full of Gloria's endless descriptions of the travel business and glances from Inga to Ted as if to tell him she understood why he had strayed.

"I tell you what," Inga said. "Why don't the two of you take a walk while I go with the kids on the trail ride?"

"I don't know," Ted said.

"That would be wonderful," Gloria said. She looked at Ted. "I'd love to have a few minutes alone with you up here."

* * *

Ted and Gloria watched as Inga and the kids waited on line and then were mounted onto horses all strung together. They waved and Inga waved back.

"She's nice," Gloria said.

Ted nodded.

"Is she a good student?"

"I've had better," Ted said and wanted to bite his tongue off afterward.

"Is she the one who called last night?"

Ted didn't know how to answer. Suppose Inga had already apologized for calling the house and this was just a test to see if he would lie. "Yes," he said.

"Well, she called you Professor Street today," Gloria said. "Maybe she heard some disapproval in my voice last night. You think?"

"I don't know."

"The kids like her," Gloria said. "Maybe we've found a new baby-sitter."

"No," Ted said quickly, perhaps too quickly. "I mean, we don't really know her yet. And she's a graduate student. You know how they come and go. The kids will get attached to her and then they'll miss her. I mean, why do that to them."

Gloria laughed. "From my experience, a lot of these graduate students hang around for a long time."

"I suppose," he said.

"Don't you like her?" Gloria asked.

Ted shrugged.

They crossed a stream by walking on a fallen tree, then stopped to observe a Steller's jay on a low branch.

"Do you think she's pretty?" Gloria asked.

Ted was in hell, that was all there was to it, in burning, stinking hell. "Not really."

"Oh, come on," Gloria said, laughing.

"Okay, she's kind of attractive."

"She has a crush on you," Gloria said.

At any second, maggots would be gnawing through Ted's shoes, into his feet and up through his legs, middle and throat to his brain, because he was in hell. He looked at the sky and the trees and the rocks and the birds and the shades of death. How could hell be so attractive?

"Big deal," Ted said.

They walked on, held hands, Gloria feeling light and it showed in her gait, Ted barely able to lift his trailing foot and with all his strength throw it out in front of him.

* * *

Gloria took the kids to get snacks before they took the tram back down the mountain, leaving Ted alone with Inga in front of a display of a rattlesnake eating a field mouse.

"What are you doing here?" Ted asked. "How did you know?"

"I followed you," Inga said.

"Followed? Are you crazy?" Ted tried not to look like the frightened man he was as he caught people staring at him. "Followed? What do you think you're doing?"

"I had to see her for myself," Inga said. "Oh, Ted, I feel so badly for you. She's a very sweet woman, but she's not for you. And such lovely children."

"Precisely," he said. "Those are my children with her. She's my wife."

Inga shook her head. "You're so sad. I can see it. I could see it all through lunch. Was that the most boring conversation you've ever heard or what?"

"Please, Inga, please don't do this."

"I love you, Ted."

"You can't love me. I'm a married man."

"But I can fuck you, is that right?"

Ted could see Gloria pause, waiting for Perry to tie his shoe. "That's not what I mean," he said under his breath, though Gloria was much too far away to hear.

"I'm going to tell her," Inga said.

A hot flash of fear washed through Ted's stomach and he felt unsteady. "Inga, please."

"You're living a lie," she said.

Ted was near crying. "Please."

Gloria and the kids were on them now. Emily moved in close to Inga and offered her some of her potato chips.

"Was it crowded over there?" Inga asked the children.

"Too many people," Perry said, then laughed as if he liked saying the words.

The tram car came and Ted contemplated knocking out the window and throwing either himself or Inga out onto the rocks below. He stayed close to Gloria to ward off any approaches by Inga, but the woman stayed on the other side of the car with the children, pointing out the window and giggling with them.

They parted in the parking lot and Ted felt lightheaded as they started their drive home. Gloria noticed his discomfort and asked him if he had a headache and he told her he did. Both kids fell asleep quickly and Gloria leaned back into her seat and hummed a tune softly. Ted would have to tell her that he had been putting his thingie in Inga's thingie receptacle. If Inga told her first, she would leave him for sure, but if he told her that he had been weak and cowardly and that he knew he had slipped up and that he was sorry and that it would never happen again and that he loved her and the kids, then maybe, just maybe, she might poison him or shoot him or stab him, but not leave him.

So, that night, he entered the bathroom while Gloria sat soaking in a hot bath. He put down the toilet lid and sat.

"I'm out of shape," Gloria said. "I can feel the walking we did. Tomorrow I'll be stiff for sure."

"Me too," Ted said.

"Do you think I'm getting fat?" she asked.

"No," he said and he was telling the truth. "Gloria, I need to tell you something." He watched her face open to him. "It's about Inga." Gloria looked like a deer caught in his headlights and he knew she knew there was no finding the brake pedal in time.

"What about her?"

"Gloria, I slept with Inga."

Gloria looked away, then grabbed the soap and began to bathe.

"Gloria," he said.

"Don't say my name."

"I'm sorry. I love you and I slipped up and I want you and I love the kids and I love you and I'm sorry, I'm sorry."

She dipped under to wet her hair and came up reaching for the shampoo. "Would you mind closing the door on your way out?"

Ted did, but as he shut the bathroom door he wondered if that was indeed the door she meant. She didn't say anything to him that night, didn't yell, didn't cry, didn't tell him to sleep out on the sofa or anywhere else. But she slept in her terry-cloth robe and in socks, with her back to him, her knees to her chest.

* * *

Gloria had not left Ted for his infidelity and she had not asked him to leave. She made him crawl and to Ted's dismay, he found he was good at it. He begged her daily for forgiveness until he felt empty. But it was not this loss of pride which had caused him to seek exit from life, it was the same stuff which had led him into his affair with Inga—a belief that he was bored, that life was over anyway, that he made no difference to anyone—all selfish and indulgent thoughts, whether true or not, but his thoughts nonetheless.

And now here he was, in the very tub Gloria had sat in that night, with his head put back on his body and his life put back together no less crudely.

CHAPTER THREE

SEX WITH GLORIA HAD never been uninteresting, though Ted, in his infrequent and uncharacteristic moments of second-order reflection, would have been hard pressed to say what he thought interesting sex might look like. They had put their parts together and stirred things around and they both admitted to orgasms and general, if imprecise, satisfaction. Before his affair with Inga, Ted and Gloria had regular intercourse in the usual and standard positions and occasional oral sex. Once he had begun his adulterous foray, the frequency of his sex with Gloria first ballooned, then dropped rapidly to nil. He'd found it surprisingly easy to generate excuses and even became slightly disappointed that his excuses were so casually accepted and honored. After his confession in the bathroom, what they could have been said to have was anti-sex, an active non-participation in the act which resulted in a gradual but undeniable diminution of his once, if not proud, not unproud organ. Slowly, things got better; as Gloria forgave him, they found their way back to sex, first as an act of repentance and contrition on Ted's part and then as an act of base gratification.

On the afternoon of his resurrection, just like the night of his confession about his affair with Inga, Gloria crawled into bed wearing several layers of clothing. She did not, however, turn her back on him as she did before, but lay facing him. He looked at her face and wanted to tell her he was sorry, not sorry for the affair and all his other pitifully atrocious behavior through the years, but sorry that he was now submitting her to this torture, confusion.

"Is it really you?" Gloria asked.

"I think so," Ted said. He touched her face.

"I'm so scared," she said.

"Me too."

"Kiss me," Gloria said, but it sounded liked a question.

Ted leaned over her and placed his lips against hers. Never did a kiss feel so much like a first kiss, not his first kiss with Gloria when they were in college and not his very first kiss with thirteen-year-old Meg Tollison when he was twelve. Gloria's lips felt electric, fat, full and moist and her tongue barely touched his own, sending a wave through and over him. He loved her at that moment because he had always loved her, but he especially loved her because she was not running away from him. He felt like a monster, a re-animated ghoul, but Gloria was kissing him, kissing him in spite of her fear and uncertainty, in spite of the hideous and ghastly reality of his presence. She touched his hair and moved her hand down over his ear until she was tracing the sutures on his neck. Her nails suggested a tugging at his stitches and Gloria moaned.

"Take me, Ted," Gloria said. She had never said anything like that and it sounded foreign and outlandish, but strangely correct. "Take me," she said again.

Ted buried his face in his wife's neck and together they wrestled through the wardrobe she was wearing until finally she was naked and he was inside her. They moved together, slowly at first, her hands pulling his hair, then returning to his neck, rubbing his shoulders, then returning to his neck. Finally, her fingers stayed there on the line which held him together and she moaned and moaned and bucked and bucked and had what must have been a dozen orgasms. She lay spent. Ted came with her during her last climax, happy that she was so obviously satisfied, but feeling strangely jealous that so much of her attention had been directed to his deformity.

"Oh, Ted," she whispered. That was all. *Oh, Ted.*

"Did you like that?" he asked stupidly. His question was in fact more stupid than vain, as he did not feel responsible.

"You were wonderful," she said. "I felt you everywhere inside me." She closed her eyes.

Ted studied her face and decided he liked the feeling of having pleased her so, decided it didn't much matter what about him had excited her. Then, he felt genuinely good about himself, realizing that the old Ted could not have been so selfless, that the old Ted would have worried about his manhood and passive-aggressively taken his feeling of inadequacy out on her. Ted closed his eyes and drifted, he hoped, only into sleep.

* * *

In his dream, if indeed it was a dream and not some other, as-real reality, Ted's head sat, as much as a head can be said to sit, at the head of a heavy oak table in a heavily oaked boardroom. Several figures sat around the table. To Ted's left there sat one head shared by two bodies, each body seated in a separate chair, each torso wearing a tee-shirt, one reading Hegel, the other Heidegger. Opposite the single-headed-two-bodied Hegel and Heidegger sat one body bearing two heads, the elbows on the table, the right hand supporting the chin of the left head and the left hand supporting the chin of the right. Though the body was wearing a dress shirt with no label, Ted somehow knew that the heads were Paul Althaus and Karl Heim.

The heads of Althaus and Heim spoke in unison, their dissimilar voices scratching against each other. "What do we know of immortality? There can be no such thing. That would mean a denial of death."

"Pure being and pure nothing are the same," the mouth of Hegel and Heidegger said.

Ted's head was confused by the apparent non sequitur.

"You are alive and dead," said Hegel and Heidegger.

"You are not alive," said Althaus and Heim. "You are resurrected and resurrection is not of the soul, but of the whole being, the whole person, body and soul."

"You are nothing and so you are pure being, the two being absolutely different, each immediately disappearing into the opposite." The Hegel half of Hegel and Heidegger sat up straighter in his chair.

The heads of Althaus and Heim nodded with frowns. "When we die, we pass into nothingness, of course," they said. "Everything dies, so then how is the person reconstituted?"

Of a sudden there was another form at the end of the table, a body with no head, but an open neck in which there was only blackness. There was no voice, as there was no mouth, but the figure said, "Will not the reconstituted person be only an imitation of the original? And so, how can one look foward to the things that would happen to the reconstituted person as things that would happen to the original?"

The head of Hegel and Heidegger shook. "The thing is destroyed, but continues to exist as nothing and so still *is* and, therefore, can be reconstituted as itself."

"Then it has not been destroyed," the headless form said. "The new person is an imitation. The original person is gone. There is no more Ted. There is only Ted-prime."

* * *

Ted awoke with a start. He sat up and put his feet on the rug by the bed, held his face in his hands and found his neck. He got up and walked into the bathroom. He looked at the mirror and studied the face that looked back. Was he indeed himself? And if he was an imitation, knowing all that he knew about the original and feeling all the guilt that he felt, what difference would it make? His question was, Was he himself? And his answer was, "Who else could he be?" Not a very satisfying answer.

* * *

Gloria was up shortly after Ted and together they walked down to the kitchen. The excitement of the day must have been a lot for the kids to handle, as they did not stir. It was nine o'clock when Ted looked from his seat at the kitchen table to the clock on the stove. Gloria was pouring herself a cup of coffee.

The phone rang and Ted crossed the floor to answer it.

"Let it ring," Gloria said.

Ted paused at the phone, looked at her face, then picked up. A man's voice spoke to him. "You're the devil," he said. "You are Lucifer come among us. God will strike you dead."

"He tried," Ted said and hung up. He was certainly amazed by the call, but equally amazed by his immediate response. All his life he had come up with his pithy comebacks hours after they would have been effective or any good.

"Who was it?" Gloria asked.

"Just some nut," Ted said. "I'm afraid we're going to get a lot of calls like that one."

"What did they say?" Gloria sat at the table, tried to calm herself by blowing on her coffee.

Ted sighed. "He said I'm the devil."

"Oh," Gloria said. "Are you?"

Ted looked at his wife's eyes and realized that the question was not completely silly. "I don't think so, honey. I think I'd know if I were the devil."

"I guess so," she said.

"Who knows, maybe I'm the son of you-know-who?" Ted laughed.

Gloria, who had always—if not secretly then privately—felt some pull to a belief in a god, did not offer up a chuckle. Before they had children, she'd brought up the subject of church a couple of times, but was silenced by Ted's ridicule. However, superstition and the supernatural seemed not so strange in the face of their current predicament. Ted wanted to tell her that his sitting there was proof that there was no god, though he would have been unable to articulate such an argument. But he didn't tell her that, exercising his newfound prudence and circumspection, not wanting to hurt her feelings needlessly. He was, in fact, kind and he liked thinking that about himself. He had certainly been nice to others, friendly, even open and sometimes understanding, but now he was a kind man, a generous man and he hated his old self because he realized that the one person he had never been terribly kind or generous to was his wife.

The phone rang again.

"I'll get it," Gloria said. She walked over and picked up. "Oh, hello, Ethel." Ethel was Ted's sister, to whom he had not been close since their mother's death over ten years ago and their father's subsequent admission to a sanitarium because he had Alzheimer's disease. Ethel had always been rather stiff, pushy, in a bad way, advisory. Ted never called her and she never called him, except when she had some news concerning their father's ever-deteriorating condition. "We missed you at the funeral."

Ted was tickled by the comment.

"Well," Gloria said into the phone, "I guess the news was fairly accurate in that regard." She looked at Ted and shrugged. "Oh, he's sitting right here." She brought the receiver to him.

"Hello, Ethel," he said.

"I understand you're not dead," Ethel said.

"That's more or less the case," he said.

Ethel was silent on the other end.

"How are things in Baltimore?" Ted asked.

Then Ethel let it all out. "What the hell is going on? One minute you're dead and the next you're on CNN and every other network. How can you be alive?"

"Let me get this straight," Ted said, calmer than he expected. "You don't care enough when I die to come to my funeral, but you call because I come back to life."

"Is there something I should know?" Ethel asked.

"Know about what? You mean, is this a family thing?" He wanted to tell her to go cut off her head and find out, but instead he said, "It's pretty scary for all of us. I'm kind of busy right now. Tell what's-his-name I said hello." He hung up.

The front doorbell rang.

"What now?" Ted said. He and Gloria marched to the door in their robes. They looked at each other and then Ted opened the door. They were blinded by bright lights and there were many back-lit heads and microphones coming at their faces.

"Tell us, how does it feel to come back from the dead?" a barking voice asked.

Ted closed the door. They could hear the hubbub outside. Emily and Perry appeared at the top of the stairs, rubbing their eyes, asking what was going on.

"There are a bunch of trucks in the street in front of the house," Perry reported.

The phone rang.

"Ted?" Gloria said, her eyes showing new fear. "What are we going to do?"

Ted's first thought was that they should sneak out of the house and flee, but that was, of course, ridiculous. He was a college professor and knew nothing of how to disappear in the streets, much less how to survive and take care of his wife and children. He'd often imagined that he would pose a terrible problem for the Witness Protection Program, which would be unable to place him and his family in any community because of his inability to do anything other than what he did, namely teach and attempt to write obscure articles. He would never survive a job in a hardware store and he wouldn't fit in with construction workers and he'd no doubt kill someone if placed at the controls of a crane or any kind of heavy machinery. Trying to clandestinely relocate an English professor would be like changing a professional basketball player's name and trying to hide him on another team.

"Let's just stay cool," Ted said. In fact, he *was* cool—cooler than he had ever been. Perhaps it was simply that without a pulse, there was nothing to race, but he knew that it was more than that. And he knew that it wasn't that he had seen the worst—namely death—and survived it. He understood something now, though he had no idea what it was. Deep in his being he was calm and knew, knew something, knew he knew it.

The phone was still ringing.

"Isn't anybody going to answer that?" Emily asked.

Ted went to the phone on the table beside the stairs.

"Yes, this is Ted Street," he said.

A woman on the other end was telling him that she was not concerned with his sudden fame, but with his medical condition. "My name is Dr. Timmons and I'm from USC Medical School, where I do research in cryogenics."

"You freeze people?" Ted asked.

"No, actually, I've only been interested in freezing tissue and organs up to now," Dr. Timmons said. "But since we sort of work at the same institution, I thought—"

"You thought I wouldn't mind becoming a guinea pig," Ted said.

"Mr. Street."

"No, I don't mind," Ted said. "I want to know what's going on as much as you do. Come over tomorrow morning and bring your stethoscope, not that you'll need it."

"Thank you," Dr. Timmons said.

As Ted hung up he heard a commotion in the kitchen.

"There's a strange man coming in through the window!" Perry screamed.

Ted ran in to find a man's legs and rear end stuck through the window over the sink. Gloria and the children stood frozen by the breakfast nook. Ted ran to the sink, pulled a fork from the soapy water and plunged it into the man's bottom, causing him to howl in pain and disappear into the darkness outside. Ted pulled down the sash and bolted it locked.

"That's it," Ted said. "I'm calling the police." And so he did and learned that there were already police there controlling the crowd and he told them that the news people were invading his home and would they please keep them off his property and they said they would try. He hung up the phone and then removed the receiver from its cradle and left it that way.

* * *

In a world still combating the heresies of Voltaire, Darwin and even Robert Ingersoll, a man returning from the dead was hard to take. In most cultures this would have been the case, Ted admitted, but his own, with its appeal to so-called reason and scientific method, promised to behave as badly as his imagination would allow. He had put Gloria and the children to bed, all in his room and was now seated downstairs in the living room watching CNN. They had a spanking-new logo for the story, his name written above an open passport bearing his driver's license photo with a cross over that and the caption read, "Back from the Dead."

There was a detailed discussion, though not terribly informative, about the nature and constitution of death itself and when that got too boring they would repeat the footage of the riot in Long Beach. Then it was back to the experts.

"Dr. Dume," the news anchor said, "tell us again just what death is."

"Traditionally, we have viewed death as when the heart stops beating, but biologically speaking, death is not a disjunctive event, but is an ongoing process that concludes with the irreversible loss of function of the entire organism. Lawyers and doctors look upon death very differently. For the medical profession, death is not a precise moment or instant, but a continuous process. A heart might stop, but cells and tissue might continue showing signs of life for days. As the cells and other parts are deprived of oxygen and nutrients, they die as well."

"Oh, my," the anchor said. She was a pie-faced brunette wearing hoop earrings. "You mean that in fact we often bury our loved ones while parts of them are still alive?"

"Technically, that's true," Dr. Dume said. "But certainly we can't wait around for every single cell to die. Obviously, since we revive people whose hearts have stopped and since often we even stop the heart intentionally for certain procedures, we cannot hold on to the definition of death as the ceasing of the heart's function."

"I guess not," the anchor said.

"So, now, we pronouce a person dead when the brain dies," Dr. Dume said.

"So, to the point, Dr. Dume, is Ted Street alive?"

The camera moved in close on Dr. Dume's face and he said, "Seeing as his head was severed from his body and that even if we were to see his heart pumping and his neck spewing blood everywhere, we would consider him dead, then he is indeed dead. How could he be alive?"

"But apparently he is alive."

"I can't help that," Dr. Dume said, a little agitated now. "The Talmud even makes reference to such a thing. It says, 'the death throes of a decapitated man are not signs of life any more than are the twitchings of a lizard's amputated tail.'"

"But he walked and talked," the pie-faced woman said. "Those could hardly be said to be death throes."

"Who's to say what a death throe is?" Dr. Dume gestured excitedly. "Perhaps this is all mass hysteria."

"But we have a brief ten seconds of Mr. Street on camera when he opened his door," she said. "Do dead men open their front doors and then close them?"

"Then he's not dead!" Dume shouted. "All these questions. I think it's obvious that this is a hoax. Maybe he was never dead."

"Are you telling us that medical science is capable of successfully reattaching a human head back onto its body?"

"I didn't say that!"

Then it was back to footage of the riot and the ten-second clip of Gloria and Ted in their robes at the front door, wide-eyed like roadkill. The camera zoomed in on Ted's neck.

"There," the anchor said, "we can see the crude sewing job done by Mr. Alden Ash of the Iverson, Ash, Graves and Shroud Mortuary in Los Angeles. Mr. Ash is reported to have said, 'I didn't do anything special. I just sewed his head back on.'

"This just in," she said. "There was a mass suicide off the Hancock building in Chicago just minutes ago as thirteen members of the You-Know-He's-Coming-Back Cult leaped ninety-six stories to their deaths on the street below. Some were heard to call out 'Teddy, Teddy,' as they approached the pavement."

Ted switched off the set and felt sick. But he knew that he was not responsible for the action of those nuts in Chicago. He had not chosen to come back from the dead, if indeed he had. He would not have chosen it had he the option.

* * *

Ted's father had been diagnosed with Alzheimer's two years before his mother committed suicide. The first time he got lost was in a shopping mall. Ted's mother, Irene, paused to look at a table of watches in Macy's and when she turned back to Harvey, he wasn't there. She and the mall police, two fat men with small flashlights, scoured the place twice, one of the guards finally finding Harvey in the housewares department of J. C. Penney comparing the weights of cutting boards.

"Do you think it's better to have a thick, heavy board or an easily stored, light one?" Harvey asked the man.

At first, he did not recognize Irene, but winked at her and asked her if she was married. Irene would tell this story later and smile at the knowledge that deep inside him, in his unconsious, Harvey still found her attractive, but it never served to erase the sadness of his vacancy.

After the mall incident, Ted flew out to Baltimore and sat in the doctor's office with his mother and sister, Ethel. The physician, an exceptionally large man, came into the room and hovered over them.

"How is he?" Ted asked.

"Not good," Dr. Cumbersome said. "I'm afraid he is in the early stages of Alzheimer's disease."

"Is there anything we can do?" Ethel asked.

"No," the doctor said.

"No? Just no?" Ethel asked.

"No," the doctor repeated.

"What *do* we do then?" Ted asked. He reached over and held his mother's hand.

"Well, the problem is that the episodes like the one last week will not be frequent at first and so, institutionalization can be very difficult." The doctor sat on the edge of his desk. "In short, he's not going to want to be there. On the other hand, since we can't predict the next event, he could get lost or hurt or, well, you get the picture."

"He's always been so strong," Irene said.

Dr. Cumbersome nodded.

"What do you recommend?" Ted asked.

"It's a tough call," the doctor said. "He'll have to be watched pretty much all the time. It only takes a couple of seconds for something bad to happen."

"That's so true," Irene said.

"And he'll resent being watched," Cumbersome said.

"That's so true," Irene said.

"He should be in an institution," Ethel said.

"No," said Irene.

"I agree with Mom," Ted said.

"Doctor?" Irene complained.

"You don't have to rush into a decision," Cumbersome said. "Take a few days, think things over."

"What's there to think over?" Ethel said. "He could black out at any second and walk off, never to be seen again."

"We'll watch him," Ted said.

"The hell you will," Ethel snapped. "You're going to fly back to sunny California and leave the watching to me and Mom."

Ted didn't say anything, since basically she was correct. He looked at his mother and at the doctor and they looked at him. "I have to get back to my family and my job," he said.

They said nothing, but stared at him, stared at him as if to say, *Oh, you talk a big game, but what are you going to do to help?*

"It's okay, Teddy," his mother said, squeezing his hand. "You have kids to worry about."

"Jesus," Ethel muttered. "It's the old kid card. Man, do I hate that. And you don't even have to pull it. She pulls it for you."

"That's enough, Ethel," Irene said. "Let's take your father home and make him feel comfortable and loved."

It was a reasonable and sweet thing for a person to say and mean and Ted was impressed by his mother's strength. He knew that she would never put his father away in a hospital, certainly not with the slightest hint of disapproval from one of her children. She would try to watch him and deny to him at every turn that that's what she was doing.

And so she tried. She watched her husband's episodes, as the doctor called them, become more frequent, but hardly regular. Harvey twice locked her out of the house and peered at her through the blinds, having no idea who she was and telling her to go away. And seven times he disappeared and had to be found by police, once ending up in a rough section of town and another time under a pier at the docks, his nose bloodied and his palms shredded. That time, Ted flew to Baltimore and tried with his sister to persuade Irene that it was time for Harvey to go to an institution. Still, she refused, but her face had changed. There was not a hardness in her eyes, but the sweetness was gone. And though she was not a drooling mess like their father, she wore a very similar expression, one perhaps of resignation, but as it turned out, of mission. Shortly after Ted arrived back in California he received a call from Ethel telling him that Irene had shot herself in the head with their father's old pistol.

"It's all your fault," Ethel said.

Ted did not argue with her.

* * *

Ted showered at daybreak while Gloria and the children continued to sleep, amazingly. The lawn and street in front of the house were teeming with people. Photographers and cameramen stood around smoking and pointing to the house. Reporters stood in the morning dew and broadcast their impressions of the house, the neighborhood, the situation inside. Ted not only imagined that that was what was coming out of the mouths stuck in the middle of the unreal faces, but with his new ears, he could actually make out their reports. The police had roped off the house and three stood guard in the front yard. Gloria came down in her robe and looked out the window with him.

"How long will they stay?" she asked.

"I don't know," Ted said. "The kids still asleep?"

"Yeah," Gloria sighed. "They're really wiped out. I'll bet you're tired too. Were you up all night?"

Ted nodded. "I don't feel tired." He looked at Gloria and smiled. "The man from Channel Thirteen thinks we're aliens. He hasn't said so on the air, but that's what he said to that makeup guy."

"Aliens, eh?"

"Yep, and I don't think he means from Guatemala," Ted said. "That doctor is supposed to come this morning. Perhaps she'll be able to tell us something."

"Do you really think so?" Gloria asked.

"Not really."

* * *

Dr. Timmons did show up, but was stopped at the yellow tape by a policeman. Ted could hear the discussion and asked Gloria to go out and bring the doctor in. Dressed now, Gloria did go out and the cameras all turned to her and started clicking and rolling and the reporters barked questions, but she stayed her course to the doctor. Ted was proud of her strength. She brought in Timmons and her assistant, a little, fat fellow with a notepad in his hand.

Timmons stopped on seeing Ted standing in the foyer and swallowed hard. "Mr. Street," she said and extended her hand for shaking.

Ted took the hand and wondered if his touch would feel cold to her. It certainly had not felt so to Gloria the night before. "Dr. Timmons," he said. "I'm glad you came."

"Thank you for letting me come," she said. "This must be a very stressful time for you."

"Short of dying," Ted said and watched Dr. Timmons try to decide if she should laugh. "I'm not sensitive about this," Ted told her. "The truth is, I hope you can help us understand what's happened."

"I'll do my best," Timmons said. "Oh, this is my assistant, Richard Lilfaman."

"Pleased to meet you," Ted said.

Lilfaman nodded hello to Ted and to Gloria.

"Where can we sit?" Timmons asked.

"Let's go into the dining room," Ted said. "Would you like some coffee? Tea?"

"Coffee would be wonderful," Timmons said.

"Coffee, please," Lilfaman said.

Timmons sat at the dining room table next to Ted and Lilfaman sat opposite them, taking notes. The doctor took out her stethoscope. "Would you mind opening your shirt a bit for me?" she said.

Ted unbuttoned his light blue denim shirt and turned slightly toward her.

"Just relax," she said.

Timmons placed the instrument on his chest and moved it around, then looked at Lilfaman. "No sounds at all," she said.

"I was going to tell you that," Ted said.

Timmons continued to listen. "Nothing," she said. She took a blood pressure kit from her bag. "Is there any point in my using this?"

"I don't know."

"We'll try." She closed the cuff around Ted's arm and started pumping it up.

Gloria came in with the coffee, set down the tray and walked back into the kitchen.

"I don't know why I'm doing this," Timmons said. "I can't find a pulse in the first place." She stopped squeezing the ball and listened while she watched the gauge. "No blood pressure," she said to Lilfaman, who dutifully wrote it down.

Ted looked at the woman's face and could see her fear. He could in fact hear her heart beating, just slightly less fast than Lilfaman's heart. He could also see the very small twitch in her lip and he felt bad for her. "What now?" he asked.

"I really can't tell anything here," she said. "I need to find out if there is any brain activity."

"My speaking to you doesn't count," Ted said.

"As odd as it sounds, no," she said. "An electroencephalogram will tell us that."

"I'm pretty sure there's brain activity," Ted told her. "Do you have any theories?"

"None. I suppose the mortician could have accidentally sewn

your head on so that all the nerves reconnected, but that doesn't account for the fact that your heart is not pumping blood to your brain. Cells need oxygen to function."

"Apparently not," Ted said.

"Maybe we don't really understand cell life," she said. "Maybe cells don't need the things we think they need. I don't know."

Gloria was standing at the door now, watching, listening.

"It seems I'm dead," Ted said to his wife.

"Obviously you're not dead, Mr. Street," Timmons said.

"Then what am I?"

Lilfaman put his pencil down. He offered, in a high, grating voice: "The ancient Greeks and Romans, the Thracians too, used to wait three or more days for putrefaction to begin before they disposed of the dead. This was just in case they were still alive. In fact, the Romans would call out the name of the dead person and even cut off a finger to see if they still bled, to be sure."

"I breathe when I talk," Ted said. "Does that mean anything?"

Timmons shrugged.

"But I don't have to breathe. I mean, if I'm not talking, then I can sit for hours without breathing. I can walk across the room without breathing. I really want to know what's going on."

"I'm sorry," Dr. Timmons said.

Ted watched her put her things back into her bag. "So am I," he said. "Are you done looking for an answer?"

"I'd like for you to come to the hospital so that we can run some tests, but I'm afraid I already know what they will show. They'll show that you should be dead."

"And then I'll say something and ruin everything," Ted said.

Timmons let out a short laugh. "Basically."

Gloria stepped to the table and stood behind Ted, put her hands on his shoulders.

"Are you a religious person?" Ted asked the doctor.

She paused, then said, "No, I'm not."

"Neither am I," Ted said. "I never have been."

* * *

Ted watched from the window in the living room as Timmons and Lilfaman were swarmed upon by reporters and cameras as they crossed the police tape. Timmons was frightened by the horde and Lilfaman tried gamely to shield his supervisor. Finally, however, they were completely encircled and the darting questions found their mark.

"Are you a friend of the family?"

"Are you a doctor? That is a doctor's bag, isn't it?"

"What were you able to determine? Did you get to examine Mr. Street?"

"Is Street in good health?"

Timmons was stunned. She stammered out sounds, but was unable to form those sounds into words. Lilfaman stepped in front of her and spoke. "Dr. Timmons has no comment for you right now." Again, he tried to move the doctor through and past the crowd of media.

"Dr. Timmons, what kind of doctor are you?"

"Yeah, just what kind of doctor are you?"

"How is it possible that Mr. Street is still alive?"

"Is this a hoax?"

Then, as if reaching the end of her rope, Timmons said to them, "The man is dead, yet he is still alive. His heart is not beating, but his brain continues to function. I don't understand it. I don't have any answers for you. He's frightened, I think. I too am frightened." Then her voice seemed to turn inward. "Maybe we should all be frightened."

CHAPTER FOUR

HAVING WATCHED THE DOCTOR leave and the milling news crews purchase paper-wrapped sandwiches and cans of soda from vendors, Ted decided that being caged in his own home was not a good and desirable thing; at least it didn't feel particularly good. So, he gathered Gloria and the children together, got them bathed and dressed in fresh clothes and informed them that they were going out to take care of business. Gloria was obviously terrified by the thought, her hands moving in small quivers at her sides, but she seemed more disposed now than ever to have and show confidence in her husband, and expressed trust in his judgment. Emily, however, began with a wide-eyed stare at her father, not so much of surprise but of rage and anger, a fiery anger which found air with a screaming fit and a dash up the stairs to her bedroom.

Ted had throughout Emily's few years been conspicuously incapable of talking with her on anything but a superficial level, in spite of his conscientious performance of the bedtime-story-reading ritual and his constant readiness to crawl on hands and knees about the floor when she was very young and to run about the yard with the child and her pals a couple years later. When, at age eleven, Emily's routines were interrupted by the early and necessarily rude coming of her first period, Ted, having been called into the bathroom by the terrified child—Gloria being away from the house—slowly fathomed what had happened and standing there, staring at the bloodied panties in Emily's little hand, was unable to say anything, comforting, informative or otherwise. Gloria returned home to find Ted sitting on the edge of the tub (the tub had seen so much) trying to get Emily to converse with him about soccer. Tonight, though, Ted found himself sitting quickly and confidently beside the child on her bed and asking,

"What are you feeling, honey?"

"I'm ashamed," she said.

"Ashamed of me?" he asked.

"Not ashamed." Emily shook her head. "Embarrassed. I feel embarrassed." She scooped up one of her stuffed animals, a blue dolphin, and hugged it.

"I'm sorry," Ted said. He tried to feel the nubs of the chenille bedspread with his fingertips, but could not. "I'm not embarrassed, but I am really scared."

"I'm scared too," Emily said. She looked at her father's eyes and held them, perhaps longer than she had ever before and he could see deep into the brown of them, to that obstinate streak which he actually loved and which used to frighten him. "Did you die, Daddy?"

"I don't know, honey." Ted reached over and, with the tips of his fingers, touched her hand. Though he could not feel the softness of her skin—his skin must have been icy or rough, but whatever it was, it was different from the way his skin had felt or from the way his skin should have felt, because it erased any closeness his brief chat with the girl had created and sent her into a screaming, limb-swinging tizzy. She ran from the room, banging around the door-jamb like a marble in a pinball game, and down the stairs. Ted followed after her, meeting the expectant eyes of Gloria and Perry at the bottom of the stairs. Together they dashed into the kitchen and discovered the open door. The world outside the house seemed so incredibly vast and foreign and they stopped at the sight of it.

"Oh, my God," Gloria said.

Ted ran to the door, looked across the uneven lawn of the back-yard and saw the distraught child being encircled by the coffee-and-cigarette-breathed news vultures. "No!" he shouted and ran full speed toward his daughter.

The news people, reporters and cameramen, multiplied like rocks in a field and spun to face the approaching man, frantically readying their equipment.

Ted reached Emily, but again the touch of his hand caused the same unfortunate reaction as she kicked and screamed and caused several adults near her to do a rational thing; they removed the child from the source of her fear. People fell in between Ted and his daughter and he called to her. Then he called for Gloria, not so much for assistance, but out of distress. The news crews from the front of the house spilled into the back and the space between Ted and Gloria became replete with cameras and bodies, voices and commands. He saw his wife pushing toward him, slapping at micro-phones and camera lenses. Questions pierced the din to find his hearing and Emily was gone into the sea of legs and waists, away from his sight. There was no sign of her and he called out her name over and over. Then he heard Gloria scream. Ted fought his way back to his wife, hoping that Perry had remained in the house. He reached Gloria and she fell sobbing into his arms. Then there was a policeman helping them, a short Hispanic man who would not look directly at Ted, but he supported Gloria as they climbed the back steps. Ted and Gloria finally made it back to the house. Once inside, they leaned against the closed door and breathed sighs of relief as they saw Perry sitting under the table.

"Where's Emily?" Gloria asked.

"Out there," Ted said. He looked at the shaking, crying boy. "Perry, come here." Perry crawled out from under the table and ran to his parents. "Are you okay?"

"Ted," Gloria said.

"I'll call the police," Ted said.

* * *

Outside, Emily was sitting out of sight of her parents, crying in the midst of a huddle of ostensibly concerned adults. For whatever reason, the news people decided that it would be best for the child to be with women and familiar women at that and so the women anchors of the local newscasts tried to comfort her. The child looked at their made-up faces and yes, they did appear familiar, but they also looked unreal, more like ghosts than even her father.

"Emily, right?" Barbie Becker from Channel 5 said.

Emily nodded.

"There, there, everything will be just fine," Yvonne Yashimoto from Channel 4 said. "Would you like a glass of water? Some ice cream, candy, maybe?"

Wanda Washington from Channel 13 took the child's hand and stroked it.

"Somebody ask her what it's like in there?" a man called from behind the women. "When can we get a camera on the kid?"

Emily looked at all their faces and sipped now from a red plastic cup of water. She tried to look back at her house, but was unable to see it. "I want to go back to my mom," Emily said. "I want to go back in!" Emily said.

"Are you worried about your mom?" someone asked. "Why your mom and not your dad?"

"Somebody get a camera on this."

"Is your father different?"

"Is your mom okay in there?"

"Are you getting this?"

Emily was crying.

"Emily, can you tell us why you were running from your father?"

"Emily, are you afraid of your father?"

"Emily, is he behaving strangely?"

"Emily, do you believe your father is alive?"

Ted was on the phone with the police. Gloria stood beside him and Perry held on to his waist, his small hands bunching the fabric of Ted's shirt while he used the wall unit in the kitchen. The first officer put him on hold and so did the second, and when the third came onto the line he screamed, "Put me on hold and I'll come to your house personally. Yes, I'm the dead guy and I want some service."

"What's the problem, sir?"

"My daughter is lost someplace and I need your help. I think the news people around my house have her."

"Actually, sir, Child Protective Services have your child now."

"What?"

"You'll have to call them to have your questions answered," the officer said.

"Where is my daughter?"

"I'm not sure, sir." Then, after a pause, the woman on the phone said, perhaps covertly, "Why don't you turn on your television?"

Ted hung up.

And so Ted and the family turned on the television. There was Emily, her face not made up like the woman sitting beside her and so she looked wan and anemic, her eyes red and puffy from crying and her bottom lip quivering pitifully. There was another woman standing behind her and she wore a light blue shirt with a patch stitched onto her shoulder.

"Why did you run out here?" Barbie Becker from Channel 5 asked.

"I was scared," Emily said.

"What were you scared of?"

"I don't know. I want to go back to my mom," Emily said.

"But not your dad?" Barbie Becker asked.

"Yes, my dad too," Emily said.

"But you didn't say your dad."

Gloria moved closer to Ted on the sofa and took his hand. The coldness of his touch didn't seem to bother her. She held Perry around his waist. Ted swallowed hard, and as he did he wondered if he was actually producing saliva and if he was, where it was going, but his wondering was a way of avoiding the painful reality in front of him. His daughter's words and perhaps her perceptions were being distorted and so was his relationship with her.

"Can I go back to my house?" Emily asked.

"Let's ask the nice lady from Child Protective Services behind you," Barbie Becker said, turning her heavily made-up eyes to the woman. Ted studied her powdered face and darkly outlined eyes and thought she looked more dead than he.

The officer in the blue shirt with the patch cleared her throat when presented with the microphone, then said, "Actually, we've received some complaints that perhaps this girl has been abused and so we'll have to take her into custody until we can get the matter cleared up."

"So, little Emily here has been abused?" Barbie Becker said.

"I didn't say that," the officer said. "The matter has yet to be investigated." The woman put her hands on Emily's tiny shoulders and turned her away from the camera.

"There you have it," Barbie Becker said to the camera, her eyes staring right through the screen and into Ted's face. "A poor abused child, rescued from her living-dead father. I'm Barbie Becker, Channel Five."

Ted and Gloria didn't know what to say or do. Perry wanted to know where the woman, whom he considered a fireman, was taking his sister, but Gloria said only for him not to worry. Gloria asked Ted what they were going to do and he said he didn't know and then she started to cry. Ted decided to call Channel 5. Ted did call Channel 5 and in short order he was on the air live with Barbie Becker. The woman's voice was excited and thin, not quite a whine, but it grated on Ted's dead nerves, like a scratching across the sutures which held fast his head. He collected his breath and his composure and spoke to her as evenly as he could, finding as he attempted such calmness that he was indeed that calm.

"Our daughter ran from the house and we would like her returned home," Ted said.

"I'd love to help you," she said.

Ted could see her, sitting in a canvas-back chair, a bib clipped around her neck, an attendant standing by with a powder puff at the ready. He could hear her popping gum, not presently, but in her history, in the back of her mouth where all the answers to all the questions her high-school teacher asked her seemed to stall.

"I would. I would truly love to help," she said. "But, you see, I can't. Those Child Protective people have her."

"Where do they have her?"

"Oh, I can see her now. She's not twenty feet from me," Barbie Becker said.

"Help me," Ted said, but there was no begging in his voice. It was almost a command and it gave Barbie Becker momentary pause, but he could hear the effect evaporate immediately.

"If you help me," she said, softly. "Give me an exclusive interview and I'll see what I can do."

Ted tried to hear what was happening behind the woman over the phone, but his heightened senses failed him. Ted didn't need a lot of time to consider her deal; he wanted his daughter. "Okay," he said. "Can you have our daughter with you?" Ted listened to his use of the plural possessive *our*. In the past he would have been inclined to say *my* daughter and he wondered whether then it had been his unconsciously trying to dismiss Gloria or just base selfishness at the root of it.

"I believe I can manage that," Becker said.

"Good," Ted said. He hung up and looked at Gloria. "I told her

I'd talk to her, give her an interview. She said she'd try to get Emily back for us. Which one is Barbie Becker?"

"She's the one on in the morning," Gloria said. "The one with the hair, who used to do the traffic from the helicopter."

Ted nodded, but he still didn't know which one she was even though he'd just seen her on television talking to his child. "They all run together," he said.

"I'm hungry," Perry said.

"Come on, honey," Gloria said and led the boy away to the kitchen. "Let's see what we can find."

"Where's Emily?" Perry asked.

"She's on her way home," Gloria said.

* * *

Barbie Becker and the Channel 5 news team arrived unceremoniously, with a rather timid knock at the front door. Barbie Becker's hair had been several different colors through her television career and Ted remembered this as he recognized her in the foyer. Now her hair was red and it fought with her blond lashes and brows, but all of that was quieted by the brilliance of her smile, a hundred teeth, whiter than any teeth Ted had ever seen. He could not for a few seconds take his eyes away from her teeth, finding each one and then all of them collectively. He considered that he should be too embarrassed to smile in her wake, but of course he was in no mood to smile anyway.

"Mr. Street, I'm pleased to meet you," Barbie Becker said.

"Where's my daughter?" Ted asked.

"She's coming. I promise," Barbie Becker said.

The crew and Barbie Becker moved into the living room like a storm of activity, all talking their special technical talk, setting up lights and umbrellas and sound booms. Two men hovered around Barbie Becker like bees, patting down her brow and brushing her hair while she sat this way and that on the sofa, crossing and uncrossing her legs. Ted watched her, Gloria under one arm, Perry wrapped around his waist. He saw great sadness in Barbie Becker and then he was seeing more.

Barbie Becker is standing in front of a large bathroom mirror, over one of a pair of shell-shaped sinks, having just peeled off the layer of paint that is the face she is on television. Her skin appeared sallow, her eyes sunken and poorly defined, flesh sagging at her temples; she had added fifteen years and she looked at the woman she is on television every night, the woman the station and the networks no longer want, a woman looking every bit her age, skin soiled and wounded by years of makeup, eyes vacant from years of denial and lack of confidence. Her husband reads in the bed just beyond the door, in his pajamas. He is younger than she but is still aging. Because he is a man, however, his receding hairline counts for less than her sagging breasts, the padding around his waist is nothing compared to the cellulite on her thighs. She will want to make love, to hold him, but especially have him hold her, when she slides into the bed next to him, but he will continue to read his magazine, to turn pages while she lies there staring at the side of his face. She will think her feet are too big. She will touch his arm to hear him sigh, and wonder if he is still sleeping with that woman he met in Phoenix three years ago. She sees a new line around her mouth and remembers that crying does not help.

"Mr. Street," Barbie Becker said.

Ted looked at the woman's eyes.

"Come and sit beside me on the sofa," she said.

Ted walked away from Gloria and Perry. He glanced to the door, expecting to see his daughter. The cameras should have been making him nervous, would certainly have in past times, but they were not, though the crew and Barbie Becker, to a lesser degree, were keeping an extra inch or two distance from him, just far enough away that his gravity would not pull them into a terminal orbit.

"My daughter?" Ted said.

"She's coming," Barbie Becker said.

"We want to get a sound check," a man said.

"Say something," Barbie Becker said. "Say anything."

"There was a young man at Nunhead

Who awoke in his coffin of lead;

'It was cosy enough'

He remarked in a huff,

'But I wasn't aware I was dead.'"

The crew became completely quiet and Ted tossed a pained, puzzled glance to his wife, then said to all of them, "It just came out. How's the sound check?"

The sound man cleared his throat and said, "Fine."

A man wearing a headset and standing between the two cameras counted down from five and pointed at Barbie Becker.

"I'm Barbie Becker of Channel Five News and I'm here with a special, live, exclusive interview with Theodore Street, who yesterday shocked the world by sitting up at his own funeral. Thank you for allowing us into your home, Mr. Street."

Ted looked at the woman's eyes, ignoring the rolling cameras, and he talked to her. "If my daughter doesn't walk through that door in the next five seconds, there will be no interview and I'll choose another reporter to do this with."

"We'll be right back," Barbie Becker said to the camera.

"And we're out," the director said.

"We were live," Barbie Becker said to Ted.

Ted listened again to her words, then forgot them. "I want my daughter."

"Hal," she wailed to the director.

"I'm on it," Hal said and he had a cellular phone to his ear.

"I can't believe you did that," the anchor said to Ted.

Ted held her eyes again, sensing her nervousness but feeling no sympathy for her. "I'll do it again," he said. "Would you like to pack up now?"

"Are you threatening me?" Barbie Becker asked. "Because if you're threatening me, I'd like you to know that you're threatening the entire news media and therefore the very fabric of our society."

"Shut up, lady," Ted said.

"Get that camera on," Barbie Becker said sharply, her skinny finger pointing to the director.

"If it comes on, I'll say how you pine for attention from your husband and worry every evening before bed about that new wrinkle beside your mouth." Then Ted added, "It's not so sad to age."

"Do you want the camera on?" the director asked.

Barbie Becker raised her hand and shook her head.

"We've got to do something," the director said. "They're dying trying to fill air at the studio."

"What about his daughter?" she asked.

"They're having trouble finding her." The man grimaced as he said the words.

Ted stood up. He could sense not only Barbie Becker's concern for the airing of the interview, but her fear of what Ted could see. She threw him a sidelong glance as she rose to snatch the phone from the director's ear. In a stage whisper she said, "I don't care what it takes, you get that kid through that door now."

Ted knew that the bravado was for his benefit and he also knew that the front door was not about to open with his daughter coming in. He started picking up cable, unplugging couplings and handing the entrails of the equipment over to the crew.

"What's this?" Barbie Becker asked. "What are you doing?"

"When you have my child, come back," Ted said. He walked back to Gloria and hugged her, kissed her forehead. "Out, please," Ted said to them all.

The crew obeyed and so did Barbie Becker. She stopped at the bottleneck at the door and turned, her hair swinging in a deliberate way to communicate her displeasure. "You realize how humiliating this is for me," she said.

"Don't let yourself be humiliated the same way next time," Ted said. "I'll wait an hour before I call Channel Eleven."

Ted felt as though he had not exercised control in the situation, but that he had some. He was concerned for his daughter, concerned that a gulf was being made between the two of them, perhaps between all of them. He was more worried, however, by the fear he saw in Gloria's face. She was stunned and somehow, perhaps merely because she didn't know what to do, was allowing her dead husband to handle the matter, something he would never have been able to do when alive. And Perry. Perry was just floating, lost and probably so confused that no damage was being done, at least immediately, but Ted believed that if he could get Emily back into the house soon, they would all be all right.

Two hours passed, during which time Ted read novels he had read before but now seemed to understand more fully, finding more resonance and feeling a new joy in having marks on the page become meaning in the world. Gloria played a couple of board games with Perry. Outside, the television crews and reporters had diminished slightly in number. Ted turned on the television and saw news concerning other places, floods in Malaysia, tornadoes in Alabama, football games and imploded skyscrapers, but still there were periodic returns to the front of his house.

The phone rang and on the other end was Barbie Becker, her voice bright and cheery as if nothing had happened and she said, "We've got it all worked out. I told Child Protective Services that I mistakenly reported a situation of abuse and that I was sorry, but I was wrong and so Emily can be returned to you. Isn't that wonderful?"

"Did you make such a report?" Ted asked.

"What?"

"Were you the one who filed the complaint?" Ted's voice was even and did not betray any anger and for that very reason he knew that he sounded all the more threatening.

"No, it wasn't me," Barbie Becker said. Her lie hung like static over the wire for a brief, fat second and then she came back. "So, when are we on?"

"You may come in now," Ted said. "As long as my daughter is the first person through the door."

"We're coming now," she said. "You're really going to talk to me this time?" She made it sound as if Ted had been the problem with their first attempt at the interview.

"I'm really going to talk to you. Do you think you're ready, Ms. Becker?"

His question threw her and she was silent for a few fat seconds. "Yes, I'm ready."

* * *

Ted could hear the feet on the walk outside, the rattle of cameras, the dragging of coiled cord, and especially the wheezing of his daughter's lungs. She was not crying, but she had been and so the labored breathing. Beside her or behind her was Barbie Becker and she was telling the child that she was sorry, that she hadn't meant for her to be separated from her family and asking if she would "act nice" to her once they were inside the house, saying, "I really need this interview. It means the world to me. I might have a shot at the networks. Oh, why am I telling you, you're just a child."

As promised, the first person through the door was Emily, and Ted allowed her to dash past him to her mother. The gravity of the situation was driven home by the girl's uncharacteristic hugging of her little brother. Barbie Becker was next, asking if they were still on, obsequious and truckling instead of forward and bullish.

"I'm so sorry about the misunderstanding earlier," she said, taking Ted's left hand in her two and letting it go as quickly. Her face registered no surprise or displeasure at the touch of him, but she dropped it just the same. Ted stepped over and greeted Emily and she did hug him, but she kept her arms well away from his neck and his bare skin.

"Okay, let's get started," Barbie Becker said, pacing the carpet of the living room before settling into her same seat on the sofa.

Ted sat next to her. This time he was rigged up with a microphone clipped to his shirt. A wire led from the mike to a box that the sound man left on the sofa cushion by Ted's leg. The sound man asked Ted to move the microphone up on his shirt a couple of inches and he began to fumble with it and so Barbie Becker reached over to help him. Her hand touched his and Ted saw another flash of her life.

Ted watched as she sat in the front seat of a red Dodge Dart and lied to the man who would become her husband. His hands were clamped onto the steering wheel, his eyes locked on the lights of whatever city lay sprawled before them while he listened to Barbie Becker tell him that she was pregnant. She was in fact not pregnant and Ted knew in the scene as well as she that she was not pregnant and the lie fixed in place the life of the man sitting behind the steering wheel and Barbie Becker was satisfied. But Ted felt less interested in the scene itself than with where he was spatially in relation to it. He was not inside Barbie Becker's head, he was not the dashboard of the automobile, he was not the air around her, but he was there. He was there in much the same way he'd often felt he was throughout his life—unweighted, uncentered—but at least in this scene from this sad woman's life he understood what was going on. And as he came back to the voices and cameras aimed at him, he was all too aware of what was going on.

The red light of a camera flashed on. "I'm Barbie Becker of Channel Five News with an exclusive, live interview with the recently resurrected Theodore Street. Mr. Street, I'd like to thank you for allowing us into your home."

AMERICAN DESERT

Ted nodded to her, then, as a second thought, to the camera.

"My first question is simply, Are you dead?"

Ted looked at Barbie Becker, at her eyes, and saw a person who was not so unlike the person he used to be; having no sympathy for himself, he could find none for her. "Ms. Becker, I'm here talking to you. Could a dead person talk to you?"

"Well, I don't know," Barbie Becker said. "It is true that your head was severed from your body. We saw that on tape."

"I'll take your word for that," Ted said. "But I am indeed sitting here, talking to you, am I not?"

"So, you're alive then?" she asked.

"You tell me," Ted said, offering a smile, "if a man's head can be cut off and he can remain alive."

Barbie Becker leaned toward Ted and whispered, "Stop answering my questions with questions." Then, back to work, she said, "Your revival, if we can call it that, sparked a huge riot through the streets of Long Beach. What do you have to say about that?"

"I really didn't witness it. What was it like?"

Barbie Becker's neck muscles tensed into cords. "Stop it." Then, "How do you feel about all this attention?"

"Why did you lie to the police about my daughter?" Ted asked.

"Mr. Street," Barbie Becker complained.

"Are you a liar, Ms. Becker?" Ted asked.

Barbie Becker's face lost all color and whatever vacuum that was sucking in her pigment also pulled in her makeup and so she was left looking like a ghost, her mouthparts working to no discernible effect.

"You lied about my daughter, I know that, but what about other

85

lies? How did you explain to your husband that you weren't pregnant after all? Was Cindi Culler really sick the day you sat in for her twenty years ago, your first on-air job? How often do you lie to yourself? When you look into the mirror at night before bed, do you really believe those lines will be gone in the morning?"

The room was painfully silent and the dead air was just that, but no one was dashing to resuscitate it. Barbie Becker called upon her years in the business, her professionalism, her steely control and said, "You're mean," and dipped her face into her hands and cried.

"No, Ms. Becker, I used to be," Ted said. "I used to be just like you and I guess that's how it is that I see so much of you. I didn't intend to be cruel, only truthful. This truth thing is new to me." Ted looked at the camera, seeing behind it how excited the director was, how happy he was to zoom in on Ted's face. "I don't know if I'm dead or alive," Ted said. "I'm told pictures don't lie. I saw the picture of my head on the ground. But here I am. Perhaps the picture lied. Perhaps this picture is lying. Perhaps I'm not here talking to you at all. But I'm not lying. I'm not lying anymore. Please, leave me and my family alone. I'm asking the media to leave our house and I'm asking you to find your own lives."

"And cut," the director said. The room became filled with the sound of applause and Ted looked over to see Gloria beaming at him like she had never before. Barbie Becker was still holding her face and sobbing. Ted put a hand on her shoulder, but she jerked away from his touch and came up, staring at him with her face behind bars of running mascara.

"Don't touch me, you devil," she said. "You've ruined me."

Ted said nothing more to her, but removed his microphone and then walked over to Gloria and the children. He was, unlike everyone else in the room save Barbie Becker, not so charmed with his small and modest speech, but instead he was impressed by his capacity to feel such overwhelming and disparate things, his intense love of his family, his need for knowledge of their safety and his dread of the dangers which awaited them beyond the walls of their house.

BOOK TWO

CHAPTER ONE

IT USED TO BE that when one was caught sleeping with the wrong person or misappropriating public funds or dying and coming back to life, one could just move to another town and start over, maybe suffer a career and/or name change. Now, Ted thought, even if the media would leave him alone, his face was permanently etched in the minds of the entire world, a ceaseless, monotonous, insipid lodging in the public mind that appeared to have nothing but compartment after compartment for the storing of useless images and pointless, meaningless synaptic events.

The number of people making camp outside their house seemed to have diminished, but only slightly. That even one had grown tired and given up was encouraging.

While Gloria was upstairs putting the children to bed, Ted sat on the sofa in the living room staring at his death notice in the newspaper. There had been no obituary, only the sterile, no-frills public announcement offered by the funeral home, which really served more as an advertisement than anything else. At least they had spelled his named correctly. Ted gave a thought to going up and kissing the kids good night, but decided to let this day slip past. He could hear Gloria telling Perry "sweet dreams" the way she always did, followed by the sound of his door being shut, then the sound of his lamp being switched back on. Perry read at night and believed no one knew, but they all knew, even Ted, despite his general self-absorption.

Gloria came down the stairs and sat down beside Ted. She looked down at the open newspaper and he closed it. "Life's weird, isn't it?" she said. They looked at each other and laughed at her understatement. "Ted, I have to ask you something and I want you to tell me the truth."

"Okay."

"Where were you going when you had the accident?" Gloria was staring into his eyes as if she knew the answer, but was simply looking for confirmation.

"I was on my way to kill myself," Ted said. "I think. I thought that was what I was going to do."

"Oh." The fact that the answer had been expected made it no less painful to her. "Were you so unhappy?"

"I guess I was. But not with you." Ted thought about that. "That's not true. But my unhappiness with you was because of me. I just didn't like myself. I was unhappy with you because you made me face that fact."

"Ted," Gloria said, putting her hand on his.

"I'm a fuck-up, Gloria. Hell, I can't even die right." He laughed. "I couldn't make it to my own appointment with suicide and then when I died by mistake I couldn't stay dead. Look at what I've caused."

Gloria's eyes grew wet.

Ted heard his own words and noted the same pitiful voice he

had always despised and caught himself. He had reflexively slipped back into his old selfish, indulgent shell and it sickened him, but at least now he could spot it. He understood that evolution was labor. "I'm sorry, Gloria. That was the old me talking. I see a lot better now. I know that I love you. I always have. I've just been too weak to show it, to admit it. You know, I'm not a bad man, but I'm a lazy one."

"It's been hard the past few years," Gloria said.

"I'm sorry about that." Ted touched Gloria's hair and recalled when there had been no gray in it. "You know, I like the gray in your hair."

"You're joking."

He shook his head. "I do. It's sexy."

"I don't look old?"

"You look older. Don't you think you should?" Ted tugged at his collar and felt his stitches.

"You know it's not so bad having the phones unplugged," Gloria said. She snuggled up against her husband.

As she fell close, Ted remembered how terrified he had been during the days of his affair, how when Gloria had come near him, he would flinch or try to run, out of guilt no doubt, but more out of fear that she would be able to smell another woman, if not her perfume or facial astringent, then the scent of her body, her saliva, her vagina. And of course she could, did, every time. Only she'd never said anything, deluded herself, trusted her husband rather than her own senses.

Ted felt Gloria's eyes close. He was going to make it all up to her, going to make it up to the kids and himself if it took the rest of his life. Then it hit him. What was the rest of his life? Would he be alive forever or was he in fact already dead? Was he the equivalent of the beheaded chicken scurrying around the barnyard, propelled only by a storm of nervous impulses?

He remained on the sofa, not asleep but not awake either. His eyes were closed.

* * *

The next morning, Ted got down on his knees and plugged the phone into its jack behind the table in the foyer. It rang immediately and he watched it. He answered it and it was his sister. "Are you okay?" she asked, her voice stressed, if not shaking. She was talking to her dead brother.

It was a reasonable question and Ted felt no quarrel with her in his heart. "I'm good. Thanks for asking."

"So, what's going on?" she asked, an attempt at normal conversation.

"I don't know," was his honest and no doubt unsatisfactory answer.

"There are news people outside my building," she said.

"I'm sorry." He didn't know what to tell her. "Is Dad okay? Does he know about any of this?"

"He doesn't understand anything," she said. "Hey, the doctor told me a good one. The nice thing about Alzheimer's is you get to meet new people. Sweet, eh?"

"Listen, I'm going to try to get there soon. I'd like to see Dad and you. Would that be all right?"

"Yes."

. . .

The phone rang again and it was Hannah, Gloria's sister. "I've been trying to reach you guys. The phone just rang and then I drove over, but your house is surrounded and I couldn't get through. What the hell is going on? I saw you on television. Are you all right?"

"I think so. Gloria and the kids are okay." Ted knew that she must be very worried. "What about you?"

"My arm is broken," she said.

"I'm sorry."

"It happened in the riot."

"Let me get Gloria for you."

* * *

The next call was from a man with a high voice who said he was with the government, though he would not say which agency, not even after Ted pressed. "Just tell me where your office is," Ted said.

"I'm afraid I can't do that, sir."

"Then why are you calling?"

"We'd like to meet with you."

"How can I meet with you if you won't tell me where you are?"

"I can come to you."

"I don't think so."

"I think you should reconsider."

Ted looked at Gloria. She had been standing nearby through the conversation and had no idea what was being said. "Some government guy," he whispered to her.

"A few minutes of your time," the high-voiced man said.

Ted looked again to Gloria, shrugged and hung up.

"I'm going to unplug it again," Gloria said.

"Forget it," Ted said. "I'm sick of hiding out. How are we doing on food?"

"Not so hot."

Ted looked up the stairs, then to his wife. "Get the kids. I refuse to be held prisoner in our own house. We're going shopping."

* * *

Stepping through the door from the kitchen into the garage, Ted remembered the awful feeling he'd had when they'd first bought the house. It was a two-story mission-style, heavily wooded testament to middle-class values. It had at one time been a two-family dwelling, but it was now one single temple to the fifties. He'd hated it then, but was also proud that he'd been able to buy it. On some level, however, even his pride sickened him. He feared becoming "one of those guys" who always lived across the street, a piece of Americana, a simple, grease-needing cog in the machine. He had become what he'd vowed never to become and it had been so easy to become it; that was the worst part. Now, as he stepped into the dusty garage, he looked at the minivan they had found they couldn't live without, but even that didn't bother him. Now it was a symbol of the children, though people didn't use to need such things. He looked to Gloria and asked about the Lancia. "How badly was it damaged?"

"I don't know." She shrugged. "They towed it away. I didn't give it another thought. I think it was totaled."

"It doesn't matter," Ted said and he meant it. He had loved that car as a kind of lifeline to his past, connoting some stupid notion of a free existence. He had no need for that kind of sentiment now.

They climbed into the van and Ted hit the switch to open the garage door. It was much like the undocking of a space vessel, he thought. The light of the outside world was harsh but welcome and they rolled out slowly. The eyes of the news people found them and quickly they were pointing their cameras and flipping toggles, but none of them was ready for the Streets' simple act of driving away. Their support vehicles had become planted and now they were stranded at the house. There was a certain amount of satisfaction in seeing them so flummoxed, so lost to action. Ted drove across the lawn to freedom. The kids responded gleefully and for the first time in the past days things seemed like they might be on the mend, that this *familiar* trip to the grocery market might make them more familiar. Ted thought this while he tugged at the collar of his turtleneck and felt the slick sutures around his neck. There was some perverse comfort in the tactile confirmation of his present circumstances, a grounding that perhaps had been missing throughout his life.

At the market they parked in the lot the way people park in lots, locking up the car by habit and falling together in formation to make their way to the door.

Ted grabbed a cart and then let Perry push it. They made their way to the produce section while people steered a wide path and stared. The Streets could not help but feel the attention and so they clumped together and did not venture away to their favorite foods as usual. They studied the apples together, the bananas, the grapes, the lettuce, peas, squash. A clerk ducked behind the melons and slowly came up for a longer glimpse.

Emily was badly affected by the attention. She was shaking as she walked and at first pulled away when Gloria reached for her hand, then allowed the contact. Ted and Perry pushed the cart together.

"What are we going to do?" Gloria asked.

"Let's just go about our business," Ted said.

And so they did. They walked down the aisle of teas and coffee, Emily and Gloria taking the point. Past the heads of his womenfolk, down the long aisle and out the window, beyond the working-mouthed gawkers, Ted could see the gathering of news people in the parking lot.

"My God," Gloria said. The front of the store was filling with human bodies and cameras and lights and chaos. "Ted," she said, without looking back at him.

"I see," Ted said. "Just back up, all together. We're going to slip out the back. All right?"

"Daddy, I'm scared." Emily looked past her father down the aisle, then at the ceiling.

In spite of the current distress, the fact that Emily had chosen to call him Daddy was not lost on him. "It's going to be okay, honey. Come on, just pretend we're still shopping." He reached down and took her hand.

The family walked along the back of the store, past the dairy products and meats, a section that held some resonance for Ted. He made a note to himself to giggle about it later. Between the eggs and the meat was a swinging door with a round porthole of a window and Ted ushered his wife and children deftly through it.

The storeroom of the market was not as brightly lit as the sales area. In fact it was downright dim and made more dark by the stacks and stacks of brown cardboard boxes strapped to pallets. A couple of dirty, yellow forklifts sat quietly, side by side, like sentries. There was no one back there, no doubt because they were all out front trying to get a glimpse of the dead man instead of working.

"This way," Ted said, sensing which way was out. He was listening for street sounds which might give him a clue, but there was such a din—voices, music, metal scraping against metal, everything inside and out—inside his head that he could not distinguish a car horn from the scratching at a stubbly beard on a cameraman's face.

But there was noise closer to him, whisperings or searchings for breath that he could not make out. They were slowly moving between towers of pork 'n' beans and dry dog food when the voices became shouts, indiscernible, though soon his family's screams joined in. Ted could not see, but he felt cloth cover his face, his arms wrested behind his back. He felt a brief tug at his shirt and he knew that it was Perry, but soon his son's hands were gone. Ted was horizontal, his head engulfed in a sack, though this time still connected to his body and he was being carried by several people, big men by the feel of their arms and strength. Ted squirmed, twisted, afraid for his family. He called to them. He could hear Emily's voice and then Gloria's and Perry's calling to him, yelling, "No, no!" and, "Bring my daddy back!" and, "You put him down!" And then Ted was outside, feeling the warmth of the sun through the sack, smelling the diesel fumes of passing trucks, the rotting food in a nearby Dumpster. He was thrown onto a surface so hard his head bounced. He hoped it would stay attached. He was in a truck or a van, that much was certain, and when he heard the engine fire up he stopped kicking and tried to think what he should do. He tried to relax so that the thoughts would come. Ted listened; the people who had abducted him had not spoken even to each other yet and all he could hear was their labored breathing. The one nearest him wheezed deep in his chest.

"You should see someone about that asthma," Ted said, righting his body so that he was leaning against the wall.

"Shut up," a voice from forward in the vehicle said. "Shut up, you devil."

CHAPTER TWO

ONE THING BEING DEAD had taught Ted was that it didn't pay to struggle uselessly. And so he accepted the fact that he was blindfolded and bound and let his body go limp, feeling the bouncing of the tires, the right rear was a little low, smelling the sweat of his captors and the fumes of the exhaust. He could hear an exhaust tick. He could feel the temperature rise inside the truck, could feel the sun through the side window and knew from its movement over the course of an hour that they were headed east. They were probably at that moment passing the city of Riverside, sitting in its private bowl of smog. They kept going. Ted was sitting more comfortably now, his back having conformed to the wall of the van, his legs having adjusted to the lumpy carpet beneath him. They turned off the freeway. Ted could feel the curve of the off-ramp and the left turn that had them headed north, into the desert, probably somewhere around Morongo Valley, Desert Hot Springs or even farther east.

Hours had elapsed. There had been little talking the entire drive and only one stop for gas. There was at least one woman among the five of them and she spoke in clipped sentences.

"Stop here," she ordered. "Back in a minute," she said. "Gassed up," she said. "Too hot," she said. "Window down," she said. "Not breathing," she said. The observation about breathing concerned Ted and he moved his legs to quell their fears (?) that he might have expired. Again. "Turn here," she said. For all her two-word commands and observations, she did not appear to be the leader of the small band.

The leader was, Ted believed, driving the van. He spoke evenly and frequently, reminded all of them to remain calm. "When we get back to the compound we'll just give him to Big Daddy and he'll take care of everything. He'll take care of this devil."

Ted found himself worrying about Big Daddy and what might be in store for him. He did try to convince himself once or twice that he was already dead and therefore had nothing to fear, but the truth of the matter was, he had no idea whether he was planted in the world of the living or teetering on the edge of nonexistence. One nudge from Big Daddy and Ted might never see his family again.

"You can take the blindfold off him now," the woman said.

When Ted's eyes focused he was looking at a thick-shouldered woman with short sandy hair and dark eyes. She was sitting cross-legged in front of him, her back straight, her eyes boring into his face.

"Hello," Ted said.

"Devil," she spat at him.

"Where are we?" Ted asked.

"Never you mind that," a big man said. His face was in shadow as he sat in the passenger seat. "We'll ask the questions."

"Okay," Ted said. The more they tried to bully him, the calmer he felt and he remembered the advice he'd always heard about surviving quicksand, relax and swim out. So, he relaxed, and the more he relaxed, the more anxious his captors became and the more relaxed he became still, until they were nearly shaking and he was nearly asleep.

"Big Daddy's going to take you apart," said a wiry man from behind the woman. He shifted his position so that he could see out the windshield, avoiding Ted's eyes.

"Who is Big Daddy?" Ted asked.

"Who is Big Daddy?" The driver laughed. His voice was gravelly and resounded in his chest and though Ted couldn't see the man, he imagined that he was of considerable size.

"You didn't hurt my family, did you?" Ted asked. But of course his family had been hurt by his being taken. Perhaps.

"We'll ask the questions!" the big glaring man in the passenger seat shouted.

"Is Big Daddy his real name or is that some kind of title?" Ted asked.

"Big Daddy has a pipeline to Jesus," the woman said.

"Don't answer his stupid questions," the man in the passenger seat said to her.

"It doesn't matter, Gerald," she said. "Big Daddy's going to take care of him."

"My name is Ted."

The woman didn't say anything.

The van ground to a halt on loose gravel and sand. The door opened and Ted breathed in the dust, the smell of a fire, cow manure. He looked across the dry yard to a long building. An owl beat its wings across the violet sky. The man who had been driving did have a large chest, but he was short, very short, though easily bigger around than Ted. The short man stepped close to Ted, looked at his bound hands and then up at Ted's face.

"You don't scare me," the short man said.

"Good," Ted said. "I wouldn't want to scare you. If I scared you, you might try to hurt me."

"Shut up," he said. Then, as if some power grabbed him, he closed his eyes, turned his face to the night sky and began to pray, his words fast and running together:

"LordJesusIbegyouforstrengthinthefaceofthisdevilhereinfront ofmewhathashisheadsewedonlikethedevilhesurelyisJesusGodChrist almightywhatmadetheheavensandtheearthandalltheanimalsand eventhepoliticaldogswhathuntusdownlikethelambsweisintheir blackhelicopterswhileweGodfearingwhitepeoplehideoutinthe desertawaitingourtimetostrike."

He paused and sucked in a breath.

"LordJesusGodalmightyinheavenwithyourdaddyandyour selfandtheHolyGhosttheDivineTrinityLordLordLordkeepmesafe fromthedeathinfrontofme."

Ted stood looking at the man and when he stopped praying and looking at the sky and was again looking at Ted, Ted said the only thing he could think to say, which was, "Wow."

Ted's expression of at least some kind of awe was not well received and resulted in the short man's barking out the order, "Kick his devil's butt and get in to see Big Daddy." Between the time of the order and someone's acting on it, Ted was able to see the sad, short man, all four feet eight inches of him furtively trying on pants in the boys' husky section in Sears, the pained and angry expression when asked if he needed help by a salesperson and when pointed to by innocently brutal children trying on similar garments.

The man whose name was Gerald kicked Ted's rear end not once but twice and though Ted winced at each coming blow, neither blow was painful. It wasn't that Ted was numb, without tactile sensation; he sensed the kicks, but the strikes to his body did not hurt him. He only felt them. Ted was pushed and dragged across the baked-hard ground by Gerald and the woman, the short man leading the way, the other men having already disappeared.

At first the voices crying out in unison seemed to be chanting, but then Ted heard it as singing. There were about twelve or so voices at work inside the nearest structure, cranking out a slow rendition of "Michael, Row Your Boat Ashore," a song which Ted had long associated with Christians, but had no idea why. He'd never been able to figure out who Michael was or what was awaiting him on shore. He wanted to cry out Who was Michael?

Inside, there were indeed about twelve people, singing and seated in a circle around a very round man wearing a red blazer held fast with a wide black belt and a silver buckle. A look from the sparkling eyes of Big Daddy halted the singing and they turned tutti to regard Ted at the door. Big Daddy did not rise but sat there, his huge belly swallowing most of his lap. He stroked his long, white beard and seemed to be measuring Ted, looking him up and down, finally issuing a hum of sorts which caused his disciples to all stand. His shock of white hair was unruly and stuck out from his head like a halo. He pointed a fat finger at Ted and said, "Bring him to me." His voice was surprisingly mellifluous and for a second Ted wanted to hear him sing. But the fat finger was pointing and the hands on Ted's back were pushing and soon he was just three feet from the black-booted leader.

"I'm Big Daddy," he said.

"I'm Ted."

"Dead Ted," he said. "Dead Ted."

Then the room was filled with chanting. "Dead Ted, dead Ted, dead Ted, dead Ted, dead Ted, dead Ted."

Big Daddy stopped his sponges with a raised hand, then said to them, "Sponges, behold before you a symbol of our Lord's power. That he has allowed us the strength and resolution to capture this devil must surely be seen as a miracle to any child of God, whether he know he be a child of God or not. Our Lord and Masterful Savior, Godalmighty, who art in heaven, thank *You!* for delivering unto us this fallen being, this flesh carved from the flesh of your fallen one, Satan. Look upon the devil, children, see him for what he is, power-less in the face of a true soldier of God."

Ted leaned close to Big Daddy and said, "I have to pee."

"You what?" Big Daddy asked.

"I have to pee," Ted repeated. He was perhaps even more sur-prised at his statement than Big Daddy. This was the first such urge to pee that Ted had felt since losing his head on Ocean Boulevard and for it to come at a time like this was more peculiar, to say the least. The absurdity of his having said this to Big Daddy on the heels of the pronouncement about being a true soldier of God caused what Ted felt to be a hint of a smile to form at one corner of his mouth, but he fought that off and offered to the zealot as earnest a look as he could muster.

Big Daddy, on his part, could not have looked more disappointed.

Perhaps the devils of his imagining did not need to urinate, but kept their waste and filth inside them to fester into even more foul evil, or perhaps it was simply that he saw such a human request as a diminishing of the enemy he was holding up before his wide-eyed followers and therefore diminution of his own power and message.

"Mister Mander!" Big Daddy called out and Gerald from the van appeared at the ready. "Take this demon to the toilet and stay with him." Big Daddy looked at his disciples and warned: "But do not look at his organ nor his excretions directly. Observe them, if you must, through the safety of the mirror."

The congregation oohed and aahed, amazed that Big Daddy should not only have thought to protect Gerald from a head-on sighting of demonic waste, but that he possessed such knowledge about how to safely witness the evil. Big Daddy had recovered nicely and salvaged some face.

Gerald walked Ted by a pair of identical, blond twin women near the mouth of a corridor. They walked past three doors and turned left into a moderately large bathroom. A shell-molded sink sat beneath a counter-length mirror. The tub was a cheap vinyl inset, with a yellow nonslip mat on its bottom and no shower curtain. The toilet was black and looked relatively clean. The counter was littered with crocheted doilies of pink, yellow and green and a basket of similarly colored soaps.

"Go ahead," Gerald said, looking at Ted in the mirror. When Ted looked into the mirror back at his eyes, the man turned away.

"I'll need my hands," Ted said and showed his bound wrists.

Gerald groaned, then untied the knot. "Hurry up."

Ted unzipped his trousers and began to pee. He watched himself and was saddened to find that in the black bowl of water he was unable to see the color of his urine. He could hear Gerald's breathing catching in his throat as well as his accelerated heartbeat.

"Do you have to go?" Ted asked, zipping his pants.

"No. You done?"

Ted flushed and stepped to the sink to wash his hands, an action which caused Gerald to step back and register surprise. "Devils are actually very clean," Ted said. "You'd be surprised how fastidious Satan himself is. He won't talk to anybody until he's washed his face in the morning."

Gerald was shaking now.

Ted stood straight, his hands wet and hanging like a surgeon's, and looked for a towel. Gerald grabbed a frilly pink rag from the rack and tossed it into Ted's chest, told him again to hurry up. Ted looked at Gerald's red, tired eyes and detected the slightest trace of whiskey deep in his mouth.

"Are you all right?" Ted asked.

"Let's go."

"I'm really no devil," Ted said.

Gerald opened the door and stepped aside to allow Ted to pass through. They walked back down the corridor and into the main room, where Big Daddy sat with his boots off and was having his feet massaged by the twins. The fat man indicated for Gerald to sit Ted down in a folding metal chair facing him. He moaned at some favorable pressure and then looked at Ted. "God has blessed me with good-smelling feet," he said. "It's not that they do not stink, but they actually smell good. Don't they, twins?"

"Yes, Big Daddy," the twins said.

. . .

Ted saw Big Daddy as a boy. He was a fat little boy and he was running around a suburban yard, the trees just more than saplings and
the lawn near death. "Come on inside, Little Daddy," the boy's
mother called to him. Little Daddy waddle-ran on his tiny, good-
smelling feet across the yard, through the back door and into the
kitchen where his fat mother stood at the stove and his fat, white-
haired father sat at the table, his hands tented in front of him preparing for the pre-meal prayer.

"Sit down, Little Daddy," his father barked. Then when the boy
was seated, his father stared at him and said, "Did you wash your
stinkin' hands before you sat at this Christian table, boy?"

Little Daddy made to move quickly from the table, casting a
glance his mother's way, only to find her back fixed to both of them,
when his father caught him by his hair.

"I don't care if your feet smell like perfume, you little heathen,
you will not defile this Christian table with your filth! Do you read
me, you little peckerwood piece o' shit?"

Little Daddy winced and some of his hair gave to the pulling.
"Yes, Big Daddy," the boy said.

"Now, go wash yourself," the man said and threw the boy
headfirst toward the doorway to the rest of the house.

Little Daddy's mother smoothed her apron and turned to set a
bowl of mashed potatoes on the table.

"Hurry up!" his father shouted.

But the boy slipped and caused a stack of *South Bend Tribunes*
which were piled on a stool by the door to fall over. He cringed even
before he heard the squeaking of his father's chair's feet against the

linoleum, tried desperately to collect the newspapers back into their former structure. The first blow was accompanied by a scream from the boy's mother's throat, the scream serving oddly to abate the sting of his father's belt across his back. At least, and her face showed it all so clearly, his mother cared enough to scream, if not to stop it. The belt kept coming, the stinging sliding into numbness, though there were no further screams from his mother. He felt his back rip open in the place where it had been opened a few days earlier, felt his striped shirt sticking to the blood, felt his father's breath by his ear when the man leaned close and said, "I beat you so you'll be a good, God-fearin' man. I hope you appreciate that, boy."

"I do, Big Daddy, I do," Little Daddy said.

* * *

"Carlos," Big Daddy said to the short man who had been driving the van. "I'm hot. Have somebody fetch a pail of water so the twins can wash my feet." Big Daddy looked at Ted. "Nothing cools you down like cool water on your feet."

Carlos sent a skinny man with a sleeveless shirt and a tattoo of a Volkswagen on his forehead to fetch the water.

"God has blessed me as sure as anything," Big Daddy said to Ted. "You can tell your devil that, when I send you back to fiery hell. But I"—now he was addressing his sponges—"I am going to heaven and all who follow me shall indeed follow me into the kingdom of the LordJesusGodalmighty. *Forsitan ad hoc aliquot condiciones pertineant.*" The disciples chanted amens and made worshipping sounds. "So, you see, you don't frighten me, devil."

The man returned with the water from the kitchen and set the pan and rags between the twins. The women wet his feet.

"I'm not going to kill you yet, however," Big Daddy said. "I want to show you around first. I want you to take a full report back to your master. And to show you just how Christian I am, I will show even you, devil, kindness and love. Are you hungry after your journey?"

Ted shook his head.

"But I'm sure you're tired. Cynthia, you and Gerald, take our question to his cell, rather room. Make him comfortable. Give of yourself."

The woman from the van and Gerald stationed themselves on either side of Ted and escorted him out into the yard and across it. The night was much cooler now and though the drop in temperature registered in Ted's perception, he was in no way made uncomfortable by it. Cynthia, however, was without a jacket and her bare arms showed goose bumps in the moonlight. They walked past a barn and to a small shed with one barred window. Cynthia switched on the single bulb by pulling the chain that dropped from it in the middle of the room. The cot was narrow but made neatly with one flat pillow and an olive drab blanket folded at the foot. Gerald stood by the door, facing the night.

"This is it," Cynthia said.

"Thank you," Ted said. "What if I have to pee?"

"There's a bucket in the corner," she said. She was harder than Gerald, her jaw set in an exaggerated way, almost an underbite. Ted could hear her teeth grinding away in her head.

"Thanks again," Ted said.

The door was closed and Ted was left to sit on the cot. He thought of Gloria and the children.

CHAPTER THREE

GLORIA DIDN'T WANT TO talk to the police, but she had to. There were a lot of things she'd had to do lately that she would have preferred not to. She'd had to make that drive to the morgue, had to view her husband's head in that stainless steel bowl, had to make funeral arrangements with her children fidgeting in the stale coffin showroom, had had to watch her ostensibly dead husband become undead. Most difficult of all, she'd had to hold her family together. But through all this, including the needlesome close re-gard of the likes of Barbie Becker, she'd learned she could depend on Ted. And now he was gone. She couldn't help wondering, no doubt, whether things would have been better if her husband had remained extinguished through the supposed last ceremony of his life.

The precinct station was not busy the way Gloria thought it would be. There was a man dressed as a woman sitting against the far wall of the large room; he had the biggest Adam's apple she had ever seen, standing out from the thirty feet that separated them. The transvestite stared at Gloria and the children as if he knew them and it dawned on Gloria that he probably did, probably had seen them on television or in the newspaper. Gloria was sitting beside the iron desk of a thick-necked, ex-Marine detective named Tara Benoit.

"That lady has a mustache," Perry whispered to his mother, then squeezed himself closer to her when Detective Benoit glanced at him.

"You say your husband was abducted," Benoit said, her voice not so deep for a woman but lost somewhere back in her throat.

"He *was* abducted. Two hundred people saw it happen," Gloria said. She looked at the trace of hair on the woman's lip and then at the detective's hair; it fell about the woman's ears to her neck, but sat atop her head like an aubergine beret.

"They witnessed the abduction?"

"Well, no, we were trying to slip out the back of the market to avoid the news people and they took my husband." Gloria squeezed tighter the children who were on either side of her.

Emily did not look at the policeman, but out the window beyond her, into the thick brown haze she knew to be the sky.

Another detective came over, leaned close to Benoit's ear, whispered something, then walked away laughing. Benoit didn't laugh, in fact looked unfamiliar with or incapable of laughter. "Do you know who took him?" Benoit asked.

"No."

"Was it the news people?"

"No, it wasn't them," Gloria said. "At least, I don't think it was news people."

"Did you see their faces?" Benoit asked. She sipped from a can of diet cola. "Can you describe them? Were they short or tall, men or women, dark or light hair?"

"No," Gloria said, flatly. "I don't know."

"What did you see?" Benoit asked Perry, leaning forward and showing him her lip hair.

Perry could not find it in himself to talk to her. All of the excitement was working on him and against him, his little hands trembled.

Benoit put the question to Emily.

"I didn't see anything," Emily said. "I just heard shouting and then my dad was gone."

Benoit nodded and typed into her terminal. "Name is Theodore Street," she said as she entered the information. "Height?"

"Just under six feet," Gloria said. "You've seen my husband on television."

"Weight?"

"One sixty, I guess."

"Any identifying marks?"

Gloria was growing steadily more impatient, her foot starting to tap. She said, "He has a scar which runs completely around his neck. He's all stitched up."

Benoit typed.

"His head was recently severed from his body, but has since been reattached."

Benoit typed.

"There is a pronounced and noticeable lack of bodily sound and function." Gloria shook her head. "My God, you know who the hell we're talking about." Gloria took a second to privately object to her choice of the word *hell*, she not knowing whether Ted had been there briefly or was visiting there presently. She and the children were certainly living through a version of it.

Benoit typed.

"What are you typing?"

Benoit typed.

Gloria stood and started away with the children.

"We're not quite done," Benoit said.

"We're done," Gloria said.

* * *

As Perry was following his mother out of the station, he saw the smile of a young officer and returned it. He looked at the revolver on the man's hip, the shining blue-black metal, so clean-looking and polished and neat and he wondered, at his young age, having never broken a bone, what it would feel like to die.

* * *

Ted's dream made no pretensions to being anything but a dream, however painstaking the realistic rendering was. Gloria and the children, Ted's father and Barbie Becker all done up in red, sat on wooden bleachers, seven rows up in a line of twenty, watching as Ted played volleyball on the beach below them. Ted's teammate was the president of the United States, who was dressed in red, white and blue Speedo trunks. Together they stood on the opposite side of the high net from Big Daddy and a man named Vernon Howell. Big Daddy's belly was flopping over his red trunks and his meaty legs shook like jelly as he tried futilely to run and hit the ball only to wind up the target of Howell's shrill complaints.

"Run, Mister Fat-ass," Howell said. Howell was medium in every way, sickly average, unforgettable because of his absolute forgetta-bility.

"Screw you, Mister Retardo," Big Daddy said.

"Don't call me that," Howell barked.

"Retardo," Big Daddy said.

"You're just jealous," Howell said, running a thumb around the inside rim of his trunks.

"Why would I be jealous of you?" Big Daddy said.

"Because I'm chosen," Howell said. "Because I took fifty with me. Because I'm a martyr. Because I am Jesus Christ."

"I'm Jesus Christ," Big Daddy said, stepping his fat form closer to Howell and looking him in his painfully average face.

The president said, "Come on, let's play. It's our serve."

"You leave us alone," Big Daddy said.

"Yeah, back off," Howell said. "Call off your dogs! Call off your dogs! Call off your dogs!" he chanted.

The president served, hitting the ball high into the air. The ball went higher and higher until it was just a speck against the sky. Ted looked over at his family and watched them as they watched the trajectory of the volleyball. Higher and higher. Then the speck became fixed, hanging in a position in space for what seemed a long time before starting to come down.

"It's a trick," Howell said and he produced a pistol from his trunks. "Let me shoot you," he said to Big Daddy. "It's our only way out."

"Shoot yourself first," Big Daddy said.

Ted looked at the bleachers to see Gloria grab the children and squeeze their faces into her sides. Ted's father was still watching the approaching ball. Barbie Becker was taking notes.

"The ball is coming," the president said and adjusted himself in his tight swimwear. "It's coming. Get ready."

Howell put the muzzle of the pistol to his head and pulled the trigger, his head splitting like an egg carton, his blood finding the sand and the ample front of Big Daddy, his brain more sliding than flying from his cranium and seemingly pulling him off balance so that he fell on his back to the sand.

"He's dead," Big Daddy said as if he hadn't expected it. Looking through the net to the other side, he said, "And you killed him."

Ted's father made a noise and the volleyball landed with an impressive, ground-shaking thud just out of bounds.

"Daddy! Watch out!" Perry called out.

Ted turned to see that Big Daddy had pried the pistol from Howell's dead hand and was pointing it across the net at him. The president ran for cover. Ted faced the gun and felt unafraid. Big Daddy squeezed off a round and though the report bothered Ted's ears, as did the screams of his family, the bullet did no harm. The projectile passed through his body and left him standing with no discernible ill effects. Ted was alive, very much alive. He fell to his knees and cried.

* * *

When Ted awoke it was still dark outside. A rooster crowed somewhere. He didn't like the sound. Recalling the dream did not bother him greatly, if at all, but the thought of it as a dream made him remember a friend he'd had in graduate school. His friend had been a pretentious sort, fond of quoting that insipid story from Zhuangzi about the man who dreamed he was a butterfly dreaming he was a man.

"So you see Zhuang Zhou's dilemma," Alfred would say back then, puffing on his pipe. "The question becomes for all of us, 'Are we dreaming or are we dreamt?' "

Ted had heard it all before, but still was unwilling to tell Alfred to just shut up. Besides, he was busy contemplating whether he should go through with his wedding to Gloria.

"This could be a dream you're having right now," Alfred said. "Imagine that. I'm just a character in your dream."

"Alfred, my dreams are better than this," Ted said. It was one of the few immediate responses of which Ted was genuinely proud. Most of his heady retorts presented themselves to him some time after being needed, leaving him to think, *If only I'd said that then.* His life had been full of those delayed responses and it was a great sadness for him, he viewed it as an uncorrectable inadequacy. But lately, as the only dead guy around, he'd been more disposed to the utterance of what he, in the past, would have called gems. He stood and walked from his bed to the window, looked out at the dark yard and wondered if his dreams were ever better than reality.

* * *

The following morning, Cynthia and Gerald came to the shed to collect Ted. He was ready to go, having washed his face in the small basin and put on the clean tee-shirt which had been left for him on the room's only chair. Unlike his carefully chosen turtleneck the tee-shirt did not conceal the sutures around his neck and so when Cynthia and Gerald opened the door, they were a little bit taken aback. They were in fact horrified and had to be reminded by Ted that they were supposed to be on their way to Big Daddy. "Take me to your leader," he said, only half humorously.

They kicked across the dusty expanse of yard toward the house, the two disciples keeping a markedly wider distance between themselves and their captive than they had the previous day. Several chickens pecked at the ground near a windmill and a little spotted dog carried a dead something with his head held high. Again there was singing coming from what Ted took now to be the main or central house of the compound. "Michael, row your boat ashore/Hallelujah!" they sang.

The sidelong glances of the singing disciples graduated to full-blown stares as they too saw Ted's neck for the first time. The music sputtered and faded into courtroom muttering.

Big Daddy, to his credit, did not miss a beat, but launched into prayer. "Our dear, sweet, forgiving JesusChristGodalmighty, please protect us from this demon standing in our worship chamber. Thank you for the strength you have given me to shield my flock from the evil of the world. This crusty-necked subject of Lucifer shall see your blinding light, shall hear of your power and glory and shall feel the wrath of goodness against the sick evil of Satan's hell. Who knows what evil lurks even here in the hearts and minds of men?"

"*Umbra scit,*" Ted said.

The Big Children, as Ted had suddenly thought of them, cringed and drew back as if he had spoken Satan's foreign tongue at them.

"That was a joke," Ted said.

"I'm sure it was," said Big Daddy and he, with the help of the twins, hoisted his girth from his chair and stepped toward Ted. "I should simply kill you where you stand." The disciples muttered approval. "But I have things to show you, things I will need for you to report back to your evil master." He stared into Ted's eyes for a few seconds, then barked, "Come with me."

* * *

Ted's father sat in a bentwood rocker in his private room in the nursing home in Baltimore. The front of his white shirt was stained with Tabasco, one of the orderlies having determined that the old man liked his eggs "spiced up." He sat there and he rocked. His daughter brought in the *Time* magazine with Ted's picture on the cover and put it on the tray beside him. Ted's father did not know who the woman sitting on the blue-cushioned chair beside him was, though somehow he knew that she no longer cried every time she came to visit. He looked at the face on the magazine and he said, "Ted, there's something on your neck."

* * *

Big Daddy was standing close to Ted and together they watched the disciples sitting at long tables, eating from red plastic plates. The bulbs suspended from the ceiling on cords were lighted but to no effect, as the large windows let in lots of sunshine. The room was actually cheery and the mood was reflected by Big Daddy, who was dressed in a red sleeveless tee-shirt, red shorts and his patent leather over-the-calf boots.

"Look at them eat," he said. "They eat, but not like me." He patted his belly and smiled. "I am the ravenous bird." He watched Ted as if for a reaction. "You know, 'Calling a ravenous bird from the east, the man that executeth my counsel from a far country?' "

Ted smiled to himself, then asked, "So, you think of yourself as Cyrus?"

"What? No, I'm the ravenous bird," Big Daddy said. "I am a bird for God, a winged angel of the LordJesusGodalmighty."

"A bird?" Ted said.

Big Daddy was annoyed and covered it by saying, "Do you remember when those cosmonauts said they saw the angels?"

"No."

"It was back in eighty-five. The Russians were in space and they looked out the window and saw angelic beings. Well, I saw them too." Big Daddy looked softer for a second, his eyes even closed, showing his splendidly long, white lashes.

Ted believed that the man believed he had seen angels. "You saw them?"

"Yes."

"Where did you see them?"

"In Death Valley. Can you believe that? In Death Valley."

"Where in Death Valley?" Ted asked. "In Echo Canyon? At Dante's View? On Funeral Peak?" Ted guessed, dredging up places he knew in Death Valley.

Big Daddy shook his head. "I saw them sitting in the snack shop in the Furnace Creek Inn. Six of them. Six angelic beings."

"What did they look like?" Ted asked.

"Not like you," Big Daddy said, his voice coming back, his edge returning, his eyes opening fully. He smiled at Ted and said, "Come, I want to show you things."

Big Daddy's minions were again engaged in song, now singing

the *Michael* song in a minor key a fifth higher than before as a kind of after-prayer for their meal and all straining the muscles of their eyeballs to catch furtive glimpses of Ted and his neck. Ted looked at Big Daddy's pale blue eyes and saw that somehow they had grown weaker since last night and he wondered if the presence, or simply the perceived presence, of the demon was sucking the energy out of him. Ted felt compassion, and at the same time of course disgust and repulsion, when he considered the pathetic, fat zealot. If Ted was indeed the devil, and who was he to say that he wasn't, then he would be the opponent of this man's god. Ted looked away from Big Daddy's eyes so as not to suck away his ability to merely stand and said, "Remember when David said to the sons of Zeuriah, 'What right do you have to play opponent against me?'"

"That's from the Book of Samuel," Big Daddy said. He might have been literal minded, but he knew his Bible and he believed that Ted's knowing the Bible was only further evidence of his being in league with Satan, because only a devil could know the holy book so well. Big Daddy looked at Ted with renewed energy, generated by fresh dread, mistrust and hatred. "Do you know the Book of Isaiah?"

Ted's education was serving him well, but to his detriment and possible harm. Still, he said, "Yes."

"Of course you do," Big Daddy said. "Of course you do."

Big Daddy led the way out the door and through the brown dust and heat, his black boots whitening more with every step until they were the same color as his legs. Gerald followed them, but not too closely, though Ted could hear the man's breathing.

. . .

Big Daddy's little man, Gerald, had made a trip to Israel when he was twenty-three, after dropping out of junior college and taking a job as a welder's assistant for two years and then as a guy who did front-end alignments at a Midas shop in El Paso. When he got to Israel all he could do from the time he stepped off the plane was worry about eating, afraid of being a glutton. He would go for days without a bite, then eat everything in sight. He too considered himself the "ravenous bird" and he too thought literally, thinking himself a dove for the Lord. He could not get over the fact that Mount Zion turned out to be little more than a mound and he predicted that when the time came, when the day of reckoning arrived, that God would cause a geological event to alter the size of the hill. While camping under the very sky the baby Jesus had looked up at from the manger, Gerald dreamed he was having a discussion with Ellen White and the sister was dressed in the finest, whitest religious cloaks of the nineteenth century.

"I have been to a world that has seven moons," Sister White said and she touched Gerald's face.

"You're an angel," Gerald said. "But where are your wings?"

"Angels don't have wings, my sweet child," she said. "What people think are wings is really only the light from the spaceship. The ship travels by the refraction of light. 'The chariots of God,' Gerald, 'are twenty thousand, even thousands, of angels.' "

"Oh," said Gerald.

"Read the Book of Isaiah, chapter six, verses one through four," she said.

"Yes, ma'am," Gerald said and when he opened his eyes and left the dream, he was hungry. He ate his way back to Tel Aviv and onto the airplane and back to the States and found Big Daddy in a little storefront church on Crenshaw in Los Angeles. Big Daddy told Gerald it was okay to eat, that it was okay to be afraid, that he didn't have money because the devil didn't want him to have money, that it was okay with LordJesusGodalmighty if he didn't have money and that he, Big Daddy, would channel the Lord's love from heaven, through his chubby body and good-smelling feet right into the God-fearing soul of Gerald Mander, the lost and wondering Gerald Mander.

* * *

"This is Bunker Number One," Big Daddy said, stopping at the entry to what Ted saw as a tornado shelter, double doors laid at a thirty degree angle to the ground and raised about three feet. Gerald stepped in front of them and pulled open the doors, releasing musty but cool air.

"After you," Big Daddy said, gesturing for Ted to climb down into the shelter.

Ted did. The steps were concrete and lights were already burning inside, perhaps triggered by the opening of the doors, like a refrigerator—and like a refrigerator, because it was underground, the shelter was cool.

"I would tell you to watch your step," Big Daddy said. "But I don't care if you fall." He laughed and commented to Gerald simply by looking at him.

Ted laughed with them and that gave them pause.

The shelter was very large, lighted by long rows of fluorescent lamps suspended from the drop panel ceiling. Ted estimated that the back wall was nearly one hundred feet away and the room was forty feet wide easily, but the most striking thing was that the entire space was filled with cannons, old cannons, clean cannons, fat and skinny cannons. Ted looked at Big Daddy as if to say, "What now?"

"What do you think?" Big Daddy asked.

"Cannons," Ted said.

"Lots of cannons," Big Daddy said. He looked lovingly at his weapons. He stepped to a group of four identical guns. "This is a German breech-loading siege cannon with a five-inch bore. It's on a field carriage instead of a naval carriage, but it works just fine that way." He stepped down the line. "And this, this is a Civil War, U.S. Army six-pounder with a smooth bore. A handsome gun, don't you think?"

"Why do you have these?" Ted asked.

"I have them because they still work and because nobody expects me to have them. I've been collecting them for years and nobody can trace a single gun, a single shell, a single ball. This one is the oldest, but nothing is dated after 1920. Beautiful, isn't it? The idea, I mean."

Ted followed the man down the aisle.

"I've got twelve of these," he said. He uncovered a shiny gun, narrower than the cannons. "This is a forty-five-caliber Lowell battery rapid-fire gun on a field carriage. Of course it's crank operated."

"Why do you have these things?" Ted repeated.

"For the war that's coming, the war against evil, against you, against the government, against the black helicopters." He twirled his fat body around as if dizzy from enjoying his toys. "I've got Hotchkiss five-barrel rapid-fire revolving machine guns and Gatling machine guns and three-inch steel-muzzled rifled cannons and you know what? They'll kill you as dead as an M-16. Just as dead, dead, dead. Right, Gerald?"

"Right, Big Daddy," Gerald said.

"Dead is dead," Big Daddy said.

"So they say," Ted said. The black, brass and chrome shimmer of the guns was in some way beautiful—perhaps for their ancientness they looked less harmful, even quaint—but as Big Daddy had pointed out, they were not. Ted imagined agents of the ATF and the National Guard almost laughing as they saw these guns lining the ridge in front of the compound, only to taste suddenly the cordite or ballasite or whatever aged blasting gelatin the shells contained.

"How did you get these things?" Ted scratched his head.

"They're guns," Big Daddy said as if that were an answer. "Guns are easy to get. Especially old guns that nobody cares about. But I love them. I love their simplicity. I love the craftsmanship. Look at the tooling on this barrel." He ran his hand along the length of the rifled cannon.

Ted asked, "What good are they down here?"

"Oh, we can get them topside in plenty of time," Big Daddy said. "I'll know they're coming before they know they're coming." He rocked back and forth on his heels. "I've also got two hundred and fifty Whitney Navy revolvers and seventy-two Pettingill Army revolvers."

"How old are they?" Ted asked.

"Eighteen-sixties. I've even got seventeen cases of Confederate Perry carbines. Fifty-two-point-seven groves caliber."

"Will they fire?"

"Oh, yes," Big Daddy said. "The weapons which once cut this land in two will do so again. But we also have newer guns. We have 1914 English Enfield rifles and Austrian Mannlicher rifles. Killing is killing, whether it's slow or fast. In fact, slow is better, gives the heathens a chance to find the LordJesusGodalmighty and repent. And who knows, if somebody standing near the muttering, praying, dying man hears his pleas to the Lord then maybe he will be moved to lay down his arms and find the Light. Because God knows we're not laying down our arms. We are the soldiers in His army until the spaceships come to take us to the Holy City. Are you getting all of this?"

Ted nodded. What Ted was getting was that somehow this *man of God*, who seemed a demon himself, considered Ted the devil. Ted felt the man's need to kill in order to affirm his own life and to give his existence meaning. So, he did again the only thing he could think to do, the only thing that made sense. He nodded.

CHAPTER FOUR

GLORIA'S SISTER WAS THE only one in the room who was not pacing. Gloria, Emily and Perry were single file wearing a trail in the tan carpet. Hannah, who had always been fond of birthdays, especially her own, felt no compunction saying, in midst of all the working of feet, "Isn't anyone going to wish me a happy birthday?" With a marker she signed her own name to her cast.

"Happy birthday," Gloria said without breaking stride, but managing a sidelong, cutting glance at her sister. Her brown eyes had grown weaker and she felt she was having to attend to focusing more than ever. She watched her feet strike the nap of the rug.

"You always told Mom and Dad that Ted was going to do something in this world," Hannah said, lighting a Pall Mall and shaking out the match. "I wish they could be here now to see what he finally turned out to be. Did he make full professor? No. Did he win an award? No. Did he turn into Frankenstein in front of the whole world?"

"That's enough." Gloria walked into the kitchen, her children behind her like ducklings. She could feel Hannah behind them. "Hannah, I can't believe how selfish and cruel you can be. Think of Emily and Perry."

Hannah seemed caught surprised by her sister's response, look-ing sheepishly at the children. She walked to the sink and ran water over the glowing tip of her cigarette, as if that somehow helped to right her wrong. "I'm only talking because I'm nervous," she said. "I'm worried about him just the same as you guys."

Gloria grunted something unintelligible, pacing now across the black and white linoleum tiles.

"I'm sure Ted's okay," Hannah said, shifting to a reassuring tone. "Ted can take care of himself. We've seen that."

Gloria cut another look at Hannah.

"Sorry."

Gloria sat down at the table next to Perry and looked at his little face. "Aunt Hannah is right," she said. "Daddy is good at taking care of himself. So, I don't want you to worry anymore. Okay?"

Perry nodded.

Emily walked to the refrigerator and opened it. The cold air made her cry.

Hannah, who had never even bordered on sensitive, was still not close. She pulled a Snickers candy bar from her pocket and began to unwrap it. "Gloria, you have a death certificate, don't you?" She didn't wait for her sister to answer, but continued, "I think you should collect the insurance. What is it? Three, five hundred thou?"

"I can't believe you," Gloria said as she held Emily close to com-fort her. The refrigerator door was still open and the cold air reminded her of Ted and she realized that it must have had the same effect on the child. She shut the machine and walked Emily to a chair at the table.

"The insurance company owes you the money," Hannah said.

Gloria sat and stared at Hannah. "You're a genius," she said. "If I try to collect, then the insurance company will hire a detective to find Ted. They'll do anything not to pay. That's a great idea."

"Oh, Christ," Hannah said.

* * *

The disciples were sitting in a circle, a complete circle and, all being there, they were stacked, to Ted's surprise, three deep. Big Daddy was dressed in his red jacket and red pants despite the baking midday heat and he was pouring off sweat, as were his followers, there being no shade for dozens of yards. Ted's nose told him that they stank, but he was not as offended by their odor as he was undisturbed by any of the other extreme sensations he felt. Big Daddy paced and turned and looked at each sappy, feeble, infirm face, then looked at Ted the longest before he sat between Cynthia and Gerald with the short man behind him. Ted was overcome with concern that the little man's view was blocked.

"When I was a boy," Big Daddy said, "they told my mama that I was retarded, that I was slow, and the poor woman, having had little education, this because she was just poor white trash, a trailer park floozy, they didn't care that she didn't believe them. My daddy believed them though. He'd point at me and say, 'Look at that retard,' then excuse me with, 'But he can't help it.' My daddy would beat me, beat me to within an inch of my life for 'being a sinner,' he called it. He said that God didn't love me and so he made me a retard, a reject. When I went to school, they put me in a special class and all the other children who weren't in that class would point and say, 'Here comes Mr. Retardo.' I began to believe their taunts and I began to think, 'How can God be so cruel to me, to make me retarded and let these other children pick on me?' I would cry and run home and my daddy would yell at me, tell me just because I was retarded didn't mean that I had to be weak. And because of him, I had no pity for myself. What is more pitiful than a wretch with no pity for himself? Imagine me, sitting in the high-school theater, watching that play, *Romeo and Julia*, and at the end I'm crying, weeping at the deaths of these two people, because they died for love, but yet not weeping at my own death, the death I was living because of my lack of love for God, for the LordJesusGodalmighty, bread of my inner strength, light of my heart, against whom I had committed the sin of fornication, for to love this world instead of God is an act of fornication, to weep at those silly teenagers' deaths was a sin against the good and great Lord. Oh, LordGodJe-susChristalmighty, let my spirit not faint under the weight of the task you have placed on my mortal shoulders, let me not collapse beneath your discipline, and let me not faint in confessing to you those acts of mercy of yours by which you have drawn me from all those evil ways that were once mine, drawn me like a poultice draws out infection." Big Daddy was sweating streams and making a pattern of wet in the sand. "Drawn me from those ways that you might become something sweeter than all those alluring pleasures that used to haunt. Oh, yes! I used to love to find a sweet young thang! and take her home with me, squeeze her little ass and plow her deep with my manliness. Oh, how good that felt, to feel those smooth thighs and smell that nectar which rose up from between her legs. But now, oh LordGodChristalmightyMakerofallthings, I am a servant to the spiritual pleasure which now replaces all that lust. I used to do drugs for pleasure, to find an escape from this world, but now, aside from the pills I take to control the pains in my back and side, and to help me sleep because I remain up so often keeping vigil over my flock, I do not take drugs. And I do not lust now, but love and I do not have sex to satisfy my carnal cravings, but to comfort my frightened sheep, to initiate them into the world of complete surrender to the Godeverlasting. I am the light of my Lord and he is my guiding light, the Son and the Father, the Spirit and the Flesh. I drink of his blood and eat of his flesh. I am just a cracker until I put that cracker that is His flesh into my undeserving, white trash mouth and then, Then! I am a soldier of the good GodJesusalmightyChristLordSavior! Say Amen, my babies!"

"Amen!" the sponges shouted. Ted studied them, looked into each and every one of their blank faces and saw that they *believed*. They believed because it was a thousand degrees out there and there was nothing else to do. They believed because in that heat nothing else made sense. Believing was easy. It was quick, like sitting. One minute you're standing and the next you're sitting, active up until the time it is done and then it becomes passive, but unlike sitting, believing has nothing which stands analogous to standing, no action which will undo it. The only thing that stops believing is believing something else, and that leaves one still believing and therefore still a believer. Best never to start. This was what Ted concluded beneath that hot sun which fortunately did not trouble him, but was reducing the disciples to puddles of God-fearing salty water.

After the midday sermon, the believers were allowed to return to whatever shady place or task awaited them and to contemplate what they had just heard. Ted however was tied and staked out in the hot sun, made to sit cross-legged and stripped of his shirt. Gerald made fast the last knot on the rope which held Ted's hands behind his back and stood away, next to Big Daddy, who looked drained, his red clothes soaked. He certainly worked hard for whatever it was he got from all this, Ted thought.

"We've decided we'll torture you for a while," Big Daddy said. "I've always wanted to torture the anti-Christ, to lacerate a reaching limb of the devil himself. I bet you'd like some water."

Ted looked at his knees and the dusty earth below them. The heat couldn't hurt him, he was sure of that. He wasn't thirsty yet and he was fairly confident that he would not get thirsty. But he was saddened by Big Daddy's sickness and his words, not only as they related to him, but by his message to his sheep who were now off trying to make some sense of it all. Ted considered how sheltered his life had been, how he had complained daily as he rolled into campus, worrying about having plenty of handouts for his students, concerning himself with whether his teaching evaluations were enough to counterbalance his lack of scholarship, obsessing over parking. Here were people in real trouble, sick people who because they were in real trouble were in fact *real trouble,* people to fear. Still, he did not fear Big Daddy, but instead saw through to the shattered, fearful, disturbed bully that he was and Ted knew that no mirror was true enough to reflect back to this man what he threw out. He was small, minuscule, Lilliputian. But, thought Ted, so was a virus, a germ, a bacterium. He could not look up at Big Daddy because he did not want to look down on him.

"Let him fry," Big Daddy said.

So, Ted sat there and fried, to no painful end, to no injurious result, but he fried nonetheless. While he sat he watched disciples make periodic trips from the main lodge across the grounds, past the cell in which Ted had slept and into a bunker, the doors of which were like the bunker sheltering the cannons and munitions. Each trip they made with trays or jugs or both. Two or three of them. Never one alone.

* * *

Deep in the recesses of the main lodge, Big Daddy was talking to a disciple. Ted could hear the footfalls of the fat man's boots as he stepped, the crunching twists of his toes as he made turns to continue his pacing. "I'll tell you why we have to kill the devil," Big Daddy said. "Every time the Hebrews showed mercy to their enemies, God got mad. Read Judges two. The LordGod-Jesus is a tough mother. So, you see, we have to kill the devil. Read even back to Exodus twelve, verse twenty-three. Read Isaiah six. Read all of Samuel. Read Luke ten, verse eighteen. Read Matthew twelve, verse twenty-eight. Read Revelations nine, verses one through three. Read John twelve, verse thirty-one. Are you getting all of this?"

The disciple's pencil scratched loudly in Ted's ear.

"Read the Word of God and the Word will set you free," Big Daddy said. "The devil's ass is mine. We'll keep him for a couple of days and then we'll shoot him with a cannon, blow him to smithereens. Won't that be something to see?"

. . .

Dusk came suddenly and seemed to hang on forever, shading the desert sky lavender to red. Ted was amazed at his comfort, at how the heat had not affected him, at how the dropping temperature now was of no consequence. His mouth felt dry, but he was not thirsty. Cynthia walked from the main lodge toward him, her long, flowered housedress catching the breeze and revealing thick calves and ankles. He noticed that her left foot turned in slightly and her toe kicked up sand with each step. She stopped in front of him.

"Big Daddy told me to come here and tell you that no water is coming," she said.

"Thanks," Ted said, but the quality of his response was not sarcastic. He looked at her eyes and she looked away. "Cynthia, right? Do I look like a devil to you?"

"I don't know. You could be a devil. I've never seen a devil."

"That's fair enough," Ted said. He saw another tandem of tray-toting sponges making the trip from the big lodge to the bunker. "What's that all about?" he asked.

"What?"

"All the trips with food to that bunker."

Cynthia grew more nervous than before and didn't answer.

When the two disciples opened the bunker doors, Ted heard the sounds of children's voices, speaking in painful whispers and whimpering. He recognized the sounds so well. He recalled the sound of his daughter crying herself to sleep when he had so disturbed the family balance that the girl thought the house was falling apart. He later understood that her crying had been because he would not leave and save them all the pain.

"There are children down there," Ted said.

"No water," Cynthia said and started away.

"What are you afraid of?" Ted asked. "You're not afraid of me, are you?"

Cynthia pivoted and looked at the devil's face. Even in the near dark Ted could see that she was near tears.

"Why are you here?" Ted asked.

"I'm here because the world is so screwed up. Poor people live on the streets and eat out of filthy garbage cans and super-rich people control the government and television networks and everything that people think and something's in the water in cities that makes us all believe that everything is the way it's supposed to be and so we all follow the almighty dollar like drones."

"So, you're against capitalism. You're a socialist?"

"I hate socialists too. I believe in a church state. I believe in a benign dictator who has been ordained by the LordGodJesus to rule over this planet and lead us into the next world free of suffering and without the pain of artificial competition." Her eyes were slightly glazed, the words coming readily, but not exactly fluidly.

Dear Mom and Dad,

Well, I'm finally sitting down to write this to you. Gerald says I've been putting it off too long, but here it is. How long has it been now? A year and a half? Two years? Anyway, here I am.

I had my first week in the emergency room and I learned a lot. I didn't know there was so much to dressing a simple

*wound. Much less the bad ones or burns. Like with the burns
you have to clean the wound with a scalpel. And if you do it
right, then you don't hurt the patient very much. A lot of the
nurses don't care and they hurt the patients without caring.
On purpose in fact. I love helping people. The world though
doesn't seem to want me to do that.*

*I'm glad I'm at the hospital because at least there is one
person there who really cares whether the patients are comfortable. Some of the nurses don't even give pain medication
or shots to the patients when they ask for it.*

*Gerald and I went to a meeting the other night. There
was this really cool guy talking all about helping people. He
doesn't have any money. He gives it all away to the poor and
homeless. He knows the Bible like the back of his hand. He's
a wonderful speaker and we're going to a smaller gathering
of interested people tomorrow night. He's not that old, but
he looks old, if you know what I mean. He has age in his
eyes. He goes by the name of Big Daddy. I have to admit that
I was put off by his name at first, but that's really what he is
sort of. Big Daddy. Kinda jolly and comforting.*

*Anyway, Gerald finished his welding course and I'll be
through this practical nursing program pretty soon. Gerald
said he might want to go to Israel. Then I don't know what
we'll do. We don't want to stay in Los Angeles. Maybe we'll
move up to Vegas and be closer to you guys.*

Gerald sends his love. Write soon.

Love,
Cindy

Dear Janie,

Just writing to thank you for the gifts. I hope you're doing okay. The robe is really neat. I wear it all the time. Gerald says I should wash it once in a while. Then he laughs. And thanks for the massage oil. I traded it with Sophie because I like frangipani.

I've stopped working at that awful clinic and now I'm helping with the patients at Big Daddy's shelter. The other nurses here are not as well trained, but they are far more caring than the ones at the hospitals I've worked at. Anyhow, work takes up most of my days, but it's very satisfying. One of the women here used to work at Ukiah General up in San Francisco and she says it was awful, that all they cared about was who was going to pay the bill. We're the richest country in the history of the world and we can't even take care of our sick.

Gerald is working as a security guard. He has to carry a gun and walk alongside bags of money to armored cars. He hates it. Big Daddy says it's a good experience for him though. He leaves for Israel next month. I wish I could go with him, but my work here is important.

Well, I got to go. Write soon.

Love,
Cinders

Ted paged through the letters of Cynthia's past and he was confused, not by the easy tracking of the woman's fall into Big Daddy's cult, but by his ability to see the words of her history at all. He saw before him a kind woman, a sad woman, a ripe woman, a sucker being born again every minute. She was the kind of soul you'd like everybody to be and not. She was good but a fool, capable but stupid, searching but hopelessly lost.

"Tell me about those children," Ted said.

"You're dying in the morning," Cynthia said, her whole being shutting down, her face blanking, whatever light there was behind her eyes switching off. "They're going to shoot you with a cannon."

"I know," Ted said. "How do you feel about that? I mean, you're a decent person, a kind person. You like helping people. You're a nurse, right?"

"How do you know that?"

"Do I look like a devil?"

"Again, I don't know what a devil looks like," she said. "You've got those stitches in your neck." The ice behind her eyes was breaking. "You should be dead."

"Apparently that will be taken care of in the morning. Did you see my daughter's face when you kidnapped me?" Ted didn't wait for her to answer. "Did she look frightened?"

"How did you know I'm a nurse?"

"You look like a nurse," Ted said.

Cynthia backed away on her toes, frowning with fear, her hands shaking by her sides as she no doubt actually did see the devil sitting on the ground just feet from her, then turned to run back to the lodge. It was important, this gesture of running, it demonstrated the proper fear of the demon. Once inside, she was greeted by Big Daddy. The minions were singing the *Michael* song again, getting just a little closer to the shore and that was a backdrop to the voices of Big Daddy and Cynthia.

"How is our devil?" the fat man asked.

"Are you sure he's a devil?" Cynthia asked.

"I'm sure," he said.

"He knew I was a nurse," she said. "I didn't tell him. How could he know?"

"See, that's how a demon works. He slipped up. Only a puppet of Satan can know things like that. Come here, Cynthia, let Big Daddy hold you. Let Big Daddy put his arms around you. Let Big Daddy comfort you. Let Big Daddy feel your soft innocence melt into his divinely touched body. Can you feel the power of the Lord-GodJesusChristalmighty?"

"Yes, Big Daddy."

"Michael, row that boat ashore."

"Hallelujah!"

"Hallelujah! Hallelujah! Hallelujah! Hallelujah! Hallelujah! Hallelujah! Hallelujah! Hallelujah! Hallelujah! Hallelujah! Hallelujah! Hallelujah! Hallelujah! Hallelujah! Hallelujah! Hallelujah! Hallelujah! Hallelujah! Hallelujah! Hallelujah!"

* * *

When Gloria had first told Ted on that chilly spring morning that she was pregnant, his heart sank and he stared at his toes as he sat on the edge of the bed. How could this have happened? But of course it was all too obvious how it had happened. How was he going to support a child? He tried to smile, but said, "What are we going to do?" Gloria couldn't believe his response and began to cry. Ted, however, being the Ted he was back then, pressed, asked, "How could this have happened?" Gloria just stared at him. "Did you forget to take your pill?"

"I'm going to have a baby, Ted," she said and rolled out of bed onto her feet and stepped to the bathroom.

Ted met the closing door, stopped at it, letting the side of his face push against it. "I think we should talk about this."

"What is there to talk about?" she said.

Ted listened to her open the sticky window over the tub. The sound of the neighbor's barking dog wafted in. "I think we should discuss the matter," he said.

"The matter is settled," she said, in a voice that settled it. Then she opened the door and stared into his face. "The matter will be a boy or a girl. Get used to it."

"Don't I have any say in this? I mean, it's my body too." He knew it was a stupid thing to say as soon as the words crawled piteously from his wretched mouth. And the look Gloria gave him—it was a cross between "Who the hell are you?" and "I just knew you'd behave like this, you pig."

"I'm sorry," Ted said and in fact he was, for several things. "It's just that it's all such a shock. A surprise, rather. I have to get used to the idea. I mean, are we ready for a kid?"

"We'd better get ready," Gloria said.

Ted put his arms around her, finding her so thin, wondering how she could contain another person, and told her that they would be ready, told her he loved her and though saying it couldn't have been enough, Gloria accepted it and melted slightly into him.

But Ted felt like a liar, was in fact a liar, for as he lay there in bed, he considered that he did not love Gloria at all, cursed himself for not having weaseled out of their marriage before it happened. He could not bring himself to think about getting ready for the child, didn't know how to think about that. He could think only that he had nine more chapters of a ten-chapter dissertation to write and that his professors were not disposed to having great confidence in him in the first place and so it had better be good. Even then, Ted recognized immediately the loathsome selfishness of his thinking and of his words to Gloria, but he couldn't help himself. This was how he excused it. He suffered from congenitally weak moral fiber, a condition which could be remedied neither by medical science nor an appeal to reason. He wondered what kind of bad prenatal diet his mother must have had while he was forming and then he had a fleeting thought that they should see to Gloria's diet. It being perhaps the first decent thought he'd had in a while, he was slow acknowledging it.

He looked over at his sleeping wife, her mouth shaped in a tight grimace, a dream no doubt bothering her, and resolved or resigned to be happy with the situation.

The next morning, sitting at the table in the kitchen, at the breakfast table so-called, as they never sat with any custom or routine, they shared bagels and silence. Ted finally sighed a sigh of notably different quality and caused Gloria to say, "What?"

"I'm glad we're going to be parents," Ted said.

"Really, Ted?"

Ted nodded. "It will bring us even closer," he lied. "I know you're going to be a great mother. I worry about me, though."

"You'll be great too," she said, wiping a little more cream cheese on her blueberry bagel, the very act of spreading a comment. She was smiling, but not at Ted. She was smiling into the air in front of her.

Three weeks later, Gloria miscarried in the bathroom at a motel at the Outer Banks.

Ted waited for her in the empty lobby of an upscale urgent-care clinic. It was just after eleven at night and the receptionist was talking unabashedly to her boyfriend on the telephone and listening to easy-listening rock music turned low on the radio.

The woman hung up and sighed loudly, dreamily. "Relationships," she said.

Ted nodded.

Then Gloria came out. Ted knew what had happened and he, for the first time in his life, said the right thing, which was nothing. He held her and she cried. Over Gloria's shoulder he saw the receptionist, who nodded understandingly. But as was Ted's way in those days, his good sense, however noted at the precise moment, never was long-lived and when he was putting Gloria into the car, he said, "I know this is tough, honey, but maybe this is best. Maybe we weren't ready."

Gloria waited in the car while Ted went slump-shouldered back into the clinic to have his index finger seen to and bandaged, it having been mangled by the slammed car door.

* * *

The next morning began hot and the congregated disciples seemed unsure about the heat and their mission. Gerald and two other men rolled out a bright and shiny cannon and locked its wheel in the middle of the open area. Big Daddy strolled a wide circle, his fat legs and good-smelling feet giving him bounce, making him seem happy with his sweat-sticky body and matted hair.

"This," Big Daddy said, stopping and indicating the weapon beside him with a sweep of his hand, "is a Civil War bronze six-pounder, smooth-bore cannon. It weighs eight hundred and eighty pounds. But it weighs so much more. It was a weapon of the Union that the Confederates took, much as we are taking this weapon of Satan. Isn't it a handsome gun?" He rubbed his hand along the barrel, caressing it.

Gerald and Cynthia had taken the time during his words to get Ted to his feet. From Cynthia's touch Ted could tell she had softened toward him, though he was unsure what such softening meant. Did she want somehow for him to be spared or simply that he not suffer greatly? Or did she, in her sad, religious haze, desire only that he not take her with him into the depths of hell? Little did she realize that they were already sharing hell, hers all the more profound for her oblivion.

Big Daddy turned to Ted and pointed a fat finger at him. "Put the devil in his place," he commanded.

Ted loved the sound of it, the weight of his words. *Put the devil in his place.* The sentence made him smile in his mind and had the unfortunate effect of actually pushing up the corners of his mouth so that he wore, however briefly, a peculiar smile which all the sponges noticed and from which they recoiled in unison. Ted was tied to a wooden stake about twenty yards from the cannon, his hands behind his back, his chest facing the dark muzzle. Looking into the seemingly bottomless mouth of the weapon, Ted experienced a fleeting prick of fear and, though when the twinge was gone it was indeed gone, he appreciated that he had felt it. In fact, he wanted it back, was exhilarated, enlivened by it, wanted it back as soon as it was gone. Then Ted was made angry by the loss and when he looked at Big Daddy, he found him deficient and for that reason alone worthy of his choler. "Okay, Fatso, shoot me," Ted said.

The complete lack of anxiety in Ted caused Big Daddy discernible consternation. He stood behind the cannon while the twins packed the cannon's barrel with wadding, tamped it, then added the six-pound ball. Using a lavender disposable lighter, Big Daddy lit the fuse and stood away, putting his chubby hands over his fat-lobed ears. The disciples did likewise, many of them shutting their eyes and grimacing in anticipation of the coming boom. Ted watched the fuse sizzle its length and pause silently while nothing happened, while the cannon seemed to be deciding whether it should fire, then it exploded with a great noise, a flash of white and black smoke.

Ted watched as the black tube spit the ball at him. At first the iron sphere appeared light blue in color. It darkened as it approached, but the travel was slow, not that time was delayed, but the projectile did not so much hurtle through space as trudge. The disciples watched with appropriate horror and Ted had time to observe each and every face before returning his attention to the nearing bullet. The ball did not miss his body, but neither did it pass through him. It hit his chest with a perceptible thump and fell to the ground at Ted's feet. Ted had never heard a hush as silent and heavy as the one that fell over that dusty yard. The smoke still hung in the air along with the stench of the burned powder. Even the crows which had been issuing infrequent but consistent caws all morning were stifled, Ted thinking at first that they had been scared away by the blast, but then he saw them on the far fence, just watching. The disciples, one by one, peeled away and walked to the main building. Finally, it was Ted and Big Daddy left alone in the yard, the smoking gun between them. The zealot was shaken, his hands trembling at his sides and no words found his quivering lips. He looked away from Ted's unmoving eyes, then uncertainly at the building into which his followers had gone. He went to join them, leaving Ted tied to the stake.

* * *

Ted remained staked throughout the day, the searing sun still not bothering but giving rise to numerous flights into his misshapen past. His newfound patience extended even to himself as he was not so much embarrassed by his former self as instructed. He had time to recall the novels he had read and read again and read again and realized that he only now would be able to really read. He wanted to read Robbie Burns's poems aloud to his daughter. He wanted to read Twain to his son and cultivate a satisfying irreverence in him. He wanted to enjoy words and share their meanings with his wife. Chat-littles called as they split the coming-dusk sky. Bats searched for insects and sent out signals that Ted could hear. The sounds of the disciples were lost in the sea of desert air and the building where they were all hiding looked like a ghost ship.

Cynthia came walking toward him, her face conforming to the lines that her natural frown had created in her short life. Without speaking, she set to work on the ropes twisted about Ted's wrists.

"You have to get out of here," she said.

"Who's in the bunker?" Ted asked.

Cynthia was untying his feet. She didn't respond to his question.

"Who's in the bunker?"

"Just run," she said.

"Children are in the bunker," Big Daddy's voice rang out. He was toting a rifle. "I've been collecting them. They're my insurance. I call them my milk-carton kids."

Ted swallowed. He recalled the whimpering, the small voice. He stared at Big Daddy, a fat red smudge against the desert sky.

"Move away from him, Cynthia," Big Daddy said and he raised the rifle to his shoulder and drew a bead on Ted.

Ted pushed the woman away a step. "Get away," he said.

"Run!" Cynthia said.

Ted, out of long-standing habit and good sense, took off running. A man was pointing a gun at him. It didn't matter that the cannon's projectile had behaved so strangely or that neither thirst nor extreme heat seemed to affect him adversely. He ran. The rifle reports split the warm air and echoed off the far walls of the outbuildings. A bullet hit Ted's back and he felt that it failed to penetrate, but still he ran. His instinct was to move serpentinely to get away from the bullets and suddenly he could not see the sunset toward which he had been heading. He was in a ravine, a deep wash with a sandy bottom and side which grew steeper with each stride. The sounds of the rifle, the light of the horizon were gone and he was in a twisting secret channel which only water knew, a geological clock. Then he was spit back into view of the sunset, the ground firmer beneath his feet and looking back he saw no light, heard no sound from the compound. But still he ran, kicking up dust, keeping his eyes on the nearly sunken sun, the west.

BOOK THREE

CHAPTER ONE

TED SPRINTED INTO THE night with a speed and grace he had never known, laughing with each energizing stride, one of the pathetic undead, stretching out his legs the way he had when he jogged regularly. His running back then had not been merely for exercise, but as now, for escape, although a different kind. Just two years into his appointment at the university, Gloria told Ted, while he was doing the bills, that she was pregnant with Perry. His salary was small and the ticking of the giant tenure clock was already deafening. Ted couldn't believe that Gloria had conceived a third time and he wondered when he had in fact had sex with her. It seemed almost all of Gloria's time was consumed by their daughter and when the evening came she went right to sleep, curled into a tight ball, leaving Ted to contemplate the horrors of academe alone and to wallow in the guilt he was feeling over sleeping with a senior from Alaska with overdeveloped thigh muscles from years of snowshoeing. But the running felt good now as he fled the danger and he slowed only because he was bored, then walked to the junction of two roads and wandered onto the aged plank porch of a closed diner at daybreak. While he sat and watched the sun poke over the hills, he heard the air-chopping noise of a helicopter, far away, then closer, then very close. He couldn't see it and he didn't rise from his perch to find it in the sky. Then the machine's noise faded away.

A short, muscular man appeared from around the side of the diner, casually, as if at a party. "Hello there," he said and put a booted foot on the lowest step of the porch.

Ted nodded.

The man observed Ted's neck and seemed to smile inwardly. "Mr. Street?"

"Yes."

"I guess this is my day," the man said. His face was square and mapped out in quadrants by deep creases that seemed unnatural, wounds rather than the result of age, his pale blue eyes nearly filling the upper two zones. "I thought I was going to have to tear this whole damn countryside apart to find you."

Ted was filled with an eager, chest-tightening anticipation. This man with the carved face was going to take him back to his wife and children. But as he studied the fake-soft eyes which studied him back, his good feeling drained from his heart, spiraling into his middle and he asked flatly, "Who are you?"

"Have you ever heard of those nuts who believe in the black helicopters?" He looked up at the sky.

"You're one of those nuts?" Ted asked.

The man laughed. "No, I ride around in the black helicopters." Then he made a whistling noise like he was telling a ghost story and wiggled his fingers in the air.

Crows collected on the utility line connecting the diner to the rest of the pathetic world. Ted watched them, noting their blackness, amplified for being backlit by the sun. He glanced back at the windows of the diner, still deep and dark, offering even less promise of life now than they had an hour ago.

The man worked his square jaw, holding his chin in his hand, and Ted heard the loud cracking of his mandibular joint. Then he twisted his neck and it sounded like sand under a boot's heel.

"So, you know *my* name," Ted said. He looked the man over from head to toe, at his loose black trousers, his deep, olive green mock turtleneck sweater, his black hightop canvas sneakers. "What am I supposed to call you?"

"You can call me Clancy," he said.

"Okay, Clancy. What now?"

"You know, my father was devoted to the military," Clancy said, as if to pass time, shifting his position to suggest that if he'd had a post against which to lean he'd be using it. "He served in the big one, WW Two, and Korea. He always told me that the best army would be one that the people didn't know about. I wish he were alive now. He would love the world the way it is."

"Did he get killed in Korea?" Ted asked.

"No, he shot himself in the head with a Luger he took off a sixteen-year-old kraut on D-day when my half brother told him he was one of them homosexuals."

"But of course it doesn't matter to you that I know any of this," Ted said.

"No, just making chitchat while we wait for our ride. Hey, you're dirty. Where've you been?"

"You wouldn't believe me." Ted heard the approaching rotor blades of the helicopter. "Where am I going?"

"It's not a long ride," Clancy said. "Maybe you can even get some sleep. You look like you need it. Tell me, have you ever been in a chopper?"

Ted shook his head.

"You'll love it. It's really loud. I like how loud and noisy it is." He was already having to raise his voice.

"Do you know if my family is okay?" Ted asked.

"I'm sure they're fine." Clancy was shouting now. The blades of the black helicopter were stirring up swirling clouds of dust. "Beautiful, isn't it?" Clancy reached out a hand and Ted stood and came down the steps to stand beside him. "It's a brutal world out there, really brutal, an uncertain world!" The helicopter landed, but its blades continued to rotate. "Keep your head down now." Clancy looked at Ted and smiled a laugh. "I guess I don't have to tell *you* that. Or maybe I do. Well, come on."

As they boarded, Ted shouted, "I don't imagine you'll let me call my wife!"

Clancy shook his head. Once in the air no one spoke because of the noise. Not Ted, not Clancy, neither of the M-16 armed soldiers already strapped in. The young, vacant, order-awaiting faces pointed at Ted and though the eyes betrayed their fear, their gazes passed right through him, not cold, but robotic nonetheless. Ted did not know what their destination would be, only that they were traveling into the sun and so, east, farther yet from his family.

* * *

The insurance agent did not even pretend to recognize Gloria Street as she sat down across from him at his green metal desk. This in spite of his oh-so-friendly displays at their dining-room table when he was designing and selling them the policy. His powder blue shirt with the white collar and cuffs and his wide tie looked oddly appropriate on his lean frame. He was a tall man, even sitting, and looked like suburbia, his lips barely discernible, his face clean-shaven. There was a picture of his family, a soft, fleshy pig-nosed blonde woman and his two piggy-looking little girls.

"So, what can I do for you?" he asked, looking at the folder in front of him. "Mrs. Street."

"I'd like to collect on my husband's life insurance policy, Mr. Akers. The policy is for five hundred thousand dollars."

Akers laughed. "But your husband is alive."

"Actually, I have a death certificate from the medical examiner's office and I understand that's what I need to collect."

"But I saw Mr. Street on television."

"According to the coroner, he's dead. A cashier's check will be fine."

"But . . ."

"If you can show me my husband alive, I'll be happy to drop the matter." Gloria felt in control and liked it, having been at the mercy of the situation for so long now. "I'd rather have my husband than the money, but I am going to have one of them. I'm sure I can find a lawyer who will assist me."

"Certainly, you don't believe your husband is dead."

"All I know is the coroner, a duly appointed county official, thinks he's dead and I don't see him anywhere. Do you see him?"

Akers looked blankly at the yellow folder in front of him, then more blankly at Gloria. The sun poked through the clouds outside and poured into the room, seeming to make him hot. "I'll have to get back to you, Mrs. Street."

* * *

Gloria was pleased and somewhat surprised to find a short man with a handlebar mustache leaning on her doorbell later that afternoon. In her head she was laughing because the man didn't look anything like the television image of the private investigator, but with his appearance that was all in life she could imagine him doing. His voice was slightly high and he couldn't keep his hands from the hair on his lip. "My name is Horatio Sally," he said and presented a worn card. "Telluride Security Insurance has hired me to find your husband."

"Oh, good," Gloria said and invited Sally into the house. "We can sit in the dining room and you can ask me whatever you need to ask. I hope you can find my Ted."

"So, you do believe he's alive?"

Gloria considered the question and thought about lying, realizing that she didn't know what a lie might be. Then the truth occurred to her in all its strangeness and she said, "I don't know if he's alive. I only know I want to see him again."

Sally nodded like a man who wanted to appear like a man who had heard it all before. "This shouldn't take long." He followed Gloria through the foyer into the dining room.

"Sit down, please," Gloria said.

Sally sat at the head of the table, twirled his mustache with his left hand and tapped his pad with his pencil with his right. "I'll just ask a few preliminary questions. First, do you have children and how many? What are their ages?"

"Two. A girl, twelve, and a boy, seven."

Sally wrote that down. "You're the biological parents?"

"Yes."

"Where are the children now?" he asked.

"They're upstairs with my sister." Gloria glanced at the stairs and wondered what they were doing.

"Either of you married before?" Sally asked.

"No."

"Are you and your husband religious people?"

"Why do you ask?" Gloria scooted her chair a couple of inches from the table.

"I'll take that as a no," Sally said. "I ask because of what your family has been going through. For all I know your husband thinks that God doesn't want him and he's out trying to finish himself off. He might be ringing up priests. Who knows."

"I see. Well, he's not religious at all. He's not spiritual, either. Not as far as I know."

"He's had affairs," Sally said.

"Why do you say that?" Gloria asked.

"I'll take that as a yes," Sally said. "It was the way you said 'Not as far as I know.' People who haven't had their trust shaken believe they know their mate completely."

Gloria was shaken by the questions now, but she felt a growing confidence in Sally's abilities. He was at least very perceptive while sitting at the table.

"When was the last time you saw your husband?"

"We were in the grocery market when these people came and took him."

"Took him."

"Picked him up and carried him out," Gloria said. She wanted to cry thinking about it. She recalled being worried that they might bump him and cause his head to fall off.

"Where in the market were you?" Sally asked.

"Where?"

"Were you in the produce section, frozen foods? Where?"

"We were in the back room, the storeroom, I guess it's called. There were crates stacked everywhere." Gloria looked at his expression. "We were trying to avoid the news people."

Sally nodded.

"Anyway, we were in the storeroom and then everything just started happening and they had him and the kids were screaming." Gloria shook her head. "It was awful."

"Did they hurt him?" Sally asked.

"I don't know. A man in the alley behind the store said they drove away in a brown van, but he didn't get the license number. The police haven't been helpful at all."

"Well, that's their job."

Gloria almost laughed.

"How many people took your husband?"

"I don't know," Gloria said. "Three, maybe four. I don't know. It all happened so fast."

"Did you see any of their faces?" Sally asked.

"No. But one of them was short."

"How short? Short like me?"

"Shorter," Gloria said. "Very, very short. Like a midget."

"Do you think the children saw anything you missed?"

Gloria said, "I've talked to them and I'm sure they didn't." She didn't want the kids reliving the incident.

"A brown van and a midget. That's something, I guess." Sally put away his notepad and twirled his mustache with both hands. "Is there anything else that you can think to tell me about your husband that might be helpful?"

Gloria shook her head.

"Okay, then. Thank you for your time, Mrs. Street."

"Thank you," Gloria said.

"If you do think of anything else, just call the number on that card and I'll get back to you. Good day, Mrs. Street." He stood and glanced around the room as if measuring it.

"Do you think you'll be able to find him?"

Sally bounced almost imperceptibly on the balls of his feet. "I've been watching the news," he said. "Your husband is quite conspicuous. That's in our favor. He's also apparently very difficult to kill. That's a good thing in anybody. I think I'll find him."

Gloria walked the detective to the door.

"Well, ma'am, thanks again for taking the time to answer my questions."

* * *

The helicopter kicked up a cloud of lighter-colored dust as it set down on what Ted guessed to be a military facility somewhere in New Mexico, or so he reasoned, judging from the landscape and the duration of their journey. To his surprise he had fallen asleep in the air. Over Arizona he'd dreamed that his head had never been re-attached to his body and that Gloria had been allowed to take it home. Unaware that his head could perceive the world she'd set it on the chest of drawers in her bedroom, sent the children over to Hannah's apartment and proceeded to entertain gentlemen callers, one after another. Ted was not jealous in the dream, not angry, but only saddened when man after man failed to satisfy his wife. One man had an incredibly large penis and Gloria seemed excited to see it, to touch it, to kiss it, but it appeared to hurt her as it penetrated her, then her face went blank, as if she felt nothing, in spite of the man's bucking away. Ted wanted to shout out instructions to the men, tell them how to touch her, tell them what to say, but his mouth was inoperative. He wept while he watched Gloria cry herself to sleep, alone in their bed. He awoke to find Clancy staring at him, his eyes unblinking, but then Ted realized that the man had fallen asleep with his eyes wide open.

Now they were on the ground and the blades were whirring to a halt over them. Ted watched the guards jump out and station themselves on either side of the door, their weapons like extensions of their live-wire bodies. The mid-afternoon sun was intense, baking the metal roofs of the Quonsets and reflecting harshly.

"Where are we?" Ted asked.

"We're outside Roswell, New Mexico," Clancy said, as if saying it was pleasurable. "Let's get out." He followed Ted out of the helicopter. "This is the famous Area 51."

"The UFO place?" Ted was smiling now.

Clancy laughed. "The very same."

"So, there's truth to those stories?"

"Hardly," Clancy said. "This way." He steered Ted toward a Quonset with a flag flying on a pole standing in a circle of stones. "No little men from Venus or anything like that, but if that's what people want to think, that's just fine with us. If they really knew what we were doing here, they'd scream and die. They might anyway. Actually we fuel those UFO rumors. It makes things so much easier."

"So, what do you guys do here?" Ted asked.

"In good time," Clancy said.

Soldiers walked about rather casually everywhere Ted looked, talking, laughing, sharing cigarettes and joints. Ted could smell the pot, but no one cared, not even the stiff-backed officers who were staring at him from the porch of a two-story adobe building. The heat here was no match for what he had just left, but the sun was as bright and he realized that its intensity was causing his eyes to tire. The camp was set out on a flat and just behind it, the ground rose up to join the hills, as if the heel of some giant palm had pushed hard against the earth. Ted liked the ochre and reds of the hills and the blue of the sky. When he looked from these things and his gaze fell into an open hangar, he saw a disc that he could only describe as a flying saucer.

"Is that what it looks like?" Ted asked.

"Fake," Clancy said. "Faker than Tammy Faye Bakker's tits. But it's a good one, don't you think? You know, I've killed people all over the world. In Lebanon. In Vietnam. In Central America. Even here in the States. I don't think I'll ever get used to it. It's a thrill, though. You probably think I just say whatever pops into my head. But that ain't quite right." Clancy stopped and opened the door to the big Quonset for Ted. "After you, my friend."

The inside of the building was not nearly as primitive as its exterior. Women and men sat at narrow terminals, wearing stream-lined, high-tech headsets and typing away at curved keyboards, the screens in front of them flashing data in quickly changing colors which reflected in the glasses they all wore. On the wall to the left was a bank of five monitors, one man watching, which seemed to show the outlying terrain, empty on three screens but two showing fields of campers and motor homes, people sitting on folding loungers, bathing-suited out-of-shape people slapping volleyballs. Clancy walked over and viewed the monitors from behind the man. "They're nuts," he said, "but God love 'em, they're what this is all about. Democracy and freedom." Then to the soldier in front of him, "Any of those fuckers try to sneak in today?" The man shook his head. Clancy grunted, then said, "The next peckerwood who pokes his nose or ass through any gap in that wire, you zap the living bejesus shit out of him. You read me, soldier?"

"Yes, sir."

"Come on," Clancy said to Ted and led him toward the back wall of the Quonset where there was an elevator. None of the soldiers looked to Ted as he passed by, not at his feet, not at his face, not at his neck. But Clancy was looking at his neck. "That hurt?" he asked.

"No," Ted said.

While they waited for the elevator Ted listened to Clancy's breathing, his heart's beating, his letting of a quiet fart. And he could hear the voice of the man's father, yelling into his son's ear, "GIVE ME FIVE MORE, MISTER!"

. . .

Clancy collected his breath and did another pushup. His brother, his beautiful, Adonis brother, muscled and chiseled, wearing a thin shine of perspiration, pumped away at his own pushups, counting aloud, "One twenty-three, one twenty-four, one twenty-five . . ." "Look at your brother," the father said, on all fours, leaning into Clancy's ear, hovering over his shaking body as he pressed his arms straight once more. "HOW MANY IS THAT, MISTER?" "Fifty-three, sir." "Fifty-two," his father said. "That last one didn't count. It was ugly. I don't want ugly pushups. Not from a son of mine. Look at your brother. Look at him go." "One seventy-eight, one seventy-nine, one eighty . . ."

The elevator opened, they entered and the door shut behind them. They dropped, down, down, and Ted fancied that he was going to hell, that he had indeed died, either when decapitated or when shot by the cannon or when shot by the rifle, that he was in fact dead and on his way to what he had always suspected awaited him. He recalled the Gospel of Mark: *It is better for thee to enter into life maimed, than, having two hands, go into hell, into the unquenchable fire.* Still riding downward, Ted cursed his education. He knew there was no hell, no God, but still the words of it, the stories of it, always better than truth and so worse, with wailing and gnashing of teeth. Was Clancy Ted's Virgil, guiding him down and through the landscape that would be his eternity, and would Ted find a Lucius Brockway tomming his way through the paint factory? He wondered if there were floors between where lukewarm sinners like himself really belonged. But the new Ted, the thinking and unafraid and curious Ted, took over and Ted simply felt the dropping, enjoyed the ride, opened his eyes relaxedly and fully and waited for the car to stop.

"Here we are," Clancy said. The door opened and there before them was a multileveled labyrinth of catwalks, doors, conveyors and golf cart–sized vehicles.

"This is like a James Bond set," Ted said.

"Neat, eh?"

"I can't believe this. How much did this cost?"

"If you have to ask, you can't afford it." Clancy laughed. "This is the biggest secret in the world. This is a bigger secret than who shot JFK."

"Who did shoot JFK?" Ted asked.

"It is still a secret," Clancy said. "Just because it's less of a secret than this place doesn't mean that it's not a secret."

"Okay."

"Come on, you are down here to meet Dr. Lyons."

"Who's he?"

"She," Clancy corrected with a bit of disdain in his voice. "She is the head cheese, the queen rat, the top snot. You'll hate her guts."

They marched along a narrow metal walk above lab-coated men and women who moved with great deliberateness from points A to B, carrying boxes and trays and flasks and clipboards. Clancy knocked on a steel door with a force that should have hurt his knuckles, then walked right in. An incredibly handsome young lieutenant sat at a desk in the outer office, so pretty that Ted was momentarily blinded by him. His dark hair was short, his face chiseled with deep-set brown eyes, his skin an even mahogany.

"Afternoon, Dudley," Clancy said.

Dudley looked at him. "Good afternoon, Colonel Dweedle."

Clancy appeared to cringe at the sound of his own name. "Is the dragon lady in there?"

Dudley was looking at Ted. He showed no fear, only interest.

"Oh, yeah," Clancy said. "Here's the dead guy. Street, this here is Lieutenant Dudley."

Dudley picked up the telephone, talked softly, then hung up. "Go on in."

Clancy opened the door and allowed Ted to enter before him. Ted saw Dr. Lyons and knew immediately something that Clancy did not, something that if Clancy had known might have prompted extreme and reflexive action with harsh consequences. Ted knew by the way Dr. Lyons carried herself toward him from her desk, from the sound of her heart beating within her chest, that she was not a she at all, but a man, a narrow man with a tiny waist and slight shoulders. But the voice was deep like a man's and hard like a man's and Dr. Lyons said, "Pleased to meet you, Mr. Street. Welcome to the Re-Animation Death and Intravital Carpophoric Anaplastics Laboratory."

"RADICAL," Clancy said.

Ted shook Dr. Lyons's hand. In spite of the fact that she possessed, or at one time did possess, a penis and testicles, the doctor cut a fine example of a woman, being as striking as her aide in the outer chamber. Ted studied the office. The walls were eggshell in color and behind the desk was a painting which Ted recognized as a Motherwell, a yellow plane with a partial window in the upper middle.

"Is that a Motherwell?" Ted asked.

Lyons gave a quick glance back at the painting and said, "Yes, it is." She seemed impressed. "You like paintings?"

Ted nodded.

"What is all this sissy talk," Clancy said.

"You're probably wondering why our pit bull, Colonel Dweedle"—Lyons fondled the name with her tongue—"was sent to collect you." She walked around her desk and sat, offering the chair in front of her to Ted with an open hand, then gave Clancy a look which meant he could leave. And so the colonel did. "As you no doubt know by now, sometimes when people die, they don't stay dead."

"At least it would appear so," Ted said.

"Would you like some water?" Lyons asked.

"I'd like to bathe," Ted said.

Lyons nodded as if something of clinical interest had been revealed to her. She leaned forward, picked up a pencil and tapped her desk with its eraser.

"A shower," Ted said.

"Certainly. What you probably don't know is that people have been coming back to life, so to speak, for as long as humans have walked the face of the planet. And I'm not simply talking about burials of people who weren't actually dead yet. There's got to be a reason for this."

"And so all this UFO stuff is just a cover?" Ted asked, having already been told as much by Clancy.

"I don't know anything about that. That's for those empty-headed military buffoons upstairs. I'm a scientist, an endocrinologist and a pathologist. I work down here." Lyons leaned back. "Your head was completely severed from your body."

"I realize that."

"Do you believe a person can survive such an event?" Lyons was staring at Ted's sutures.

"Yes," Ted said.

"Well, I don't," Lyons said. "And I'm going to find out why you did even if it kills you."

"Why?" Ted asked.

"I'll tell you why"—this from Clancy, who burst back into the room—"Because you are apparently a man who can't be killed. Your goddamn head was cut off, clean fucking off and here you are talking to me. Imagine an army of men like you." He glanced at Lyons. "And women. Imagine that the Libyans are mowing them down in the desert with fifty-caliber machine guns, with mortar fire, but they keep getting up and marching forward. Imagine just a thousand such soldiers. Just imagine it." Colonel Dweedle closed his eyes and did, an orgasmic shudder passing over him. "I'm going to have those soldiers and you're going to give them to me."

Ted looked to Lyons.

"You may leave now," Lyons said.

"Okay," Clancy said, and he gave a long, hard look at Ted. "But hurry and open him up." The door actually clicked as Clancy left this time and Ted heard the door to the outer office shut as well and he knew that the colonel was finally gone.

"I hate the military," Lyons said.

"But you work for them."

"Of course I do. This is science heaven. I can do whatever I want to whatever or whomever I want and nobody complains. Nobody screams about animal or human or civil rights and safe testing. I'm God down here."

"So, you consider me re-animated."

"You, I *know* you are re-animated. You're the first one of which there is no doubt. Your head was cut off, Mr. Street. You're sitting in front of me having been sewn together by a butcher. You have no vital signs. But yet I'm talking to you and you're talking back."

"So, what now?"

"We'll do an ECG and an EEG and an MRI and see what we find in your saliva and your blood and your stools and your urine. Are you still passing waste?"

Ted hadn't thought of this, but the fact of the matter was that he had not urinated since the time at Big Daddy's compound. He found, oddly, that he was somewhat embarrassed to admit this. He simply did not answer.

"We'll check you out thoroughly enough."

"What are you looking for?" Ted asked.

"Anything. Everything." Dr. Lyons sighed. "Death fascinates me. It is the most intriguing of human life functions and that is what it is. And a necessary, inevitable one at that. When you died, when your head was severed from your body, everything stopped, everyone stopped, they stopped and looked, all sound stopped, voices, birds, time stopped. Then, that fat instant was gone and everything started up again. Death is but a dimensionless point in time, meaningless, insignificant, but it holds everything there is to know about life."

Ted smiled.

Lyons picked up the phone. "Dudley, I'd like you to escort

Mr. Street to his new quarters. See to it he gets what he needs to be comfortable." She hung up.

"May I call my family?"

"No," Dr. Lyons said, flatly. "I haven't talked to my own family in over four years, not that I want to. Ironically, you're more dead to your wife and children than you ever were."

CHAPTER TWO

PRETTY DUDLEY LED TED across a series of catwalks and through several hallways, past doors that required cards or secret codes or retinal identification, until they came to a blood red, sliding door. Dudley placed his palm flat against what Ted understood to be a sensor pad and the door opened. Dudley allowed Ted to enter first. The room looked like every hotel room Ted had ever rented, down to the tan, thick pile carpet and the hideous pastel painting over the bed.

"We hope you will be comfortable, Mr. Street," Dudley said.

"Thank you."

"Certainly. There are drinks in the refrigerator and a coffee-maker over by the sink. Your room will be cleaned daily."

"Thank you."

"There are fresh clothes in the dresser and hanging in the closet."

Then Lieutenant Dudley was gone, the red door sliding closed with a blaring hush. Ted sat on the neatly made bed and felt the cords of the spread with the tips of his fingers. There was a short bookcase where in a hotel room would have been the television and it held several volumes. Ted tilted his head to read the titles. There was a worn copy of Trollope's *Phineas Finn,* a book with the dry title of *Food in History,* Oscar Wilde's translation of *The Satyricon* and *The Occurrence at Owl Creek Bridge* along with assorted popular novels of suspense and political intrigue, but the title which made him laugh was the one that seemed to be in every used-book store he had ever been in, in every summer cottage where he had ever spent a vacation: Stefan Zweig's *Balzac.* He got up and went to the closet where he found a single red-and-gray jumpsuit on a hanger. In the drawers of the bureau he found white boxer shorts and black socks. The smell of the cedar reminded him of his parents' bedroom closet, where his father's three suits hung lost among his mother's many repetitive outfits. He would hide from his sister in that closet during games and when she was after him to get even for some offense he could never recall. He considered her a brute, a heavy-fisted cretin, and refused to believe that she was really his sister.

* * *

Neither of Ted's parents had ever found it necessary to raise a hand to him and, as far as he knew, to his sister. However, abuse comes in many forms and from varying directions and angles. Ethel, three years older than Ted—amazing how three years separation can create an irreversible social order—was what Ted, from his first day in preschool, was most terrified of: a bully. When their parents were away, if only out in the yard or in a remote part of the house, Ethel would strut in like a line boss from some chain-gang movie, chewing bubble gum and lending a scrutinizing eye to whatever Ted was doing. Ted knew then that he was being seasoned to be a coward, realizing that he could never stand up to her and never tell on her, for fear of losing his life. "You have to sleep sometime," she would say when some flavor of revenge was to be exacted. Ethel was truly wicked and vile and she was the reason that Ted turned early on to prayer as a form of hopeful defense. Every night he would offer feverish pleas to the Holy Father, as the zealots on television called him, but soon his patience wore thin and he accepted that if there was indeed a supreme being, he was supreme in reputation only and cared not much at all for a little coward in Baltimore fighting for his life against a sinister sister. And his parents were poor protectors, being certain that in winter he was bundled tightly from chin to trimmed-nail toe in coarse, scratchy wool, but being completely oblivious to the monster lurking underfoot. The most dastardly bit of luck had the upstairs bathroom, the one shared by the two children, inside Ethel's room, and to get there Ted had to wend his way through piles of the demon's clothes and belongings. This was especially treacherous at night when he could never be certain whether she was asleep or pretending, lying in wait. The piles on the floor were constantly changing in makeup and location, for reasons known only to the beast. Often Ted would lie in his own bed and try to endure the pressures of his full bladder by reading about Theseus and the Minotaur.

But one night the nine-year-old could not hold it. He walked over and stood just outside the open door of his sister's room. He couldn't bring himself ever to go downstairs and invade the closed-door quarters of his parents and that night he could hear the muffled and urgent sounds of his parents' voices. He considered the toilet way down in the back corner of the cellar, but that place was even scarier, dark and damp, full of creaking noises. He entered Ethel's lair, trying to use the tiny amount of illumination from the plug-in nightlight in the bathroom to navigate. A Barbie doll's hand dug into the sole of his foot and he suppressed a yelp and hopped in place. Then, everything was too quiet, the Gorgon's snoring was gone and Ted froze. A hand found his shoulder and he made to run, but the other hand grabbed his hair. A bony fist found his back high and between the shoulder blades and he buckled, collapsed to his knees. The beating stopped when Ted and his sister became aware of the intensified quality of their parents' remote discussion. Something crashed downstairs, a sick and unfamiliar sound of something breaking.

As Ted and Ethel ran down, they heard, one of them, mother or father, neither could tell, yelling, *something something* "heart attack." Ted expected to find his father on the floor, his mother on the phone. But he found the opposite, nearly; his mother was on the floor and his father was pounding on her chest. "Call an ambulance," he said to Ethel. But Ethel was unmoving, her mouth agape. Ted ran to the kitchen and called the ambulance number written on the wall by the phone.

As it happened, Ted's mother did suffer cardiac arrest and did afterward undergo surgery and survive. His mother and father rubbed his head as he stood next to his mother's hospital bed and she called him their *little hero*, "The way he ran to that phone and calmly dialed that number." His father did not mention the way Ethel had stood paralyzed in the doorway, but Ethel was never the same. She withdrew into herself and never again tormented her brother. The cold-turkey end to the torture was so alarming that Ted could hardly stand it. His heart raced faster than ever on his occasional night-time trips to the toilet and he wondered how suddenly the world could have become so safe. He thought he would die of anticipation and decided that this was his sister's diabolical strategy. This final persecution Ted would never overcome; he forever would believe that Ethel was bedevilling him with every kind and indifferent word.

Now, as adults, when Ethel really needed her brother's assistance, it was not there. Every time she opened her mouth, she somehow induced Ted to contrary action. It was all unconscious, her insidious and subterranean needling and his passive-aggressive resistance, though, at least, Ted thought positively, there was never any pretense that they were close or even liked each other. They dashed away from each other, if not in opposite directions, then certainly in different ones; he became an atheistic academic and she a devoutly religious nurse of sorts. Though neither turned out very good at their chosen extremes, their failures did not cause them to drift back toward some middle ground. Ethel, despite her lack of literary education, made of herself a rather fine copy of Hawthorne's Richard Digby and sequestered herself away in her own little pious realm. Sadly, they shared aging parents—shared the death of one and finally were sharing the incapacity of the other.

Ted lay back on the bed in the room where Dudley had left him and considered his father's condition, from all reports advanced enough that he recognized no one at any time. He wanted at that moment to see his father, to watch him paint the decoys he so lovingly and patiently crafted with his hands, not out of a love of hunting, but out of a love for ducks. Once joined again to Gloria and the children, Ted would go to Baltimore.

. . .

Private Investigator Sally wore driving gloves and special driving shoes, but his car was hardly special. It was a mid-seventies Ford sedan, perhaps without a model name, simply a Ford sedan, four doors, four windows, four tires, blue. He parked in the yard of his thirteenth gas station of the day, off the freeway in the town of Banning. It was early afternoon and hot. Sally bought a tricolored popsicle and ate it while he watched the mechanic bleed the brakes of a Chevy pickup.

"What can I do for you?" the mechanic asked.

"The fellow inside told me you worked nights last week."

"That's right."

"Did you work Thursday night?"

"Sure did." He yelled forward to his assistant sitting in the elevated truck, "Pump 'em up!"

"Do you remember a brown van?"

"I remember lots of vans," he said. "Pump 'em up!" He looked at Sally. "Lots of brown ones."

"This one was full of people." Sally produced a photograph. "This guy was with them. He has a pretty distinctive scar around his neck."

The man studied the picture. "Never seen him. Not in person anyway. Seen him on television. So that guy's on the run, eh?"

"One of the people in the van was really short, like a midget."

"A midget?"

"Yes."

"Yeah, he was in here. Came in to get the key to the restroom and I looked right over him. Pissed him off too."

"Ever see them before?"

"Nope. But they was going to the desert," he said, wiping his wrench off with his rag. "Pump 'em up! Feel good?"

"Good!" the man in the cab shouted back. "Bring me down! It's hot in here."

"How do you know they were going to the desert?" Sally asked.

The mechanic walked slowly to the foot controls of the hydraulic lift at the front of the truck. "They was filling jugs with water and they had two gas cans racked on the back bumper."

"I don't suppose you got a plate number?"

The mechanic laughed. "Yeah, as a matter of fact I did. It said, M-I-D-G-E-T."

"Thanks."

* * *

Gloria's younger sister Hannah had tortured a lengthy string of boyfriends, some of them twice, but was presently unattached and so she, being pathologically incapable of being alone, spent most of her time with Gloria and the kids. She talked Gloria into leaving the house for a few days, bringing the kids and coming with her on a holiday on Catalina. Gloria had initially been against it, but she agreed that Emily and Perry could do with a change of scenery and some fun.

Now the four of them sat in facing seats on the enclosed upper deck of the *Catalina Express*. The boat rocked on the sea as it eased out of the harbor. Perry was glued to the window, asking over and over how far away the island was and how long it would take to get there and if there really were buffalo in the hills. Gloria fidgeted, worrying about Ted, wondering if he had been killed or had simply finished the process of dying away from her. She held Emily's hand.

"Doing all right?" Hannah asked.

Gloria had never liked boats, was prone to seasickness.

"You look a little pale," Hannah said.

"That's kinda sad, because I feel fine," Gloria said.

A man sat reading a magazine on the other side of the aisle. Hannah, of course, not only observed that he was handsome, but that the fourth finger of his left hand was ringless. She stared at him until he became aware that she was in fact staring at him, flashed a smile and looked away, out the window at the ocean. She would glance back to make sure she still held his interest every couple of minutes, until finally the man got up, came over and asked if he might sit with them. He was a good-looking man in spite of his wide-set eyes and Hannah eagerly moved over to allow him room. His name was Richard and he had a habit of running his palm over his cropped-short, dark hair after saying something, not that he did it every time, but enough so Gloria noted it. It wasn't that he was vain, Gloria thought, but perhaps uneasy, as if being forward did not come naturally.

While Hannah made small talk with the man, asking why he was going to the island, what he did, where he lived, everything short of was he involved with anyone, Gloria detected a vacancy in Perry's face as he came back toward her. "Are you all right?" she asked.

Perry nodded, but it was no response to her question. A couple of beads of perspiration appeared on his forehead. Then, as if choreographed, mother and child got up and stepped across the aisle to the door of the restroom. The door was locked, however, and so they ran through the cabin and outside, weaving through people, Gloria's hand cupped over Perry's puffed cheeks, to the back of the vessel. The boy released his breakfast into the wake and slowly the fresh air brought color back to his face.

"Is he okay?" It was Richard, standing behind them, his large hand placed lightly on Perry's back.

Gloria said that he was fine. She knew Perry; his problem now was surviving the embarrassment of all this attention. Emily and Hannah were hovering too, but Gloria managed to police them away and walked Perry back to their seats.

Richard laughed softly. They all looked at him. "I was just remembering a time I threw up. I was twelve and I was at this dinner party that my parents dragged me to. They served all sorts of weird food, but that wasn't the problem. The problem was that, even though my mother told me not to, I ate three Mars bars and drank a questionable chocolate soda on the way to the party. Well, it turned out that there was this girl there and I really liked her. I thought she was cool and I was sitting next to her. There was this stuff on my plate. I don't know to this day what it was." He paused while Perry snorted out a laugh. "You've had it," Richard said and smiled. "So, I tasted this stuff and the girl said something to me and the next thing I knew she was covered with chocolate and everything else."

"Yuck," Perry said, but he was laughing. "You threw up all over her like that?"

"On her new dress," Richard said. "She looked right at my eyes and, boy, was she in shock."

"What did you say?" Emily asked.

"I said, 'Oops.' "

The kids relaxed into laughter, repeating *oops* while Gloria found that she was looking at Richard's eyes and he at hers. Gloria quickly looked away. Hannah noticed the connection as well and offered a smile from which Gloria also turned. Gloria thought of Ted, lying somewhere, dead or near death and was filled with guilt, not only for having shared a glance with this strange man, but also for finding the man attractive, as well as a special, separate guilt for thinking, as things can be thought in fractions of seconds, that, in all her years with Ted, she had never been unfaithful, even after his flagrant indiscretions, and maybe, peradventure, she might be deserving of just one fling. How could she be thinking such a thing? And Ted, now, after his death, was a different Ted, a calmer, dearer Ted and they, together, were different, Ted's death having brought them renewed life.

"Have you ever been to Catalina before?" Richard asked the kids.

They shook their heads. "We talked about going once," Emily said.

"Are there really buffalo there?" Perry asked.

"A whole herd."

"Richard was telling me he has a place in Avalon," Hannah said. She was staring at Gloria, trying to read her.

* * *

Later, when the kids were exploring the grounds of the hotel, Hannah said, "It's that widow thing in your face that's attractive to him."

"Thanks a lot."

"I don't mean it like that. You're beautiful, but men are drawn to that needy thing."

"Well, it doesn't matter, because I'm not a widow. I'm still very much a married woman." Gloria sat on the bed and looked at the blank television screen.

"Anyway, it was clear that he was interested," Hannah said.

Gloria picked up the phone.

"Who are you calling?" Hannah asked.

"Calling to check my machine. Who knows when that investigator might find something." But there were no messages. "So, what do we do now?"

"Go shopping?"

Gloria looked at her younger sister. "Hannah, do you think Ted is alive?"

Hannah shrugged. "Do you want him to be?"

"Yes," Gloria answered quickly.

* * *

The electrocardiogram showed no activity in the heart. The electroencephalogram indicated that, for all practical purposes, Ted was dead. There were no impulses detected by electromyography. Magnetic resonance imaging yielded no helpful information. And the isotope scan revealed that Ted was a perfectly healthy dead man. For something to do, the white-coated technicians performed angiography, laparoscopy, intravenous pyelography, sialography and administered a lymphangiogram. Dr. Lyons pushed her fingers into Ted's mouth and ears and anus, felt his armpits, scrotum and under his throat, then sat back and read the clipboard of pages in front of her. Ted was naked on the examination table, lying on his side, his eyes becoming adjusted to the harsh reflections of the stainless steel cabinets.

"What's the verdict?" Ted asked.

"You're dead," Lyons said.

"I am?"

"And you're not dead. I mean, you are looking at me and talking to me, but it seems your muscles are not relying on electrical stimuli for movement, your brain is not talking to your limbs, your heart is in a deep sleep and nothing is flowing through your veins. Yet, here we are."

"And how do you explain that?" Ted asked.

"I can't." Lyons studied Ted's eyes for a prolonged moment. "I'm going to cut you open."

"What are you looking for?"

"Anything."

Ted thought that he saw fear in Lyons's face, but then the ambiguous expression was replaced by one easily discerned as annoyance. She tapped her pencil against the chart and looked away from him. "Since you have no bloodstream and no connection between circulatory and nervous systems, I'm at a loss to know whether you can be anesthetized."

"So, I'll be awake while you perform your . . . shall we call it *mortem?*"

Lyons said, "We'll see."

. . .

How could there be a god? It, of course, could be the same god which had Jephthah present his daughter as a burnt offering in return for victory against the Ammonites. But if there was a god, it was allowing this now and, though Ted was experiencing no physical pain, the sight, sound and contemplation of what was happening killed him over and over. His torso was splayed open from his throat to his scrotum, his rib cage cracked and spread while Lyons peered into him, into the deepest recesses, her supplicant staff handing her instruments and awaiting instruction. There was a round mirror suspended from the ceiling, in which Ted's left was made right, and he watched as Lyons removed his heart. He felt a pang for Gloria, for his children, as the organ was placed by an assistant into a stainless steel dish. The room was thick with the fear of the staff and of Lyons. Ted could hear the drying of their mouths, the tiniest plops of their perspiration onto their collars. They shared frequent looks of surprise, horror, disgust and loss. Ted smelled the air and there was no smell of death, no smell of the opening of a living or once-living thing, and he knew, for these pathologists, this must have been the most frightening aspect of the whole procedure. Absolutely nothing that was expected was the case. Organs became piled high on the table, but the face on the table showed open eyes and unchanging expression.

Ted said, finally, his bladder being held by Dr. Lyons, "Will you be putting everything back?"

"If you'd like," Lyons said. "But you don't seem to need it."

"Still."

Lyons looked at the pieces of Ted and scratched at a temple with the wrist of a glove, a troubled, puzzled gesture. "I'll put it all back. You might not be quite the same."

"Still."

And so Lyons more or less stuffed the organs back into Ted's body much as one might stuff a turkey, the stomach going basically where the stomach had been, the kidneys ending up both on the same side, his pancreas falling to the floor and being kicked aside altogether. The silence grew geometrically with each step toward the end of the procedure, until the room was filled with what Ted considered "negative sound." The vibrations of the room were being sucked into Lyons and her staff, unable to actually exhale, incapable of even looking at each other for affirmation, confirmation, or shared horror, fear or confusion. Lyons did the closing herself, apologizing as she went. "As a pathologist, I'm not used to sewing up my patients," she said. "I don't know how you will heal. There might be significant scarring."

"Did you discover anything?" Ted asked.

Lyons looked at him briefly, then back at her suturing. Her demeanor had changed. The tough pretense was gone and all that remained was fear. She backed away from Ted.

Two armed guards stepped into the room, a welcome signal to the staff that it could exit. Lyons stood unsteadily between the stone-faced, black-clad soldiers.

"Back to my room?" Ted asked.

"Stay here," Lyons said. "Just for a while."

* * *

Sally turned his Ford off the main highway in Yucca Valley and drove deep into the desert. He drank from one of his many bottles of water, watching the white expanse of desolation on either side of the neglected asphalt strip. He pulled into the yard of a little diner, got out and went to the door. He was met there by an old man.

"Help you?" the man asked.

Sally looked back at the sign on the road, then at the one hanging in the window. "This is a restaurant, isn't it?"

"Basically," the old man said. "But I don't know you."

"If you only serve your friends, then it's not a restaurant, it's your house," Sally said.

"It's my house then."

"Listen, I don't want to eat anyway. I'd just like to ask you a couple of questions."

"That's too bad, because I don't know any answers."

Sally looked at the empty ribbon of road and thought that a bite to eat didn't sound so bad. "Let me ask anyway? Do you know anybody around here who drives a brown van?"

The man said nothing.

"What about a midget? Have you seen a midget around? Maybe in the van, maybe not?" Sally pulled his handkerchief from his hip pocket and wiped at the back of his neck. "What kind of food do you serve your friends?"

"All sorts of stuff. Hamburgers. Fried potatoes. Flapjacks. Steaks. Pies. All sorts of stuff."

"Do a good business?" Sally asked.

"Jumpin'."

"Really."

"I know the van you're talking 'bout," the old man said. "And the little feller. There's some religious nuts out there at Gehinnom Flats. And I mean, *nuts*."

"How do I get there?"

He pointed. "About five miles, right on a dirt road about six. The six-mile lane ain't nothin' but a suggestion, so you better keep an eye out."

"Thank you."

"The helicopters been around too," the old man said. "So, be careful."

"Helicopters," Sally repeated.

"The black ones. So, be careful."

"You bet."

"Come back and I'll serve you some food."

* * *

Gloria and Hannah sat on the small strip of bathing beach in front of the ocean-facing storefronts of Avalon. It was a warm day and the water looked cold to Gloria, though the kids didn't seem to mind it at all. Hannah had brought a couple of the awful romance novels she was always reading, having found a series which, in her words, "didn't beat around the bush when it came to beating around the bush."

"Aren't those books all alike?" Gloria asked.

"Exactly." Hannah slid her sunglasses onto her face. "The kids seem okay."

"I hope so."

"Gloria, I'm sorry about the way I was with Ted."

Gloria didn't look at her, but continued to watch Perry and Emily. "Well, maybe you'll be able to make it up to him."

Hannah fiddled with the rubber band that she'd used to secure a plastic bag over her cast.

"Do you know how ridiculous that looks?" Gloria asked.

"It'll keep the water out."

"Stay out of the water."

"This will work."

"Hello, ladies," a voice came from behind them. It was Richard. "For an island, there's not a lot of beach here."

"How are you?" Hannah asked.

He sat beside Hannah. Gloria looked at Richard's feet. He had pretty feet, short hairs on the knuckles of his toes.

"Out to catch some sun?" Hannah asked.

"Just relaxing. My house is just up that street." He used his thumb to point behind him without looking back. "The little boy seems to have recuperated."

"He's fine," Gloria said, her first words since Richard had joined them. She felt she sounded curt.

"They're beautiful children," Richard said.

Hannah and Gloria said, "Thank you." Then, they laughed.

Hannah turned to Gloria and offered a covert look, then made to get up. Gloria grabbed her arm. "I'm going to get wet with the kids."

"That water's cold," Gloria said.

"Only at first," Hannah said. She called to the children, "Here I come, you little monsters."

Richard played in the sand between his legs.

Gloria searched for anything to say.

"I'm sorry about your husband," he said.

Gloria swallowed. She looked at him, then beyond him. Then she looked at all the people around them. "Does everyone know?" Her heart was still, like her husband's, she thought.

"I don't think anyone knows. Your husband, they would recognize, but you?"

"Thanks," Gloria joked.

"I don't mean it like that," he said.

"I know. I was just teasing."

Hannah kicked herself away from Perry, splashing him while he squealed.

"Your sister's a nut."

Gloria nodded.

"That must have been something to see," Richard said.

"It was."

"Where is your husband now?"

"I don't know." Gloria was not about to discuss her private life with this stranger. She wasn't going to tell him that Ted had been kidnapped or that Ted had been a philanderer, or anything. Thinking about Ted, she began to wonder if Sally had yet called to leave a message.

"I can understand your not wanting to talk about it."

She looked at his eyes, soft eyes that seemed to understand in that general, comforting way. She at once appreciated and resented his sensitivity or display, it didn't matter which.

"I'm making you uncomfortable," Richard said.

"A little. I am still married."

"I was married once," he said, changing the subject. He pointed at a cruise ship floating far out on the ocean. "I got married on that very boat. The love boat." He laughed. "I wasn't ready and she was certifiable. It lasted a month."

"Those things happen," Gloria said.

"That was ten years ago."

Gloria nodded. "Let me ask you a question," she said. "Why are you talking to me?"

"I don't understand."

"I mean, why me? Why not my sister?"

"I'm not attracted to your sister."

"But you're attracted to me, a bag of confusion with two kids and a celebrated, resurrected husband?"

"Go figure."

Gloria was no longer thinking about the man sitting beside her. She needed to get to a phone. "Hannah!" she called. "Hannah!"

Hannah stopped playing and faced her.

"I'm going back to the room."

"You okay?"

"Fine. See you back there." She didn't say goodbye to Richard, just grabbed her bag, got up and left the beach.

CHAPTER THREE

THE GUARDS WERE INDEED stone-faced and young enough that it was all act and no act at all, standing there with the comforting stench of gun oil soaking into their fingers. They were stuck in this facility, sworn to secrecy. A secrecy the depth of which their immaturity and innocence would not allow them to fathom, a secrecy which would forever keep them from their families, which would have them, once they began to tire of the assignment, become distrustful and wary of their situation, question once too often their superiors and cause them to be quietly and *secretly* replaced by two more young men just like them. Ted was naked on the table in front of them, wearing not only the jagged stitches around his neck, but also a neat, however crooked, seam up the middle of his torso. He stood and watched the soldiers lower and aim the barrels of their rifles at him. The only thing for him to use to cover himself was the sheet from the operating table, stained with the meaningless fluids from his body. He grabbed the sheet and wrapped it about him, studied the melting faces of the boys in front of him.

"Where are you from, son?" Ted asked one of them. He had always wondered if he would ever feel old enough to call another unrelated man *son*, however objectionable the practice.

"Cheyenne County, Kansas, sir!"

"Miss it?"

"Yes, sir!"

"Expect to see it again?" Ted asked.

"I do, sir!" Pearls of sweat were breaking out on his face, on the backs of his hands. Ted could hear the man's heart, both of their hearts, like baseballs in a bucket.

"What about you?" Ted turned to the second man. "Where are you from?"

The young men looked at each other, adjusting their sweating fingers around the trigger guards of their black weapons. "Rose Haven, Maryland, sir!"

"Not far from Fair Haven," Ted said.

The man's eyes showed surprise. "Yes, sir."

"Okay, boys, this is what I think. I think that you will never see home again." Ted watched them squeeze the metal of the weapons. "I'm not the enemy, though I might look like it. Just look at this place." Ted glanced around, indicated himself by patting his chest. "Look at me. Are you going to wander into the corner tavern in Fair Haven and tell them about me, about this place?"

"We're sworn to secrecy, sir!" from the first soldier.

"Yeah, well that's the thing. Don't you understand, Cheyenne County, Kansas, that you're a liability once you leave this place? This place is not *business as usual*." Ted pointed to the floor beside the operating table. "See that? That's my pancreas. They didn't even put it back. Look at me. Have you ever seen anything like me before?"

The soldiers said nothing.

"I have a family and I want to see them. Will you help me get out of here?"

"Can't do that, sir!" Either, both, didn't matter.

"They're never going to let you leave here, boys," Ted said. "Well, they might, but they're going to fuck you up with drugs or something, then say you're crazy and you'll wind up sleeping in cartons under railroad bridges or in that special ward at the VA hospital or worse."

The men searched for footing.

"I'll be walking past you now."

"Please, no, sir!"

Ted took a step and both men fired. The bullets passed harmlessly into and out of his body, the noise of the reports more disturbing than the projectiles. He stepped closer, the men still firing erratic bursts, like coughing at a concert. They backed to the door. "I'm getting out of here," Ted told them.

The soldiers crabbed away from the door, one dropping his gun, the other holding his weapon by its barrel, letting the stock swing by his leg. Ted was amazed but not surprised by the missing effect of the bullets. Clearly, he could not be killed. Whether a function of the fact that he was already dead he could not say. Ironically, he thought, if the young men had tackled and subdued him, he would have been unable to break free. Their bullets having passed harmlessly through their mark, the soldiers fainted. Ted opened the door and stepped into a long, white corridor. Either direction was identical, the turns of the hallway about a hundred feet away.

. . .

A small sailboat motored out to sea.

"A little night sailing sounds nice right about now," Richard's voice came from behind Gloria.

She didn't turn around, but she recognized his voice. "It's too dark out there for me," she said.

"Kids asleep?"

"Yes."

"I hope I didn't make you feel uncomfortable earlier," Richard said. He leaned on the rail and looked down at the water with her. A wave of singing came from the tavern. "I hate that place," he said.

Gloria laughed. "What brings you out?"

"Couldn't sleep. This is a sweet and quaint little town, but it's noisy as hell. And these houses, they're not insulated worth a crap. Not that the windows are ever closed anyway."

"It's a beautiful place," Gloria said. "So, what do you do here?"

"Get away. I fish a lot. That's my boat over there." He pointed to a medium-sized motorboat. "It's not much, but it's fun. The house I inherited from my parents. Where are you staying?"

"Hotel Catalina."

Richard nodded.

"May I ask you something?"

"Please."

Gloria turned and looked at his eyes. "Why are you talking to me? I mean, are you attracted to me or to the fact that my husband died and came back to life?"

"You."

"Why?"

"You're attractive, bright."

Gloria was starting to smile, but not because she was flattered, but because she was finding in herself the kind of confidence she had always wanted. "Thank you for the kind words." She looked at his face and found it pretty.

"Are you a spontaneous person?" Richard asked.

"That's a line."

"I didn't mean it to be."

"So, you want to kiss me," she said. She didn't let him answer. "You should know however that the last man I kissed didn't have any vital signs." She closed her eyes. "Okay, kiss me."

"Gloria," he said.

"Kiss me, if you want to," she said without opening her eyes.

She felt his full lips press onto hers, his chest against her breast, his hands gripping her upper arms. She could feel his pulse through his thumbs and never had she felt such a dead kiss. She opened her eyes and Richard pulled back, let go of her arms.

"Good night, Richard," she said.

* * *

The hallway was like a throat and Ted had never felt more swallowed. The installation was perhaps not huge, but it was certainly labyrinthine. Except for that first step out of the elevator, no other place had yet yielded a view of anything more than a room or corridor, making it feel much like a submarine or like a tunnel. He thought he needed the light of the sun, not this artificial wash, and he contemplated the possibility that he was a reverse vampire, not fleeing the sun, but needing it. Though he breathed no air, he needed it now. The walls were closing in. He turned left, right, left, again and again, the channels endless, exceedingly well lighted and stark white, the stainless steel doors ubiquitous and identical except for varying locking mechanisms and it might have been, he thought, that he was winding in circles. No signs designated sectors, no sentries guarded portals. His dead body was tireless, but his mind, so full of life, new life, better life, he thought, was fatigued. Lost in there, searching for an exit like an animal searches for food, Ted felt less than an animal. No animal moves about at random seeking its prey; it employs a method, looks in reasonable places. Ted stopped and tried to enter a room. He pounded buttons on one keypad, offered a retinal scan to another and finally a palm sensor admitted him. Inside there was no room at all, but a passageway down, a spiraling declining corridor, as well lighted as the one he had just left, the walls a light blue now instead of white. He twisted around until he was spit out into a wide chamber, dimly lit and filled with unmanned terminals, computer screens emitting light and high-pitched whining that pierced his senses. At a desk in the middle of it all sat a man, a slightly fat man who looked up slowly to find Ted in front of him wearing nothing but a sheet. As slowly, he returned his attention to his notes.

"My name is Theodore Street," Ted said.

"My name is Oswald Avery," the man said without looking up.

"Really?"

"I'm not that Oswald Avery." Still, he did not raise his head.

"I'm trying to get out of here," Ted told him.

"Join the club."

"Can you help me?" Ted asked.

"I can't get out myself. And I work here." Avery finally looked up. "Why are you wrapped up like that?"

Ted let down the sheet and exposed his torso briefly.

"Ouch," Avery said. "So, you got loose." His comment seemed general, a thing to say. Then, "What are you?"

"I don't know," Ted answered. He stepped closer to Avery, near enough to see that he was reading a book open on his desk. "I'm Theodore Street. Haven't you heard of me?" Ted was hit for the first time with the fact that he was famous.

"I've been in this hole for eleven years," Avery said. "I don't even know who's president. For all I know, you're the president."

"No, I'm just a man who didn't stay dead."

Avery was studying now the stitches around Ted's neck. "Then of course they'd find you and bring you down here. What happened to your throat?"

"My head was completely severed from my body in an automobile crash."

Avery closed his book and leaned back and to the side in his chair. "So, you're the real thing."

"I guess so." Ted became tired of the scrutiny and shifted focus. "What do you do here?"

"You see, my dear dead friend, I have lost my funding and so I am simply waiting to learn my fate. I keep thinking that if I uncover the secret to reanimation before they kill me, that I could actually walk out of here. But without the secret, there's no point. They'd find me outside and kill me just as easily as they can find me in here." He picked up a pipe from his desk, stuck it in his face, but didn't light it.

"Why aren't they chasing me?" Ted asked.

"A couple of reasons," Avery formed the words around his pipe stem. "One, they know you can't get out. They also probably know where you are anyway. And there are only two security personnel down here. All the other gun toters are topside, keeping us secret."

"Well, the two guards passed out," Ted said. He looked around the ceiling for surveillance cameras, finding none. "Isn't there a way out of this place?"

"Maybe." Then Avery eased back into his chair. "Eleven years. Would you like to see what I've been up to for eleven years?" He did not wait for Ted to answer. He stood up and said, "Come, follow me." He led them past the terminals to the back of the big room. "Aren't you cold?"

"No," Ted said.

From a rack outside a set of double doors Avery pulled out a powder blue jumpsuit. "Here, this ought to fit."

Ted dropped the sheet and stepped into the suit.

"Did they do that to you here?" Avery moved close and almost touched the seam on Ted's torso.

"Yes, they took out my organs and threw them back in," Ted said. He zipped the suit up the front, a biting parody of his wound. "They did that to me and I'm still talking to you. Something, eh?"

"Like I said, the real thing." He keyed a code into the pad by the doors. "I want to show you something."

Ted followed the man through the doors and inside were more than twenty dark-haired, drooling men dressed in jumpsuits like the one he was wearing, sitting in molded plastic chairs around the perimeter of the room. Many of the men were badly deformed and Ted found them difficult to observe directly for more than a few seconds. A few were hunchbacked. At least three had what appeared to be a second nose pushing out over the one occupying the center of the face. There were bent torsos with only one arm and some with three. One man had three legs, while others had one and a half or none. Most of their faces were twisted, with cleft palates, crossed eyes, long drooping lobes.

"My God," Ted said.

"Close," said Avery. "Jesus Christ is more correct. You understand that we're here trying to uncover the secrets of reanimation. Perhaps the most famous reanimated person is Jesus Christ." But he didn't wait for a response before asking, "Have you ever heard of the spear of Longinus?"

"No," said Ted.

"The fifth wound to the Christ was a cut delivered by a Roman soldier named Longinus. The staff of the spear is in Rome, but the blade, well, no one ever knew where the blade was. Until about fifty years ago when Hitler's men found it in a cave." Avery sucked in a deep breath. "Anyway we ended up with the blade and on the blade are blood stains, the blood of Jesus. From the stains we isolated the DNA and using the DNA we tried to clone Christ."

"You're kidding me," Ted said.

Avery gestured with a sweep of his arm for Ted to observe the deformed men in the room.

"These are Christs?"

"They are. We haven't had much success." Avery laughed to himself. "Of course if Jesus was in fact the son of God, then maybe we're seeing the Lord's DNA as well. Something to think about, eh?"

Ted's head was swimming. What he was hearing was so huge,

yet so superficially simple. It was the simplicity that was so troubling, so mind-boggling. He looked again at the deformed shells. "Have you noticed anything Christlike about any of them?"

"No. Unfortunately, their brains are as deformed as their bodies. I've made nearly forty of them. There are twenty-seven left."

Ted posed a question with his face.

"We've killed thirteen. Needless to say, after three days they remained dormant. How long did it take you to wake up?"

"Three days."

"You don't say." Avery studied Ted again. "That could be coincidence."

"It no doubt is," Ted said.

"We've killed the Jesuses in many different ways. I wonder if mankind is that many more times saved." Avery laughed. "Hell, for all we really know it's Hitler's blood on that damn blade. Or maybe Barabbas's. We could have a whole room full of thieves here." Avery sat in an empty chair and threw his leg over the Jesus next to him. "Do you believe there was a Jesus Christ, the son of the Father almighty?"

"Not really," Ted said. "Do you?"

"I have to. My funding depends on it. Or anyway, it used to. I know that prayers don't get answered. If people topside knew what we were doing down here they'd all have cows and die. Every religious nut and his virgin mother would be crying that we were trying to play God. Of course we're trying to play God. When you play baseball you try to be Willie Mays, not Gerry Juker."

"Who's Gerry Juker?"

"My point." He studied the stem of his pipe. "What better tribute to the *Soup*reme being than to emulate him?" Avery rubbed his eyes. "Anyway, my days here are numbered. My days anywhere are numbered. I have enough money to make a couple more messiahs, then kill them with great expectations, then wait around here for one of the ever-changing youthful guards to come shoot me. Do you play chess?"

"I know how to play," Ted said.

"I tell you what. If you beat me in a game of chess, I'll help you escape this place."

"Why don't you just come with me?" Ted asked.

"They'd catch me in a second. I'd be no good underground. I would die being a homeless person inside a day. Besides, my family already believes I'm dead. I couldn't show up alive just to be found dead the next day. I couldn't do that to them."

"You could tell everybody what they're doing down here, about your experiments."

"Would you believe a fringe geneticist, presumed dead ten years ago, who shows up claiming to have made a bunch of Jesus Christs for the military?"

"I guess not," Ted said.

"I guess not," Avery repeated. "Let's play chess."

* * *

Investigator Sally relieved himself some yards away from his car off the shoulder of the road. The desert was dry and lonely and made him appreciate the city he always complained about. He got into his Ford and drove the dirt path to the cult compound. The only sign of human presence besides the road itself was a yellow fast-food wrapper blowing by with the wind. Soon, he could see the buildings of the camp, no fence, and no evidence of anyone. He stopped and watched for a while through his field glasses. He saw a woman walk from one building to another. He got back into his car and drove on. When he stopped and got out in front of the largest, most central building, he discovered that there were at least twelve men standing around him.

"Good morning," Sally called out to them.

Big Daddy stepped through the men and looked Sally up and down. "Who are you?"

"I'm a private investigator. I'm looking for someone and I thought you might be able to help me." Sally gave Big Daddy his card.

Big Daddy didn't look at it but handed it behind him to Gerald. He walked a half circle around Sally, studied his shoes, his clothes, his car.

"You look familiar," Sally said.

"Do I now?" Big Daddy said.

"I'm looking for a man, a rather odd-looking man. He has a scar around his neck. His name is Theodore Street."

"Never heard of him." Big Daddy completed his circle around the man. "Why do you want him?"

"I work for an insurance company," Sally said. "I just need to find him."

"Like I said, I've never seen him."

"Do you have a brown van?" Sally saw a couple of pickups parked behind sheds, and a blue El Camino baking out in the sun near nothing in particular.

"No," Big Daddy said.

"I hear you're some kind of religious group."

"As a matter of fact we are. Are you a Christian?"

"I have been at times," Sally said.

"Are you presently?"

Sally counted the men standing around him, felt the heat of the sun on his neck, tasted the salt of perspiration which rolled down his face and into the corner of his mouth, looked up at the sick hollowness in Big Daddy's eyes. "Yes, I am." He reached down and lifted the handle of his car door. "Listen, my number is on that card. If you see anybody like the man I described, maybe you could give me a call."

Big Daddy leaned close to Sally. Sally pulled his door open and squeezed in behind the wheel.

"Thanks for your time," Sally said.

* * *

Oswald Avery loved his knights. He loved his knights so much that his queen and rooks had fallen silent only ten moves into the game. Still his knights hopped this way and that, eluding danger and causing little trouble. All the while the geneticist spoke of what imagination it must have taken to devise such movement as was employed by the little horse. "How did it strike the inventor or inventors of the game?" Avery wondered. "One up and two over, two up and one over. How wonderfully wild, how radical. I'd love to clone that fellow."

. . .

Avery was stuck, he couldn't think of the words he needed to tell his wife that he would be gone two years and that she wouldn't be able to contact him in that time. Deep down he knew the sad truth that she really didn't care, that she had been sleeping with her psychoanalyst and that for years his absorption in his work had left her feeling inadequate and unneeded. The fact of the matter was that now, as he was heading off for work he could tell no one about, he was afraid and needed to know there was someone in the world who was going to miss him.

"I'm very proud of you," his wife said absently.

They were sitting at the kitchen table, having breakfast. The kids were to the table and gone, teenagers, a boy and a girl, he thought. Perhaps two girls. Kim and Ronnie. He watched their long-haired heads pass through the door to the outside world, a world with which they seemed more in touch than their father ever had been.

"I've been awarded a special project," Avery said.

His wife slid a plate of eggs in front of him.

"It means I'll be gone for a while."

"We'll be fine."

"It's a long stint."

"Short, long. I'll pay the bills until you get back."

"Two years. It's secret. I won't be able to call or write."

"The children will miss you."

Avery took a bite of cold eggs and looked out the window at the cold New England sky. "Have you ever wondered whether life is worth the trouble?"

"Every day," she said.

"Really?"

"Why do you ask?"

"Because I just wondered it for the first time this morning?" Avery took another bite of eggs and felt suddenly embarrassed, stupid. The eggs were slightly rubbery in his mouth and he found he could not look at his wife's eyes. He examined one of the yolks on his plate, almost firm the way she always made them almost firm, and he contemplated, as a defensive distraction, what came first, embryo or chicken, and he became amused. He must have let a smile crack through his chewing.

"What is it?" his wife asked.

"Would the children miss me if I died?"

"What kind of question is that?" she asked.

He thought her response was appropriate enough, but still she had not answered his question and he took that as an answer in itself. "I'm sorry," he said.

"Okay." She was puzzled, but did not seek clarification, turned her attention instead to the paper she was reading.

"I'm truly sorry."

* * *

"I wouldn't say that I haven't enjoyed my work here," Avery said. He was fiddling with a captured pawn. "I couldn't have done these experiments anywhere else. Cloning a sheep or a monkey, that's one thing, but a person, well—" He closed his eyes and pinched the bridge of his nose, as if to clear sleep from his eyes.

"Have any of your Christ clones been"—Ted searched—"well, divine in any way?"

"I'm not sure what that would mean," Avery said, biting his pipe and staring at the board. "They're mostly retards, if you haven't noticed. A couple have been sweet as can be. Had one who was an idiot savant, could tabulate the number of toothpicks in a jar in just seconds, but was as dumb as a post. You're trying to take my knight, aren't you, Mr. Frankenstein?"

The Frankenstein comment hit Ted like a brick. He realized he was in fact a monster, engendering fear in everyone who crossed his path—his daughter, the zealots, Dr. Lyons, the guards, everyone except the man whom he was in the process of mating at chess. The only person who showed no fear of him was a man who made monsters himself, who had taken the savior of so many in the world and carved him into discarded flesh and wasted tissue.

Ted moved his queen to a spot protected by his bishop directly in front of Avery's king. "Mate," he said.

"Nicely done," Avery said.

CHAPTER FOUR

OSWALD AVERY WAS NOT coming around quickly to explaining to Ted how he in fact would help him escape. He sat at the cemetery of a chessboard, replaying the imagined carnage in his mind and mourning his beloved knights. "That's where you killed the first one," he said, nodding sadly. While contemplating the moves leading to that loss, he said, "The problem is perhaps the eukaryotic genes. Lots of repetitive nucleotide sequences there and we don't really understand why or what for. Humans have a couple hundred pairs appearing a million times. That's an awful lot of *us*. Some people call it *selfish* DNA and say it gives us nothing, that it's just along for the trip with the chromosomes. Maybe they come from viruses. Maybe they're not junk at all." Avery shook his head and physically replayed the taking of his knight. "Maybe they're the only genes that really matter."

"How are you going to get me out of here?" Ted asked.

"I've decided I'm going to go with you." Once again he examined the wooden horse's head in his palm. "What's the difference whether they kill me out there or down here in this hell." He looked directly into Ted's eyes. "I used to be a pathetic man. Not because I was obsessed with work, but because I was afraid, afraid to live, afraid of confrontation, afraid of everything. I've never lived, have never known how to live. How could I have taught *living* to my children if I didn't know how to do it?"

"Then, how do *we* get out of here?" Ted asked. He considered that he had entertained that question so often in past days, yet not in death, not when the final door had closed on him and he wondered, if he had known that he was dying, if he could have seen his body lying headless on the asphalt, would he have tried to figure a way out. He supposedly had been on his deliberate path to suicide, but even he doubted his resolve, having never in his life been able to see any painful course of action through to its end.

"I have some things to collect first," Avery said. "You can wait with the Jesuses."

The thought of being in the room with the twenty-seven Christs was unsettling to Ted, partially because he was afraid that, despite his atheism, there might be something to the figure's divinity, that like Pascal's wager, one of the Jesuses might see him and reveal him for what he was, whatever that was. Also, was it possible that he might himself discover his own secret, some similarity between himself and these clones? If there was one resemblance, might there be others, and might he then ascend into heaven to sit at the right hand of one in whom he had never and did not believe? Ted followed Avery to the chamber and sat in a plastic molded chair just like the clones, his mood affecting his posture, and so when he looked at the shadows they all cast on the floor, his was just like theirs, hunched and sad. He made himself sit up straight and examined each and every drooling face, the deep-set brown eyes, the dark, coarse hair, the deformities, the extra parts, the missing parts, the vacant stares. But there was one, across the room, sitting just slightly more upright, his hands folded together in his lap. His eyes were soft, but not so empty, his nose was large and he had no mouth at all. Ted stared at him for a few minutes, but the man did not immediately look back. Eventually, however, his eyes found Ted's eyes and Ted was moved, not by any special magic, not by any peculiar or remarkable warmth or expression of knowledge, but by the mere fact that he was offering a response of sorts.

* * *

Hannah was pretending to be asleep, but Gloria wasn't falling for it. "You're not asleep," she said.

"How'd you know?"

"Your finger is working too hard to keep your place in that awful book," Gloria said, sitting on the edge of the bed and reaching down to unlace her sneakers. "So, what happens in this one? Does the baron promise to leave his wife for the sexy young governess or does the actress with the deteriorating career learn that her alcoholic producer husband is sleeping with her male co-star?"

"Is it a nice night?" Hannah asked.

"It's a bit cool."

"Lots of people out?"

"A few. Actually, quite a few. That bar down at the end of the strip is really loud." Gloria looked at her shoe for a few seconds before tossing it to the floor. "Did you look in on the kids?"

"Yeah, I left the door ajar for a while. Perry wanted the light.

They're fine." Hannah sat more upright, folded her pillow behind her. "What's wrong?"

"Nothing's wrong." Gloria got her other shoe off and walked over to the door between their room and the kids'. She pushed the door open and observed both children. She went back to the bed, sat, pulled off her sweater and began to unbutton her blouse, her fingers fumbling. She paused to work her hands in front of her. She often thought they were arthritic, the stiffness, the aching.

"Something's wrong," Hannah said.

"My hands hurt."

"Something else," Hannah said.

"I kissed him."

"Who did you kiss?"

"Whom."

"Just tell me," Hannah said.

"Richard."

"You didn't."

"I did." Gloria didn't believe she was saying it out loud any more than she believed she had really done it. Her heart was racing and she felt a slice of cold deep in the pit of her stomach.

Hannah was beaming. "That's great." Her voice was uncertain, as if the right words weren't readily available to her.

"It's not what you think," Gloria said, sighing. Inside, she ached, not for Ted, not for the lips she had just touched, but she ached. "And I'm not sure why I did it. I just did it."

"Did he kiss you or did you kiss him?"

"I let him kiss me," she said, as if she had not orchestrated the event, as if she could pass off some blame by claiming that she had simply allowed him his intended desire.

"I can't believe it."

"Neither can I," Gloria said. She lay back on the bed and looked at the ceiling. "I was thinking about Ted the whole time and there he was. I guess I just wanted to know if I really believe he's alive. I can't believe I kissed him. I feel like shit."

"Calm down. So, you kissed the guy. Big deal. It's not like you're having his baby." Hannah laughed. "Think about all the shit Ted did. How can you forget the affairs and the lies? Remember when that crazy woman was with your children? Recall all the things that man did and then begged you to forgive him, to forget everything."

"I can't forget the things he did," Gloria said. "I think I needed to know whether I've forgiven them."

"And?"

"And what?" Gloria looked over at Hannah.

"Have you forgiven the bastard?"

"I don't know."

"Then the answer is no," Hannah said, setting her book on the nightstand. "Where does that leave you?"

Gloria didn't say anything.

"What about Richard?" Hannah asked.

"I'm not thinking about Richard, Hannah. And I'm not thinking about Ted right now. I'm thinking about me. Finally, I'm thinking about me." Gloria considered the details of her life, realizing that the special particulars actually contained the whole, led to the exposition of the whole, believing that by ignoring the details of her life, depriving each of them the chance to develop and influence her world, she was turning each single event into a caricature of its failure. She lay back and put her head on the pillow. She fought sleep.

· · ·

After his meeting with the zealots, Sally was shaking. He'd been in some tight situations before, but one of his rules of operation was when the job turned dangerous, the job was over. This was different, however, the danger now down the highway with no promise of return. He pulled into the yard of the diner's parking lot, gave his horn a honk and stepped out of his car.

The man he had met earlier came out onto the porch, his face more relaxed now, almost broken with a smile. "Come on in and have a bite," he said.

Sally offered a puzzled look.

"I know you now," the man said. "Mind if I say you don't look too good. Something bad happen out there with them nuts?"

"I'm okay," Sally said. He met the man with a firm handshake at the top step. "I'm Horatio Sally."

"Stan Dutch. Come in and have a seat. My wife will cook you up anything on the menu."

"Thanks." Sally entered the building. Stan showed him to a table in the middle of the dim room. Sally sat and let his eyes adjust, putting his elbows on the table and rubbing his temples.

"You sure you're okay?" Stan asked, handing Sally a menu.

Sally nodded and looked up at the man, at his small eyes set far apart on his pudgy red face. "So, I'm not a stranger anymore?"

"You came back," he said. "If you come back to this place after meeting me, then you're a certain kind of person."

Sally didn't know whether he should be flattered. "I'll take that as a compliment."

"Well, look over the menu and I'll be back in a minute. Want some coffee? Iced tea?"

"Tea."

Sally rubbed his temples some more and was startled when Stan returned immediately with the cold drink. Sally thanked him and watched him disappear into the kitchen. As he turned back around he noticed photographs, about twenty of them, eight by tens, evenly spaced across the length of the wall. He got up and walked to one of them, then examined the one next to it, all of them, unable to make out just what they were pictures of. He thought that they were perhaps pictures of UFOs and remembered stories he'd heard about people living way out in the desert.

"Black helicopters," Stan said. He had come back and was waiting with a pad at Sally's table. "They come around pretty often."

"Black helicopters?"

"The government's big secret. It's how they keep tabs on us remote types. In the cities, they just watch you and videotape you while you're walking down the street. Use high-powered microphones and like that. They don't have to bug your house anymore. They just point a big wand at you and record everything you say."

"Is that right?"

"Out here in the boonies, it ain't so easy to spy. No crowd for their operatives to blend into. The helicopters come around just to make sure we ain't up to sedition and the like."

"You took these?" Sally asked.

"Yep."

Sally leaned close to the nearest photograph. "I can't really tell that they're helicopters."

"Well, they are," Stan said. "You ready to order?"

"Yeah." Sally sat down and asked for a cheeseburger, fries and a cup of chili. "I didn't mean anything about the pictures."

Stan looked at the photos on the wall and seemed to ignore Sally's remark. "It's scary when they come around. Makes you mad."

Stan went into the kitchen and Sally noticed either the dining room lights had been turned up a notch or his eyes were finally adjusting. He looked across the room and through the dusty windows. There was a face there. He got up and walked to the door, cracked it open an inch and peeked out. A young woman stood on the porch. She pressed at Sally with an anxious expression, her hands almost trembling by her sides. She wore jeans and a loose fitting black tee-shirt.

"Are you the investigator?" she asked.

"Yes."

She stepped past Sally and into the diner. "My name is Cynthia," she said as she paced to the wall of helicopter pictures and back. "I'm from Big Daddy's compound."

"The religious guy?"

"Yes."

Cynthia folded her arms over her chest and stopped pacing. "Can you help me escape?"

"Well, ma'am, I don't know." Sally looked out into the parking lot and then pulled the door shut.

Stan came from the kitchen and said, "What's going on out here? Who the hell are you?"

Cynthia seemed not to notice Sally's eyes and said, "I know something about the man you're looking for."

"You do?"

"He was out at the compound. Big Daddy was holding him

prisoner, tried to hurt him, kill him, but he got away. He ran off into the desert during the night."

"What night was this?"

"Thursday."

"Which way was he headed?" Sally asked.

"I assumed he would make his way back to the road. I don't know where he is now."

"The helicopter came on Thursday," Stan said.

"The helicopter."

"He's right," Cynthia said. She looked up at the sky she couldn't hope to see through the ceiling of the room. "It hadn't come around for a long time, but it flew over the compound that night."

* * *

Oswald Avery came back into the room struggling with five satchels and dressed in a powder blue Jesus jumpsuit of his own. The flashing red light made his uniform alternatingly lavender and blue. He didn't have to say anything for Ted to understand that the guards were awake and back at their jobs. Avery put down the bags and blew out a long sigh. "These are my notes. Don't ask me why I'm taking them, but I am. I have to. This is my life. Not bad, eh? One life in five bags. It's either a lot or not very much, depends on how you look at it."

Ted nodded. "What now?"

"Now we use the cadaver disposal chute. I call it the corpse cannon. Every house should have one." The scientist walked over to what appeared to be a louvered closet door and opened it, revealing

a stainless steel tube about three feet in diameter with a clear plastic
oval door set about eighteen inches off the floor and about four feet
high. Avery opened the door and took a step back.

Ted leaned into the tube and looked down at the perforated floor,
then up the channel at the tapering darkness. "What the hell is this?"

"We're underground," Avery said. "A long way underground.
One can't very well dispose of bodies down here. So, what this does
is pneumatically shoots the cadavers topside and into the incinerator. Clever, don't you think?"

"You're not suggesting we go up in this?"

"It's more than a suggestion," Avery said, apparently a little
annoyed. "A suggestion would imply the possibility of other options."
Once Avery seemed to feel he had let the subsequent silence make
his point, he explained, "We'll have to go up one at a time. The problem is that the cremation sequence is started by the arrival of the
first shuttled object."

"That does sound like a problem."

"The elements take a while to really get hot."

"How long is a while?" Ted asked.

"About ninety seconds."

"How long does it take to reach the top?"

"I'm not sure. It might vary. I should think no more than a few
seconds by how fast they zoom out of here." Avery looked at his
bags, went to them and picked up two. "Nineteen," he said and one
of the Jesuses, the one with whom Ted had made eye contact, the
one with no mouth, came forward. "Hold on tightly to these, Nineteen." To Ted, Avery said, "These bags are heavy, we'll need help topside carrying them."

Jesus 19 held the bags to his chest as instructed. Avery then nudged the man over and into the chute, closed the portal and slapped the big white button beside it. With a loud swoosh Jesus 19 was gone. Avery turned to the stunned Ted.

"Come on, we'd better hurry." He tossed a bag into Ted's arms. "Get in. Don't worry, just let it happen. I imagine one might be tempted to press against the walls to achieve deceleration, but I would recommend against it. You might tear or burn your flesh. Ta-ta."

Ted hugged the satchel he'd been assigned as if it might offer him some protection, then slid himself into the tube, watched as Avery did not hesitate in slapping the button. The swoosh sounded different from inside, in fact it was a sort of anti-noise, like no noise at all. A negative pressure that should have caused a pain, but was no pain at all for Ted, plowed through his head and he was gone, his toes falling to a point beneath him, his hair being pulled upward from his head. He felt himself rotating clockwise in the chute and he imagined that his insides were being rearranged, that by the time he reached the other end, to no doubt be roasted alive, his organs would be positioned where they had been originally, prior to Lyons's exploratory surgery. He managed against the thrust of the air to tilt his head so that he could look in the direction he was traveling. Time seemed to stop, the journey seemed infinite. There was no sign of Jesus 19 in the tube above him, but there was a light, a pin-prick of illumination, and he thought how ironic it was that only now, as he sought to escape capture, to embrace life, was he headed for that clichéd white light. He thought of how Avery had told him to just let it happen. Oddly, Ted also recalled vividly the smell of the coffee Gloria had made the morning after his confession of his last affair, the smell of almonds and perhaps a little vanilla in the French roast, which had been all the more striking because Gloria had never liked flavored coffees. He'd stepped into the kitchen and said, "That smells good," to which his wife had offered no reply. He'd sat at the table and watched her make enough bacon and waffles and pancakes to feed a family of twenty. The food just kept coming, platters covering the counter, bowls of Irish oatmeal and Cream of Wheat twisting dwindling braids of steam into the air. Perry had come downstairs and stood, mouth agape, at the door, then had slowly made his way to his father's side. The boy had watched as his mother made the bearnaise sauce for the poached eggs. The way she was briskly stirring the sauce must have struck him as funny, being six, and he began to laugh, looking to his father for reassurance that laughter was an acceptable response, but Ted's dumbfounded expression must have been equally funny to him, for the boy laughed harder. Then Emily came downstairs, saw all the food, saw her brother's face contorted in uncontrolled laughter, saw her father's weak chin and she began to sob and sob and sob, until Perry stopped laughing and started crying too, until Gloria stopped cooking and cried, until they were all wailing. Ted recalled this as he twisted in the cylinder. He had come to think of himself as a parody of the genetic material that was himself, but what else beyond the normal pairs of adenine, cytosine, guanine and thymine lay hidden in his DNA? Where did the normally repellant cytosine and adenine become bonded on the chain to make him the deformity that he was? Suddenly, the tube was no more and Ted was spat out into a nearly dark chamber over which stood what he knew to be a smoke stack, wide and open to the bright light of day, light which he had begun to think he would never see again. Jesus 19 was sitting in the ashes of Jesuses before him, staring at Ted. The air was hot and Ted turned to see blue gas flames jetting from elements running the length of the far wall. The chorus line of fire was growing in intensity and expanding its reach and, with its roaring hiss, creating an excruciating sonic blanket. The stillness of the room was split by the emergence first of a satchel, then by Avery through the tube. He clutched the last bag as he popped high into the air like a kernel of popcorn, much as Ted must have, but Ted didn't remember that part, and landed in the deep ashes.

Avery saw the flames and quickly said, "Let's get the hell out of here." He ran with high steps toward the big metal door.

Ted's strides behind him through the soft ashes of dead men created yet another non-sound which struck at his core, tore at his senses, perhaps at his need to hear something, anything.

Avery threw the lever, which in turn slid over the bar that was holding the door fast.

"It's that easy?" Ted said.

"This is not a concentration camp," Avery said, trying to push the door open. "This door isn't meant to lock anyone inside, just to keep the fire in. Besides, they never expected any live bodies. A little help."

Ted could feel the fire licking, almost punching at the back of his jumpsuit, the roaring hiss deafening now, as he grabbed the door and pushed with Avery. Jesus 19 stood very near them, showing no fear but staring intently at the door. It cracked open and fresh, sweet, luscious air seeped in around the hard gray metal edges, around his fingers and finally found his face.

. . .

The dream Gloria was having was one she'd had before. It began with a black-and-white photograph of the family. She and Ted were sitting on a wooden bench and the children were sitting on the picnic table behind them, their little heads higher than their parents'. Then, Gloria stepped from the photograph, then Ted, then Emily and they were no longer in black-and-white but in full color, rubbing their arms as if to help the circulation of blood. Gloria wondered aloud where Perry was. No one seemed to know. They looked back into the photograph, but the boy was not there. Gloria lifted and shook the photo as if to dry it, hoping to shake her son out into the dimension they were all inhabiting. She called his name, but no Perry shook out. "Where is he?" she asked Ted. Ted didn't answer, but was looking behind trees and rocks and sofas and under tables. Emily kept wanting to look again at the photograph. "He's not in it," Gloria told her daughter. "He's not there. He's not there. He's not there. He's not there."

Gloria awoke, sitting straight up in bed, her sister still sleep-breathing beside her. She could smell the ocean. She threw off the sheet and walked to the ajar door that separated the two rooms. Emily was still curled up tightly. Perry was not in his bed. Gloria went to the children's bathroom and looked inside. "Perry?" she asked the air. "Perry. Perry!"

"What is it, Gloria?" Hannah asked, at the door now.

"Perry's gone."

Emily was sitting up, looking around the room.

"Emily, did Perry say he was going out?" Gloria asked.

The child was still groggy with sleep.

"Emily!?"

"What?"

"Where's your brother?" Gloria asked.

"I don't know."

Hannah had her jeans and a sweatshirt on and was hopping while she pulled on her second shoe. "I'll go check the lobby."

"Come on, honey," Gloria said to Emily. "Get dressed, so we can find your brother."

"He probably went to look at the orange fish by the boats," Emily said. "He's down by the water, that's all."

As Gloria found her own clothes, the thought that Perry was *down by the water* rang in her head, *by the water*, and she began to panic, thinking of her son tripping on a gangway trying to get to a boat, slipping on slick rocks trying to get closer to the water and those damn orange fish. "Hurry up!" she screamed to Emily.

Emily was tying her sneakers. "I'm ready. I'm ready."

Gloria and Emily met Hannah and her shaking head in the lobby. "He's not down here. And I checked outside at the Jacuzzi."

"Emily thinks he might be at the pier looking at the garibaldi fish." Gloria saw the clerk come to the counter from the back room. "Do you remember my little boy?"

"Yes," the woman said.

"Have you seen him this morning?"

"No, I haven't."

Gloria wanted to scream, wanted to be at the pier that second. "If he comes back, please hold on to him."

The clerk nodded. "I will."

Gloria led Hannah and Emily out and down the hill toward the harbor. Her ears were alive for the sounds of sirens and walkie-talkie voices, her eyes tried to press around the corner for flashing lights. Maybe she'd turn the corner and meet up with a fat policeman with her child in tow. Perhaps she would discover the little devil trying to sneak back to the hotel. Her stomach was a knot, ice cold, all of her weight in the back pit of it, pulling her down the hill, trying to press her to her knees. She started to call out, "Perry! Perry!"

Emily called out too. "Perry!"

CHAPTER FIVE

GLORIA HAD PERHAPS NEVER felt a grief as profound as the one she experienced when she did not find Perry on the wharf. It was so early that there were few people at all, only a couple of fishermen waiting to walk down the plank to a rental boat, a pair of men opening a snack bar, fastening stools into the boardwalk and turning on dispensers, and one ancient Japanese woman who seemed always to be fishing from the pier. Emily and Hannah stood away, near the snack bar, while Gloria questioned a man, then moved on to the old woman.

"Have you seen a little boy?" Gloria asked.

The woman shook her head without shifting her attention from her fishing line.

"He's seven years old. And he's about this tall." Gloria startled herself with just how small her son in fact was. "His name is Perry and he's lost. Have you seen a little boy?"

The woman shook her head again. Then, as if she'd just come to understand any of what Gloria had been saying, she said, "Boy?"

"Yes."

"Boat," the woman said. She reached out over the railing and plucked at her strand of monofilament like the string of a bass violin. "The water is warmer now. Good for fishing."

"He got into a boat?" Gloria asked.

But the woman would say no more. Gloria looked back to Emily and her sister with a face so stricken that they came sprinting to her side, reaching her in time to keep her on her feet. As soon as she was steady she was walking to the counter of the boat rental, asking if they were irresponsible enough to issue a boat to a lone little boy.

The counter man did not become defensive, but said, in the collected manner of one who had heard it all before, "No, ma'am, we wouldn't consider doing that. We wouldn't do it if the boy had a major credit card and a valid driver's license."

"But that woman standing over there said she saw my son get into a boat."

The man leaned over the counter to give the fisherwoman a long stare, then returned his attention to Gloria. "Okay, ma'am, if it'll make you happy, I'll check it out." He called out the window behind him to a man below on the platform. "Hey, Pablo, make a check and see if any boats are missing." While Pablo was off counting, the man came back to Gloria. "How old is your little boy?"

"He's seven." She was scratching her arm with her nails, making tracks from her wrists to the bend in her arm.

Emily reached up and grabbed her mother's hand to stop her tearing at herself. Gloria reached down and pulled the girl close, pressed Emily's face into her shoulder. Hannah read and reread the rental options pressed under the glass on the countertop.

The man went on, "Even if the little boy did manage to get down there to a boat, which he couldn't in the first place, a little fellow like that wouldn't be able to pull-start the motor."

Pablo came trotting up the plank and met the man at the side door of the office. "Twenty-two is missing."

"Oh, my God," Gloria said.

"There's a paddleboat tied in its space," Pablo said.

Gloria and Emily were crying now. Hannah had hands on their backs, stroking them.

The man picked up the phone and called the sheriff and the harbor patrol.

* * *

There were many things that needed guarding on the military base, but the crematorium was apparently not one of them. Ted, Avery and Jesus 19 stepped from the dim chamber of ashes into the bright New Mexico sunlight. Jesus 19 was not accustomed to the light and so raised the satchels he was carrying to shield his eyes, cowering and bending forward and backward like a bad Igor impression. Neither was he used to walking in open spaces and so he staggered and stumbled. Ted took a satchel from him. The three panted, sweated, as they crossed fifty yards of gravel to the recessed doorway of a Quonset. It was evident to Ted as he looked from the shade at the passing Hummers and the lean, young soldiers who walked, talked, shared cigarettes and joints, that getting out of the underground complex had been the easy part of their escape. Beyond a row of buildings, one of them a mechanic's garage, was a high fence topped with shining razor wire and ten yards beyond that, another, identical fence. Jesus 19 was perspiring profusely, especially from the place where he should have had a mouth.

He was sitting on his satchel now, his eyes cast down to avoid the sun.

"What now?" Ted asked.

"I don't know," Avery said. "Things have changed a lot since I was last up here. There are so many buildings and people."

Ted looked through the chainlink fences at the sea of RVs and campers and tents, knowing that if they could only clear the compound, they could easily lose themselves in the crowd, shed the jumpsuits and later sneak away from the area altogether.

"The base has grown so much," Avery went on. "There used to be just four huts up here. Now it looks like a real military base."

"With real soldiers and real guns," Ted put in, then realized that he had nothing to fear in that regard. But of course he had to worry over the safety of Avery. Not only was it Avery who had gotten him out of that hole, but Ted had new resolve in the matter of protecting life in general. It was not that he owed Avery that had him wanting to make sure he was unhurt; it was that Avery represented a life, a family he'd lost—however screwed up—and needed in some way to relocate and touch, even if—and Ted suspected such—it was for the worst.

"I'm out of plans," Avery said. "Every day I've thought about using the chute. For years, I imagined climbing in and popping up here, but that's as far as I got. I'm no good at plans."

"Check the door behind you," Ted said.

Avery did and discovered that it was unlocked.

"Inside." Ted ushered the other two in and closed the door. The hut was cavernous, the only light coming through the dust-covered, translucent panels spaced evenly along the spine of the structure. It was a warehouse, a storage facility filled with rows of stacked crates and aisles between them. The air was heavy, stale, musty, hot. "We'll wait here," Ted said. "We'll just wait here until it gets dark."

"Then what?"

"I don't know yet."

And Ted didn't know, but he knew as certain as anything that he would figure a way. He had now what he had always wanted—not confidence, not competence, but resolve—and sitting with his back against a crate of canned pears, he was coming to understand this.

* * *

Sally drove from Los Angeles out the Pomona Freeway to the 215 south to March Air Force Base where he looked up an acquaintance who happened to work in the air controller's office.

"To what do I owe this pleasure, Horatio?" the man said. His light blue uniform shirt was open at the collar. Hair spiked out of the neck of his undershirt.

"I know I haven't been in touch for a while," Sally said. His tone was contrite and he found it difficult to make eye contact.

"For a while? Try over a year."

"I'm sorry, Leon."

"Sorry don't feed the bulldog, as they say. Sorry's a bit lame. I thought we had something."

"I'm sorry."

The two men had driven in Sally's car off the base and they were sitting in a Mexican/Thai restaurant called Gordo's. Leon got up and walked to the back and into the restroom. The waitress brought water while Sally sat there alone. Leon came back and drank half his glass.

"I need some help," Sally said.

Leon's anger showed on his angular face and in the way he fiddled his fork.

"I'm sorry, Leon. How many times do I have to say it? Things got crazy. Days turned into weeks and weeks turned into months. It happened. All I can do is apologize." Sally twirled his mustache.

"You think that's cute."

"What?"

"That thing you do with your mustache. You think it's cute."

"I didn't realize I was doing it."

The waitress came and took their orders.

"What kind of help do you need?" Leon asked.

"Okay. First, are flight plans of all military flights logged into one central computer system?"

Leon nodded.

"I mean, if I said a jet took off from Colorado Springs, you'd be able to confirm or deny it, right?"

"Yeah, so?"

"So, would you be able to tell me where it went?"

Leon nodded again, but he was growing nervous now. He glanced over his shoulder at the door and put his hands in his lap.

"Could you tell me if there were any helicopter flights on a particular night?"

"I don't like this," Leon said.

"Could you?"

"Yeah, I'd be able to find out, I guess. What's this all about, Horatio? You're scaring me to death." Leon was whispering.

"I want to know if any helicopters went to the Mojave last Thursday," Sally said.

"You'd like to know that, would you?"

"Yes, I would."

"Would you also like to know where they're going to send my ass after my court martial?" Leon turned again and looked at the door. He took a pack of cigarettes from his breast pocket and put one in his mouth.

"Leon, I need this one," Sally said.

"Yeah, well, I need some things too."

"I'll make it up to you."

Leon looked at Sally's eyes, then leaned back into his seat, held his face in his hand. "You're damn right you'll make it up to me."

They went back to the base and Sally waited outside while Leon went into the controller's log room. Leon came back, with even more askance looks than before, stepped to Sally and whispered from the corner of his mouth, "Roswell."

The name Roswell apparently didn't have the same significance for Horatio Sally as it did for Leon. Sally had heard the stories about the aliens and the hangar where a spaceship was supposedly stashed and all that and even the black helicopter business wasn't completely new to him. He considered it all a load of baloney and still did. But he did feel the smallest stirring of apprehension as he drove away from the base knowing he was on his way to New Mexico.

* * *

The panels along the ceiling had grown dark. Ted looked over at Jesus 19 and saw that he was asleep, his head on one of the satchels as he lay on the unpainted plywood floor. Avery was pacing, as he had been for the past four or five hours.

"Okay, it's dark," Avery said. "Now what? We need a plan. We can't stay in here forever."

"You wait here," Ted said.

"Where are you going?"

"Just wait. I'm not sure I'll be able to find what I need." Ted opened the door and stepped out. He was saddened and alarmed to find that though the sky above the base was dark, the place was lit up like a sports field. He fell back into the shadow of the doorway and looked around. Fortunately, there were fewer soldiers about. Another plus was that the yellow artificial lights shining everywhere seemed to stifle the blue of his jumpsuit and so he felt slightly less conspicuous. He walked as casually as he could across the open space toward the garage, almost breaking into a run halfway across but catching himself. At the garage, he glanced inside through a couple of windows and satisfied himself that it was empty. He walked around the building and found a small yard of vehicles, jeeps and Hummers, trucks and a tank. He didn't know how to drive a tank, so he chose an enclosed Hummer truck, got in, pressed the starter and jumped when the engine kicked over. He drove it around a couple of huts and stopped in front of the Quonset where he'd left Avery and Jesus 19.

Ted let the truck motor run while he went inside. "Let's go," he said and he grabbed a satchel. Avery and 19 followed; the three of them sat on the long bench seat of the cab. Ted waited for the area in between them and the fences to clear, then moved slowly forward, inching the vehicle more fully into the light. There was a commotion from the incinerator building. Blue-clad Christ after Christ was exiting the furnace chamber and running wildly into the open, all of them no doubt having watched the chute being operated and seeking to follow their creator, as it were. Soldiers shouted for them to stop, sirens sounded. Ted stepped on the gas and was doing forty-five when they hit the first fence. There was popping which might have been gunfire, but Ted wasn't certain. He drove on through the second fence, the razor wire scratching loudly at the roof and sides of the truck. Jesus 19's eyes were as wide as the space for his mouth. Avery let out a scream of exhilaration as they crashed through the second fence and clear of the base. Ted slammed his foot against the brake pedal and brought the truck to a sliding halt just feet from an Airstream trailer. There was a lull, a stillness for a moment while the dust settled, then everything became charged. The soldiers were unable to follow through the holes made by the truck as the UFO watchers from the outside took the opportunity to spill by the dozens onto government property. Quickly, over a hundred people with flashlights, beer cans and baseball caps were wrestling with guards, trying doorknobs, shouting into the sky. They showed no interest in the three men dressed in powder blue jumpsuits and so Ted and Avery and 19 swam through the crowd toward the middle of the camp, running about a hundred yards from the truck, where they stopped and sought to catch their breath under a large white awning. The shouting was loud and unintelligible, but the quality of it indicating glee, joy, happy excitement. Ted turned to find four young women dressed in flowing white robes staring at him, their bleached blond heads tilted like dogs as if to try to understand his presence there. Then a larger woman came from the motor home from which the awning hung, a pear-shaped, fat woman with very light blond hair, her face cream-complected, her fat hands held out as if to grab Ted's face.

"Quick, children," she said, to the smaller women, "get them into the motor home, get them out of harm's way."

Shots rang out in the compound and the flow of people was beginning to reverse direction, the tone of the shouting having altered to suggest disappointment and fear. Ted allowed himself, Avery and 19 to be led into the large motor home. They sat together, wedged into a red-vinyl-upholstered loveseat, the women standing silently in front of them, their faces as empty as the Jesuses they had left. The light inside was from candles and a couple of hurricane lamps. Incense burned.

The fat woman came in, walked directly to Ted, knelt before him, kissed his bare feet and said, "Master, I have been waiting for you."

Ted said, "I believe you have me confused with someone else."

The woman raised her head, reached forward and fingered gently the sutures of Ted's neck. "No," she said. "I would know the true Messiah anywhere. You are from the Lord God, this I know." She then pointed to a newspaper clipping taped to the wall. Ted's face, bewildered and sad, looked back at him.

Ted looked to Avery who offered a subtle shrug.

"We will protect you from the devils and disbelievers," the woman said.

Ted was pleased that she'd seen fit to make a distinction between the two. He glanced out the window to observe that there was still plenty of chaos. He looked at the woman. "My name is Ted Street."

"I know," she said. "Everyone knows you."

"This is Dr. Oswald Avery," Ted said. "And this—" He stopped, knowing that he could not identify the third of their party as Jesus 19. "This is Harold." He said it remembering a childhood silliness which went *Our Father who art in heaven, Harold be thy name.*

"I am called Negatia Frashkart," the woman said. Then Negatia rose to look out the window herself. "They will no doubt be looking for you. You must get out of those clothes."

Ted was not as certain as she that anyone would be looking for them. The secrecy of the underground compound seemed sure to stall any search efforts or even revelation to the commanders and troops topside that anyone or anything had escaped.

* * *

Ted had been elevated from devil to messiah. The irony was too great for Avery to contain his laughter as the three of them stood alone, crammed into a small bedroom in the back of the trailer. Ted was buttoning a white shirt while Avery tried to get some white denim trousers onto an even more stunned Jesus 19.

"Imagine that," Avery said. "Calling you the Messiah right in front of old Jesus Christ here." He zipped up 19's pants. "If you only had a mouth, right, old buddy?"

"I've got to call my wife," Ted said.

Ted was pausing to regard how they looked all done up in white now instead of powder blue when there was an urgent knocking at the door and the three of them were being pushed into closets and behind piles of white laundry. Clancy Dweedle's distinctive voice cracked the incensed air of the RV.

"They might be wearing blue. One's about sixty, gray hair, kinda dumpy and pale. You might describe him as fat. The other has a sutured scar around his neck. Him, you can't miss."

"We've seen no one," Negatia Frashkart said.

Ted could smell the incense in the clothes pushed up against him, the sour wood of the closet and an odor, no doubt from one of the women's underwear, which made him think of Gloria. He waited through a long, unsettling silence, imagining Colonel Dweedle eyeing items just inches from him. Without a thank-you, the door slammed and Ted was dug out and helped to his feet by two of the women.

"Thank you," Ted said.

Negatia Frashkart was watching out the window, her thick, sandaled foot tapping nervously. "The evil man continues his search," she said, then turned to Ted. "Oh, Holy One, we have waited so long for you. When news of your rising came over the television, we were here, but I knew that you would come find us. I knew if we just waited, if we just had faith, that you would come to us."

"Do you have a telephone?" Ted asked. The idea of such a mundane request from a devil or messiah struck Ted as rather funny and he fought off a smile.

It struck Negatia Frashkart as merely a question to be answered, as she said, "No." Then she turned to her cohorts and said, "Sisters, collect the others so that we might pray together before the Lord our God in the presence of his emissary, our Messiah, Theodore."

The women left the motor home and Negatia faced the three visitors with her flat pie face and smiled beatifically.

"Where is there a phone?" Ted asked.

"In town," Negatia said. She turned to Avery. "Are you an angel?"

"No, madam, I am a scientist."

She looked at the mouthless face of Jesus 19. "You, I know, are an angel. I can see it in your eyes."

Ted looked at 19's eyes and all he saw was fear. He had the eyes of a lamb headed for slaughter, sweet, stupid eyes. Ted tried to step away from Negatia, to find some room to breathe, but he bumped into the stove unit, causing a cabinet to open and pots to spill onto the floor. Ted stooped to pick up the mess, finding that the floor was filthy with a layer of grease, shoe marks and hair trimmings.

"Never mind that," Negatia said. "Come with me. Come, so that I might share you with my brothers and sisters of the Heavenly Order of Pyromantic Worship of the *Ruach Elohim*."

"How many are you?" Avery asked.

"There are but twenty-seven of us here," she said. "But who knows how many kindred souls lay waiting for us beyond the loose perimeter of our own camp." With speaking, Negatia Frashkart's deep voice had taken on a new timbre, had become mellifluous, honeyed, as if already she had launched into her performance.

* * *

Negatia Frashkart was a fat little nine-year-old girl, just slightly tall for her age but as big around as three little girls. Her father's favorite movie was the first half of *Elmer Gantry*. He was a huge man, described himself as a "huge man," but he never pronounced the "h." He had white hair and deep-set, dark brown eyes and considered himself a chiromancer.

"I don't trust that new minister," her father said, sitting in the straight-backed chair in his reading parlor. The floor lamp with the tasseled shade was lit behind him.

"Why, Daddy?" Negatia asked.

"His left hand is faceless. Haven't you seen it?"

The child shook her head.

"It's virtually without lines, unreadable. No *ligne de vie*, no *ligne mensale*. He's *without* and I'll leave it at that."

"Daddy, what do you think Jesus's left hand looked like?" Negatia asked.

"I believe Jesus had two left hands," the father said. "He, of course, had a short life line and the mensal was no doubt broken. His Saturnian line remains a mystery to me, but I'm sure he possessed a pronounced hepatic line."

"Daddy, people at church say that you're no Christian at all. They say that you're a heathen."

He took Negatia onto his lap and winced at her size. "That's because they're small and afraid of science. There's a line to be drawn between religion and superstition. Real religion allows all things, science for one, to come into it."

"Doris Wills said you're a sorcerer."

"And she might be right, but not in the way she believes it." He picked up his child's hands and studied their lines. "You have such wonderful hands, so clear, so deep. God has touched you, Negatia." He slipped his fingers under the edge of Negatia's skirt hem and scratched her fat thigh. "Like these lines here." He touched the underside of her wrist. "These bracelets, also called the zazatte and the rascette, they tell me not only that you will have a long and happy life, but one close to God, that you yourself might be chosen to meet His Son when he comes back to us." His fingers spread the fat that squeezed tight against her young vagina. "Close your eyes, child, and imagine meeting Christ. Christ with his two left hands. God loves you. God loves you, my little Negatia."

* * *

The alarm went out all over the island. Perry Street had now been missing for more than three hours. The harbor patrol and the sheriff's boats were out in the ocean and all radio calls sent back to the Los Angeles County Sheriff's Office, in which Gloria was waiting, were negative. A woman deputy was doing her best to calm Gloria's fears for the worst. Hannah stood across the room, studying a topographical map of the island. Emily seemed to have shed four years and was ensconced under the wing of her mother.

The whole town was aware of the situation and people were on the lookout. Passersby peered through the window of the sheriff's office and saw Gloria knotted to her daughter. By now, Gloria suspected, they also knew who she was and suffered further worry that Perry might be found by some nut.

"I can't sit here," she said. "I have to go out and look for my son."

The deputy placed a discouraging hand on her shoulder. "You're in no condition to go out looking for him," she said. "The best thing is for you to stay right here and let us do our job."

It all sounded fine and well coming out of the deputy's mouth, but Gloria couldn't remain still. She paced. Emily went to Hannah.

Then Richard came into the station. He walked to and hugged Gloria as if they were old friends and Gloria hugged him back. "Anything?" he asked, directing his question to the deputy.

"Not yet."

"He might be out there in a boat," Gloria said.

"Come on, we'll go out and look," Richard said.

"I think Mrs. Street should stay here," the woman said.

Richard lifted Gloria's chin and stared at her red eyes. "Do you want to wait around here?"

"No, I want to search for Perry."

"Okay, then, let's go."

Gloria turned to Hannah, then knelt to embrace Emily. "You stay here with Aunt Hannah, okay?"

* * *

The brothers and sisters of the Heavenly Order of Pyromantic Worship of the *Ruach Elohim* covered the sides of their camp with sheer white fabric backed by heavy canvas that the breeze barely disturbed. There was still much commotion back at the compound where the fences were being repaired under bright lights. People walked by on their way back to their campers and tents, sharing stories of the aliens they had nearly seen or had actually seen, the spaceship in the hangar, Elvis.

Torches burned at the corners of the area and at either side of a lectern. The whole scene felt unsettlingly ancient to Ted. He sat in the first row of low stools, flanked by Jesus 19 and Avery while Negatia Frashkart stood up to address her people, wearing that same ridiculous smile, her eyes filled with the light of faith. Her people smiled insipidly as well, their hair either blond or made blond, their faces ashen in spite of their camping out in the desert sun, their eyes vacant, their mumbles hardly mumbles at all but a constant, annoying humming of ascent.

"Even now I can see it," she said and raised her hands as if to embrace the entire light-haired mass. "A dark tunnel lit with weak torches, not like the bright ones we have ignited, but dim, and my friend, the late founder of our movement, Errol Flynn McMasters, he swayed as he went before me." For the first time, as she stood speaking between the flames of the two torches, Ted saw the silver ball on a stud through her tongue and then it was all he could see, the fire reflecting off it serving to echo her talk of the light at the end of the tunnel. She went on, "At the door stood a Christian and a Jew, both crying, both sobbing uncontrollably. He looked up as we entered and spotted on the ceiling of that great tabernacle a star, a gleaming star. Then he reached his hands out to me, just as I reach mine out to you now, and he said, 'Come closer, my child, come closer.' And I moved closer until I stood beside him bathed in the glow of a brighter flame! And his hand touched me and he said, 'Now, you must take on the burden. You must lead them the rest of the way.' And then from the tunnel came a cry of pain too great for any of us to imagine. That cry of pain has rung in my ears every day of my life and now it has finally subsided. The pain has ceased because the burden has been lifted, lifted because the Lord God has answered my prayers and completed the destiny of which my father spoke so many years ago while he molested me, while the devil filled him and led his actions. But now, here with us, here with us on this weak, sweet, sick earth we have again before us the Son of God, the Messiah our Lord God."

She paused to let her shining smile fall on the Messiah, namely Ted. Avery was doing all he could to contain his amusement, giggling through his closed lips, pressing his eyes shut against tears of laughter.

"My poor, lost soul has been on fire to solve the vexing riddle of existence and here now is the answer, my sweet Lord has come to me. But of course this is merely unmistakable evidence that we are not ready. The conclusion has come and our day of reckoning is upon us. We are now in the capable hands of our Lord God Jesus Christ Almighty. We can only hope that He will find us deserving and worthy enough to guide and escort us through these last days. Oh, Lord Christ, would You please speak to us, please give us our first glimpse of your sublime and divine light?" She smiled at Ted and stood her massive body away from the lectern, her fat arms open and begging Ted to come forward.

Ted rose and stepped to the place the fat woman had left warm. "Is there a phone near here?" he asked.

* * *

The wind pushed through the open windows of the Ford as Sally sped east into Arizona. He was tired, dead tired and his imagining that—being *dead* tired—caused him a laugh he thought he deserved, certainly needed. He also needed sleep and he would no doubt have to stop soon to close his eyes, but right now he had the stamina to keep driving. He'd stopped once for gas and left a message on Gloria Street's answering machine that things were looking up.

. . .

Gloria stood beside Richard as he piloted his boat past the long, green boardwalk and out toward the end of the breakwater. It was almost noon. They motored past a large gull standing on a buoy, so white and the water was so blue and the beauty of everything caused Gloria to cry again.

Richard reached over and put a hand on her shoulder. "We'll find him," he said.

They turned right, south out of the harbor. Richard waved to a sheriff's boat which seemed headed out to open sea. Gloria watched the boat headed in the direction of the mainland she couldn't see, wondering if Perry was trying to get back home to wait for his father.

"You don't think he could have gone out there, do you?" The wind tossed her hair and flattened the features of her face.

Richard didn't answer. He handed Gloria a pair of yellow binoculars and said, "You look out there with the glasses. Don't try to see anything, just look."

Gloria found the sound of the engine somewhat soothing. Peering through the glasses, however, all she could see was blue.

* * *

Once again the Messiah's request for a telephone went ignored. Ted was back in his same seat while the brothers and sisters made a salvo of joyous noises unto the Lord, coming to rest finally on *Michael Row the Boat Ashore.* Ted squirmed on his stool and found that his compassion was wearing thin, that he might be becoming angry. He then decided that he would control his rage, use it, and he stood and halted the singing with raised hands.

"What is it you want God to do?" he asked.

There were no answers, only an appropriately sheepish silence.

"Would you have God strike dead the evil people among you? Would you have God convert everyone to your beliefs? Would you have God accept you into the heaven you desire and leave the different-minded to burn in hell?"

Any kind of stirring among them would have been welcome, but they sat, without emotion, without reaction, all one blond collective head with empty gaze not quite focused on the object of their desire and fear.

"I need a phone!"

Negatia Frashkart broke the cooperative face and stepped forward to place a hand on Ted's shoulder. "Thank you so much for speaking to us, Lord, and showing us that we are just sinners awaiting salvation."

Crestfallen, Ted turned to Avery who was deep red with suppressed laughter by now. And when the brothers and sisters of the Heavenly Order of Pyromantic Worship of the *Ruach Elohim* broke again into a chorus of *Michael,* the scientist exploded. His laughter was taken by the disciples near and around him to be an eruption of Holy Spirit and so they sought to share his laughter, reaching out to touch him as if there could be tactile transmission of the heavenly host. Which of course caused Avery to laugh all the harder. Soon the song was lost in uproarious laughter which in the mouths of two or three became weeping. Soon they were all weeping. Avery had exhausted himself. Jesus 19 looked all around, his eyes soft and wet with what might have been concern or even compassion.

Ted collected Avery and tried to cut a path out of the camp, but at each point along the edge of the perimeter they reached they were met by two or three brothers or sisters who would not let them pass. The two men entered the motor home.

"Nineteen is out there. Is that all right?" Ted asked.

"What's he going to say?" Avery said.

"How does he eat?"

The question hit Avery as if he'd never thought of it. "He doesn't, now that you mention it. He doesn't eat. How could I have missed that? He doesn't eat and he's alive. In fact, his missing mouth aside, he's the best Christ I made. You don't think—"

Ted just shook his head. "I'm not going to think about that right now." He saw the portable radio sitting on the counter by the stove, switched it on.

A couple of pop songs played and worked to clear Ted's head of the *Michael* song. Avery had moved to sit next to a hurricane lamp and was digging through one of the satchels of his notes, dropping pages all around him. "He doesn't eat," he kept saying. "He doesn't eat."

The news came on. "And in the Mojave Desert in California, a religious cult has barricaded itself within their compound as ATF officers are seeking to remove a huge arsenal of cannons. The leader of the fringe group, a man known only as Big Daddy, has vowed that neither he nor his disciples will be taken alive. An escaped member of the cult has confirmed suspicions that Big Daddy and his followers have collected a cache of some fifty innocent children to use as hostages. Less than an hour ago, Big Daddy issued a threat that he would begin killing the children if the government officials do not back away and comply with his demands. His demands have not been made available to the media yet."

Ted forgot about needing the phone. All he could think of was those children locked away in that bunker. He had been there and he had left without them. He knew that he had to go back. Their bullets couldn't stop him. He knew where the bunker was located. He turned off the radio. "Dr. Avery, we've got to go."

"What are you talking about?" Avery said, not taking his eyes from the papers on his lap. "I can't leave. I've got to get Nineteen back into the complex and finish my work."

"I can't help you," Ted said.

But Avery was paying him no attention whatsoever. He waved Ted off much as he must have waved off his wife and children in earlier days. Ted found a white kerchief in a nearby pile of laundry and tied it around his neck to conceal his sutures. He offered another deflected goodbye and a thank-you to Avery, then went into the back room of the RV. He struggled with and finally got open a window, gave a look back, then climbed through and out. He crawled, then sidled, hunkered down, through the yards of other camps, always in full light, until he was clear of the Pyromantic followers of Negatia Frashkart.

BOOK FOUR

CHAPTER ONE

IT WAS FAST BECOMING clear to Ted that one of life's rules was "Getting almost away is easy." Spilling from the window of the RV had been, literally, as easy as falling off a log. But now he was at sea in the night, though far from anything approaching darkness, as each camp in the extensive village was flooded with light, whether from fires, batteried lanterns or strings of bulbs powered by generators. The light was many times brighter than the base he had just left. It was as if they were all afraid of the dark or perhaps they were trying to be certain that any passing space traveler could not miss them. Whatever, the place was so well lighted that there were no shadows at all in which to hide and dressed all in white as he was he felt like he was positively glowing. But as odd as he looked, he was not odd enough to attract attention among these people, many of whom seemed to think nothing of sitting and drinking beer with grown men and women dressed as aliens.

Snippets of conversations found Ted's ears as he roamed. A man dressed like an action figure Ted had seen among Perry's toys went on at length about those religious crazies over in California and how it would serve them right if the army would just go in there and vaporize them with that ultra-secret photon-ray gun they had been developing. "If you ask me," he said, "it's a fine opportunity to test the daggone thing."

Children who looked both too young and too old to be doing so ran wildly and unsupervised through the campsites, shooting each other with various futuristic toy weapons and showing off water-soluble tattoos. Portable radios blared country music and rock 'n' roll and call-in psychotherapy programs. Televisions added their eerie glow to the lightfest. Every direction looked the same and soon Ted had no idea where he was, whether he was headed toward the desert or back to the military installation. He wondered if Oswald Avery would be able to navigate and then negotiate his way back to the base and into his underground lab.

Ted walked on through endless and repetitive campsites until he could see, at the end of the field of light, darkness or what he thought was darkness. At any rate, there seemed to be less light and so he steered toward it. If the people near and in the center of the city of campers were strange, then the people on the fringe were in fact aliens. On the skirts of it all the men and women were tattooed, not just on shoulders, but up thighs and across entire backs that they exposed and showed off to their company. A woman growled at Ted as he passed by a spot between pickups she had chosen for urination, showing bad teeth and several piercings, among them her eyelids and lower lip and her tongue, through which was passed a large silver ring that kept her mouth from closing completely. Though certainly he knew by now that he had nothing to fear, he scooted away, partly as a courtesy, partly as a vestige of his old cowardly ways, but most important because getting away from her was simply the right thing to do. Finally, he stood where only dim fires offered light and bearded men and near-bearded women smoked dope and laughed and pierced each other at will. Ted found that he was exhausted, not physically, not even mentally or emotionally, but in a way that he was not sure he understood or would own up to, psychically. He crawled into a yellow school bus, curled up on the floor next to the driver's seat and drifted off to sleep.

* * *

A stretched-thin white cloud far away to the south was the only relief from the relentless blue of the sea and sky and Gloria's eyes were repeatedly drawn to it. She looked at Richard and saw the way he was scouring the shoreline as he steered.

"Has he ever done anything like this before?" Richard asked. He didn't look at her.

"No." Gloria let the binoculars hang in front of her. "But all this stuff with his father. It's confusing for me; I can only imagine what's going through his little head."

* * *

The six-horsepower motor had not been that difficult to start the first time, but now, no matter how much Perry pulled, it didn't work. He was frightened at first of the water as he drifted, but then he realized that he was being pushed to shore. He'd gotten his sneakers wet when he jumped out and pulled the skiff as far as he could onto the pebble-covered beach. The flat water he'd motored away on had become choppy and loud as it splashed against the sides of the boat and he was glad to be on dry ground, but he couldn't walk anywhere from where he was. The shallow, turquoise water of the little cove fell off quickly and became deep, turquoise water. The slope behind him was steep and high. Perry felt as lost as he in fact was and he forced himself not to cry, wondering why he had come out here in the first place, why he had sneaked out of the room, why he was so angry. He considered how frightened his mother was going to be when she discovered he was gone and the thought sickened him. He wasn't angry at his mother. He also believed he wasn't angry at his father. So, with whom was he angry? He had never been so scared as when his sister had been separated from them. Now his father was gone. Gone was perhaps worse than dead, he thought. If his father were dead, he would at least know where he was, or wasn't.

Afraid of the water now and believing he couldn't start the boat's motor anyway and being confined to that one small beach by the cliff walls, Perry started up the slope of the mountain. The dryness of the hill was amazing, he thought, given how close it was to all that water. He clawed at the ground, rocks, brush and pulled and pushed himself up. Loose dirt and stones gave way under his steps, brittle sage plants and ceanothus broke in his grasp, bees bothered him. His palms and fingertips were rubbed raw. About a hundred feet up, the wall became near vertical and Perry could go no farther. When he looked down, he panicked, his heart slamming against his chest. He didn't know where to put his feet, didn't know whether to climb down facing the mountain or with his back to it. He hugged the root of a sage, planted his feet as best he could and did not move. He hardly breathed as he stared out at the ocean. Tears streaked his face. He shouted, "Daddy!"

. . .

It was afternoon now and it was warm. Gloria still wore the jacket she'd had on earlier. Richard reached into a compartment beside the wheel and came back with a tube of sunscreen.

"You're probably burning up in that coat," he said, holding the sunscreen out for her to take.

"You're right," Gloria said. "I hadn't noticed." She took the tube, but left on the jacket. Then she noticed that Richard was slowing the boat. "What is it?"

"Over there." He pointed with his chin. On the beach of a sheltered cove was the little boat which was missing from the dock rental.

"Oh, my God," Gloria said. The boat was empty. "Where is he? Where is he?"

"Don't panic," Richard said. He pointed them toward the cove and cut slowly through the water. "There're sometimes rocks in the water here. Go look out over the bow and tell me if it's clear." But Gloria didn't move. "Gloria, please, so we can get over there."

Gloria crawled forward and tried to look down at the water, but she was having to tear her eyes from the beach and the little skiff.

"Is it clear?"

She looked down, amazing herself at not becoming queasy. "Clear," she called back.

Richard killed the engine and let the boat drift to shore. He threw the anchor onto the beach and jumped off the bow, turned and helped Gloria down. They walked over to the abandoned skiff and stared at it, as if it might give them some clue. Richard turned and looked at the ocean. Gloria ran her eyes along the beach, sniffing the air for a trace of her son. She followed the line of the slope up and into the dry brush.

"Oh, my dear God," she said.

Richard looked up the slope.

Perry was hanging on to a protruding root, one foot planted on a rock, the other slipping, kicking granite, trying to find purchase on loose dirt.

"Perry!" Gloria called. "Honey, are you all right?!"

"Mommy!"

"Hang on, honey."

Richard was already scrambling up the hill.

"He's so high," Gloria said.

Richard called up for Perry to relax and just hang on. The climbing was difficult and Richard's weight must have been working against him as he kicked free most of the rocks he sought as footholds.

Gloria watched, too afraid to scream, too afraid to cry. She didn't really understand why it was Richard who was scaling the slope, but it was okay, because she was too scared to move. She tried to think through it all. Richard was stronger than she and so he'd be able to bring Perry down. It had been several years since she could comfortably pick Perry up. And this hillside, it was so steep. Richard nearly fell and Gloria reached forward, trying to help him stay up. "Oh, Richard," she said, with an intimacy which surprised her.

"Mommy!"

"Where is he?" Richard asked, pausing on a wide spot. The face had gotten steep enough that he could not see Perry above him.

"He's right over you!" Gloria shouted.

"How far?"

"Fifteen, twenty feet. I don't know. I can't tell."

Perry shifted his weight and the foot that had been squarely placed kicked out from under him. His whole weight came to bear on the root, then it snapped. Gloria screamed. Rocks streamed down onto Richard and her son was falling, his little arms waving in the air, his legs oddly parallel to the ground, faceless as his head bounced, then his little body. She watched as he seemed to float, the rocks flying faster than his body. Then his body jerked, caught in space unnaturally, and he let out a small yelp as he stopped. Gloria made a similar sound. Richard cried out, his arm stretching beyond what should have been its limit, his fingers disappearing into a fist that held Perry by his red windbreaker. Gloria burst out with a half scream as Perry popped over the lip of rock and into Richard's arms. Richard groaned again, then fell back onto the ledge. He struggled to hoist the boy up into his lap. Perry was bleeding from his forehead, but he was conscious.

"It's okay now," Richard said absently.

"Perry!" Gloria called.

"He's hurt," Richard said. "He's hit his head."

"Mommy?" Perry said. "Mommy!"

Gloria watched as Richard, in obvious pain, slid his way down the route he had followed up, his free arm grabbing handholds and roots where he could. Then she was under him and taking the delirious boy into her own arms. "Oh, Perry, Perry, Perry."

"I'm sorry," Perry said.

Richard collapsed on the ground and held his left arm straight and close to his body. He found his feet and tried to catch his breath, looking at the water.

"You're hurt too," Gloria said. When she looked back at Perry he was unconscious. "Perry! Perry!"

"Come on," Richard said. "In the boat."

* * *

Ted came to with a dull throbbing in his head, the first real sensation of pain he had felt since his death. And, of course, it came from within, he thought. Morning was breaking and he could see the yellow-orange glow of the eastern sky through the dusty windshield of the bus. He sat up, wondering if he had slept only one night, or perhaps—since all physical laws as he understood them had been suspended—he had slept for twenty years like Rip Van Winkle. But one has to accept something on faith and so he accepted that it was only the next day, a small thing, but something. While sitting, waking and touching his sutures, he noticed that the key was stuck into the ignition of the bus. Without wasting time considering the action, Ted climbed into the driver's seat and started the engine. He heard a chorus of "What the fuck?" coming from somewhere outside the vehicle and then a barrage of shouts as he pulled away, dragging down the supports and awning of a campsite.

He drove away from the village and toward the only road he could see, followed it north, then found another little road that initially headed west but turned south. He drove this way and that until he found himself on a major highway, Route 380, and he pointed the bus west. The highway was empty. He passed a trailer truck loaded with hay and a Ford with a flat tire on the opposite side of the road.

* * *

Sally amused himself with the old line that the tire was flat on only the bottom. He looked at the problem, then looked up to see an old yellow bus tear by. He caught a glimpse of the driver's face and recognized him as Theodore Street. His heart jumped and for a second he forgot what he was about. He ran to the trunk, opened it, got out the jack and the lug wrench, the work gloves he used for such operations. Then he unbolted the spare, pulled it and dropped it to the ground. It was flat on the bottom too.

He went to the front seat of his car and pushed in Gloria Street's number. He left a message.

"Mrs. Street. I have seen your husband. He was driving a bus. More later. Horatio Sally."

* * *

The wake behind them seemed inadequate to Gloria, they weren't going fast enough. She held Perry in her lap and stroked his hair, looked forward at Richard who was rocking back and forth, urging his boat to go faster. He kept looking back at Gloria.

Perry was quiet, his eyes closed. He looked like he was sleeping. Then he screamed, his eyes opened wide, and he stared at Gloria for a second before passing out again.

. . .

Behind the wheel of the bus Ted screamed, a pain cutting through his middle. He almost lost control, but managed to stop the vehicle along a narrow shoulder just shy of a bridge. The pain was so unexpected, and because his organs were a mere jumble inside him, he could not say what it was that hurt. Then the pain was gone, but more than gone, as there was no lingering trace of the sensation. The pain sucked deep inside him where he simply couldn't feel it; so it was less than gone, because it was there.

Ted stopped at a phone booth in a rest area and tried to place a collect call to his house, but got only the machine. The operator would not let him leave a message.

* * *

The sun was slipping behind the black-and-white scoreboard of the ball field where Ted and Perry often walked in the afternoons. Emily had been a part of the outings, but since her first menstrual period she had fallen away. This was a time when Gloria's estrangement from Ted had spilled over and caused a similar dissociation in his relationship with the children. Though he was playing catch and walking with Perry, things were a bit strained, their held glances brief, their sentences short.

They were tossing the ball back and forth in the outfield. The grass had just been watered and Ted found his footing unsure. He was still wearing the leather-soled shoes he had worn to work.

"Are you and Mommy going to get a divorce?"

Ted picked up the ball from the wet grass, looked at it, then threw it back. "What makes you ask that?"

Perry shrugged.

"No, we're not getting a divorce."

"Does Mommy hate you?"

Ted caught the ball in his bare hand and felt a delicious sting. "Good throw."

"Does she?"

"Sometimes," Ted said, realizing that he hoped she hated him only sometimes. He heaved the ball high like a pop fly.

Perry caught the ball and held it. He stood there, staring past his father. Ted glanced back at the scoreboard. There was a small, black-hooded bird sitting on the fence just below the last third-inning box. Ted turned back to see Perry wind up and hurl the ball as fast as he could. It whistled by Ted's head. He followed it to its mark and watched the bird fall to the grass inside the fence.

"Why'd you do that?" Ted asked, then saw the horror in Perry's face.

Ted and Perry walked slowly toward the bird. They stood over it. Ted didn't know what to say. The bird was unmoving, looked dead, one wing folded badly, the other fanned out, showing the underside of its primaries and secondaries.

Ted wanted to ask Perry what he had been thinking, but he caught himself and sighed instead, a sigh that must have sounded to the boy like a shout. Ted was less mad about the bird now and more scared for his son. "It's a junco."

"Is he dead?" Perry asked.

"I think so," Ted said.

Perry pivoted and walked away toward third base. Ted looked back at the bird and saw the eye facing him blink pathetically. The poor thing was still alive, lying in the wet grass suffering. He looked at his son's back, his defeated posture. The bird blinked again: a plea? Ted put the heel of his shoe on the head of the junco and stepped down, felt the small creature break. He realized as he was killing the bird that he was not simply doing it to end the animal's torment; he was doing it so the killing would be his and not his son's.

Just as he was lifting his heel, Perry turned around and saw him. "What did you do?" the boy asked, marching back to Ted.

"Nothing," Ted lied.

Perry stopped and saw the flattened head of the bird. "You stepped on it."

"It was still alive and suffering, son."

"No, it was dead," Perry said. "I killed it. You didn't kill it, I killed it." Perry sprinted across the wet grass. Ted thought he could hear him crying.

* * *

"He's not breathing!" Gloria cried.

Richard could see the green structure of the pier. He rounded the buoy and continued at full speed through the no wake zone. A couple of kayakers yelled curses at him.

Gloria put Perry flat on the floor of the boat, tilted his head back and tried to breathe into him, saying "Please, Please, Please."

The paramedics' van was flashing its red lights on the pier. "There's the ambulance," Richard said. He throttled down and several men grabbed the boat and pulled her in, tied her off.

The medics moved Gloria aside and began to work on Perry. He was still not breathing. Richard held Gloria, pulling her to his shoulder while he watched.

"I've got a pulse," one of the medics said.

"Oh, God," Gloria said, exhaling with small relief. The air was electric with sound, boat motors, gulls, the voice of the woman reading off her son's vital measurements into a radio. Measurements that mean nothing until something has gone wrong. Voices became the crashing of the surf from the pier. In that din somewhere she could hear her daughter calling out her brother's name, crying, but Gloria couldn't leave to care for her then. Hannah would have to do it. A paramedic felt gently all around Perry's body. Gloria felt faint when the crew moved him to a flat board, strapped his head back, and lifted him. She was filled with anger at Ted.

* * *

Ted looked at the gas gauge and saw it slipping toward empty. The urgency of reaching those poor children held by the madman was filling him completely. He had to save them, had to get them out of the hole, had to do it because he knew he could do it, because they couldn't do it for themselves. Because they were only children.

He pulled into a gas station. A lanky attendant approached as Ted stepped down out of the bus, wiping his greasy hands with a greasier rag. He looked at the bus.

"Diesel or gas?" the attendant asked.

"I don't know," Ted said.

"Why don't we find out, then?" the man said. He walked around the bus, looking up and down, then he stopped at the cap to the tank. "I'd say gas, what about you?"

"Okay."

Ted waited while the man pumped the gas. "You don't come across too many full-serve stations anymore," he said.

"We're old-fashioned." The man spat into the dirt. " 'Sides, the Mexkins and the Indins 'round here always screw up the pumps." He looked at the spinning dial. "Big tank."

Ted stepped away to a newspaper vending machine and looked through the glass at the headline.

ZEALOT HOLDS CHILDREN HOSTAGE

Glancing back at the bus and the attendant, Ted wondered what he was going to do when the man asked him for money to pay for the gas. He didn't even have a quarter for the newspaper or a phone call. He walked casually to the door of the bus and was boarding as the man was topping off the tank. He regarded the man walking forward in the rearview mirror. He closed the door and tried to crank the engine. It wouldn't start.

The attendant pounded on the door, his face twisted in a shout of gibberish.

"I've got to save the children!" Ted shouted through the glass.

"YOU WHAT?"

Ted turned the key again. The motor tried, but failed. The man walked back into the station office and came out with a shotgun. Ted could hear the clack of the double barrels engaging. He could hear the sound of a wad of the man's spit hitting the baked hard ground. The engine started, the bus shook, Ted put the thing in gear and pulled away while the gasman discharged both barrels, taking out most of the windows on the right side of the bus. The big vehicle fishtailed as Ted bumped from the gravel to the newly blacked asphalt and he narrowly missed a vanload of wide-eyed blond children.

Now he was a thief. But not a bad thief, as he was stealing the gas to go save those poor, defenseless children. He had flinched at the sound of the shotgun's explosion, again out of habit of fear and not fear itself. The idea that he could not be hurt became a terrifying thought. Such a notion could easily become consuming, a drug, and he realized that his instinct all his life to fear power had been a correct one. And so he correctly feared it now.

CHAPTER TWO

TED'S FATHER HAD HAD an affair. She was telling Ted about it to illustrate that their father had not been the saint everyone thought he was. This seemed important to Ethel at the time, the night following their mother's funeral, a funeral that saw their father lock himself inside the hearse and refuse to look at either of them.

"He's sick," Ted said.

"I know that."

"So, what's the problem?"

"I just think the record should be set straight," Ethel said. She was sitting on the sofa in the living room of their parents' house. She was dressed in a plain black dress, had kicked off her shoes and sat cross-legged.

Ted was standing in front of the idle fireplace. He heard a sound upstairs and looked at the ceiling. "He's really out of it."

"Thank you for your observation."

Ted rubbed his face. "I'm sorry I don't live here, Ethel."

Ethel drank from her cup of coffee and then set it back on the saucer on the end table beside her.

"Why bring up an indiscretion of a sick man that happened

twenty years ago? It's not like you can confront him with it now. He doesn't even know who we are. Even if he wasn't the way he is, bringing it up wouldn't be right."

"Mother knew about it the whole time," Ethel said. "She even told me."

"She told you," Ted repeated.

"Yes, she did and I don't care if you believe me. She said she thought it was a woman at the bank, a teller. She said she caught him talking on the phone late one night. Talking in a 'hushed voice.' She knew." Ethel was near crying, but her eyes stayed firmly on Ted.

A crashing sound came from the bedroom upstairs.

"What now?" Ethel said, but didn't move to get up.

"I'll go check on him," Ted said. He stopped at the edge of the room and looked back at his sister. "You know Mom wasn't a saint either."

"What's that got to do with anything?"

"You tell me."

Ted climbed the stairs and walked into his father's room. Some of his mother's clothes still hung on the door. The room still smelled of her. His father was sitting on the bed, the covers turned back. He was wearing a suit coat over his blue pajamas. The bedside lamp was on the floor, unbroken, but the shade was bent sharply.

"Are you all right, Dad?"

The old man didn't look up. He appeared to be crying, but he was making no noise. Ted went to the bed and sat beside him, put his arm around his shoulder. "I'm sorry, Dad."

"The Orioles don't have a chance this year," Ted's father said. "No hitting. I can't fix the hitting. Can you?"

. . .

Ted had to fight the stick of the yellow bus from second gear to third every time, with an awful grinding which made him think he might not make it to California. He could hear a miss in the engine, a fried lifter perhaps, a rhythmic absence of noise which became his music, which became the heartbeat he so badly needed. Dusk was coming on, the western sky washed pink and yellow, on fire where the sun dipped below the distant mountains. Everything in him tightened each time he passed an oncoming car or when one appeared in his rearview mirror. But who could stop him? Really, only the bus could.

* * *

Horatio Sally looked at the shards of safety glass on the ground near the pumps. The attendant was telling anyone who would listen about the crazed maniac who skipped without paying a $52 gas tab.

"You get a good look at him?" Sally asked.

"Damn sure did. Weirdest lookin' dude you ever want to see. He was a nut, talkin' about how he had to save the children, like he thought he was Sally Struthers or some shit."

"Did you get a look at his neck?"

"No, he was wearin' a scarf. A white handkerchief anyway. I didn't think nothin' of it. People wear stuff like that all the time 'round here. What's wrong with his neck?"

Sally pulled a photo from his pocket and showed it to the man. "Is this the man you saw?"

"Yeah, that's the guy. Now that I see his face again, he looks kinda familiar? Is he somebody? Hey, is there some kinda reward for the guy? 'Cause if there's a reward, don't you figure I oughta get it, seein' as I seen him?"

"No, no reward. Which way did he go?" Sally asked, though he already knew the answer.

"I'm not saying anything else. I seen that guy before and I know there's some kinda reward."

"Thanks for your time."

"Thanks for my time?" The attendant was angry. "Ain't you gonna pay me for the information? Hey, we can split the reward. I ain't greedy. Hey, man."

Sally drove away.

* * *

Perry did not die, but lay in a bed far too large. Gloria studied him there, so small, so fragile, so far from her in the middle of the sheet. He looked miles away. He was conscious now, but still intubated, his eyes weakly taking her in. Gloria stroked the cast that held his arm.

"The doctor says you're going to be okay, honey," she said.

A nurse came into the room. "Mrs. Street, you'll have to come out now."

"I want to stay."

"You can't stay in the room. I've set up a cot down the hall for you." The nurse touched the back of Gloria's arm. "Okay?"

Gloria leaned over and kissed Perry.

. . .

Ted was somehow able to find the diner where he had been picked up by Clancy. He had an unusually vivid memory of the terrain, a recollection of it that even his having traversed it by foot didn't explain, as if he was meant to be in this desert, at this time. He laughed at his search for some sort of destiny. It was dark, but the desert was lit up like the military base he'd just left. Every place he went people seemed to want to erase the darkness, he thought. The diner had become the command post for the ATF and the FBI and the National Guard and the television news crews. In the parking lot each of the agencies had set up mobile headquarters complete with banners, as if competing for recruits. He parked the bus on a not-so-high ridge and looked down at the activity. He could hear their voices, low and frightened of sounding conspiratorial. Two non-black helicopters sat parked across the road from the restaurant and between them, three armored infantry vehicles. They were some miles from Big Daddy and his group. The road leading to the dirt lane that in turn led to the compound was lined with vehicles and lights. So many men. Ted closed his eyes and pictured the desert. It was anything but flat. He recalled the wash he had run through, sandy and sparely vegetated.

He climbed again behind the wheel of the bus and took it slowly off the road onto the desert floor, slowly as if to test the solidity of the sand, as if the bus might sink. He drove around the encampment with a generous buffer, his lights off, the noise of his struggling engine lost in the din of the government's machinations. He pushed on into the darkness, his heart and mind becoming fixed on his goal of saving the children. The cold night air worked friction against the sides of the bus that he imagined he could feel on his own skin. He pressed on in a general direction, not knowing where exactly he was, but only where he was going. And especially, especially, what he was going to do. He reached up and touched his sutures, an action which had become habit, a comfort, and knew that all of this had to be for a reason. At the same time, with all his good intentions, with all his devotion to the idea of saving those poor lost children, he understood that he was slipping, that he was losing his mind. Somewhere his family waited for him, but they would have to wait a while longer, wait until he accomplished what his sick brain, no doubt starved for the oxygen his nonfunctioning lungs weren't providing, had conjured for him as a mission. But wasn't it good, this thing he planned, knew he had to do, saving the little children? His fists locked about the wheel, losing all their suppleness, and so he found every hole and bump and rock and rut of the desert floor. He was tossed wildly in the seat. He found the dry riverbed and slashed through it, over greasewood and sage, the tires flattening cacti.

Finally, knowing he was near the compound, knowing because he could hear on the breeze that damn *Michael* song, he stopped the bus and killed the motor. He got out and continued on foot, hearing the voices, hearing the god-awful tune, hearing Big Daddy's voice speaking low to his sponges. He couldn't make out the words, but he knew the voice. But most important, he could hear the weeping of the children.

* * *

Gloria sat on the chair beside the cot which had been set up for her and held Emily in her lap. She brushed the girl's hair from her face and made soothing sounds. Hannah and Richard sat across the small room.

"Thank God, he's going to be okay," Hannah said.

"It's my fault," Gloria said.

"No, it's not," Richard said.

"It is," Gloria said.

Emily hugged her mother tighter.

"I should have looked in on him," Gloria said.

Richard said nothing.

Hannah cleared her throat. "I should take Emily home so she can get some rest."

"No," Emily said.

"Hannah's right," Gloria said. "You need to be well rested to help me tomorrow. Okay?"

"I'll stay," Richard said. His voice was unsure, his words hesitant.

"No, you go too." Gloria let Emily to her feet and stood as well.

Hannah took Emily by the hand. "Come on, sweetie."

Gloria faced Richard. "Thank you so much."

"Will you be all right?"

She nodded. "If Perry's okay, I'm okay."

* * *

Gloria called her house an hour later to make sure Hannah and Emily had arrived safely. They had.

"You had two messages on your machine," Hannah said. "From a man named Sally. The first said that he learned that Ted had been seen. The second one, that he has seen Ted himself."

Gloria laughed softly into the pay phone. Then she began to cry.

"Sis?" Hannah said.

Gloria hung up.

* * *

It was not difficult for Sally to put together Big Daddy's standoff with child hostages and Theodore Street's comment to the gas-station attendant about saving the children. Sally couldn't believe he'd been standing right in the middle of the nest. He drove his Ford as fast as it would go, hoping to catch up to Street before he got tangled in the mess. He wasn't sure why, it coming to him that he had actually already accomplished his assignment by finding people who had seen the man. Still, even his sighting was not material enough to satisfy Mrs. Street, the insurance company or himself.

* * *

Ted could hear the rumbling of large vehicles well away, the government agencies no doubt moving closer for an assault of some kind. He ran to the compound as he had run from it. Why had he ever run from it, knowing that those children were imprisoned in that bunker? He was running at a brisk, deliberate pace, his strides becoming the cadence he seemed to need, like the missing of the bus's motor. Though it was night, the sky was not dark, the moon being full and having its glow enhanced by beautiful altocumulus clouds which made a thin veil across its face.

He saw the compound, lit up like everything else was lit up, torches burning outside the building, all the generator-powered bulbs showing through windows. There was a row of torches along one side of the camp, facing the dirt lane which led into it and in front of each torch was a cannon, perhaps twenty of them, stacks of balls to the side and rear of each one. Ted stopped, orienting himself, remembering how he was tied in front of the main lodge and how he had watched the women carrying food from it to the bunker where the children were being kept. Then Ted heard breathing, coming closer, panting, saw a beam of light sweeping the ground. He stood where he was and waited. The light came to him.

"It's you." It was Gerald, the disciple.

"Put out the light," Ted said.

Gerald did. "What are you doing here?"

"Please don't try to stop me," Ted said. "I've come to save those children."

Gerald looked back at the compound. "Cynthia ran away," he said. "She went back and told about the kids. That's what I think. She told them and now they're here."

"Good for her."

"Big Daddy is planning to start killing them."

"He's not going to kill anyone," Ted said.

"I love Cynthia," Gerald said.

"I know." Ted touched his shoulder briefly and started toward the lights.

"He'll shoot you if he sees you."

"He can't hurt me," Ted said. He looked at the sidearm holstered on Gerald's hip. "Take that off."

Gerald didn't know what Ted was saying to him.

"Take off the gun and leave it."

Gerald obeyed, looking around as if undressing.

Ted considered the children. It was of course in their best inter-est that he should not be seen. He didn't want them endangered by bullets meant for him. He stood, watching the compound and thinking, looking at the lay of the land, the positioning of the lights, the sentries, the moon which seemed to have a life of its own.

"I can get you to the bunker without being seen," Gerald said. "Let me help you. If I help you, maybe the police won't put me away. Cynthia was right to run. I don't want those kids to get hurt. Honest."

"Okay, you get me in there."

* * *

Horatio Sally couldn't find anyone at the ATF or FBI concession booths who would listen to him, in spite of his rather excited claims that a crazy dead man was trying to sneak into the cult's compound. So, he stood along the perimeter telling his story to bored grunts who nodded that they understood, not only his story, but the fact that their superiors were too stupid to listen to anybody.

"Yeah, I was trying to tell them that one of them Civil War can-nons would blow that IFV over there to smithereens," a National Guardsman told Sally, then flicked his glowing cigarette butt out into the desert. "But they wouldn't listen. Of course the chances of them nuts hitting anything are pretty slim."

"So, you've got this place surrounded?"

"Hell if I know. Ain't nothing but three hundred miles of dry-ass desolation out there. Rocks, ravines, canyons, mountains, a whole lot of uneven nothing. I trained at Twenty-nine Palms when I was in the Marines, so I know whereof I speak."

"If you were going to sneak into their camp, which way would you go?"

The Guardsman enjoyed the question. He scrunched up his face and stared off into the direction of Big Daddy's retreat. "I don't know where all our sentries are, but this is what I'd do. I'd take off across the desert well before where we're standing and I'd find me a wash and get as close as I could, then stay low in the brush where I didn't leave depressions in the earth." He appeared proud of his plan. "I'd also be wearing tan desert camouflage and plenty of clothes. Those jumping cactus will tear your ass up out there. This ain't no pretty place, this ain't no walk in the woods, this here is the real thing."

Sally looked up the highway, twirling his mustache. "You couldn't find a wash out there and know where it was going."

The soldier seemed slightly offended, as if being doubted. "I'm telling you, you could."

"So, where exactly would you get off the road?" Sally popped a mint into his mouth, offered one to the man.

The Guardsman shook his head and glanced back at the command post. "Okay, let's go." He stepped away, Sally behind him. "You'll see even while we're on the road that this place ain't flat."

The moon was out from behind the clouds and it was easy to see the road, a black crease in the desert. Sally ate another mint and wondered what he thought he was doing. He had a feeling though. Street was nearby.

The Guardsman looked back and stopped walking after about a hundred yards. "I wouldn't want to get any closer to the command post than this, even with my lights off," he said.

Sally looked at the edge of the road. "About right here." He lit up the spot with his penlight. A clear set of tire tracks led off the highway into the desert.

The Guardsman turned on his radio. "Captain, this is Fuller. I got something here I think you oughta see."

* * *

Gerald led Ted around the compound along a well-worn trail. Ted listened as the man told him how he didn't know how he had been sucked in by the zealot, about how much he loved Cynthia and he felt he had let her down, how he should have gone with her and how much he wanted her to take him back. Finally Ted stopped him, placed a hand on his shoulder, looked at his eyes and said softly, "It will all work out. Trust me."

Ted continued to follow. He used to think that dead was dead, but that notion had been proven wrong. He used to believe that the world was on its faithful spinning course and that was that, but now he knew, things were the way they were until, simply, they changed. Now, he was going to change something. In fact, he already had. First, death had changed his concept of life. Then, resurrection had changed him as a person, made him so much more than he ever had been in life. And now, living after death had altered him yet again; he had turned a corner in his mind, accepting his remarkable station, coming to understand his immortality, his place. There was a change in his eyes, the way he tilted his head when he observed things in the world, a change in the way he pointed, turned, walked. His voice had become softer, his words fewer and more carefully chosen.

Morning nudged against the darkness. Just beyond a metal shed was the bunker. Without a torch in front of it, the step down to the door was completely dark, black. Ted could hear the voices, the weak little voices, crying, questioning, praying even, but the prayers made no sense to him. He turned to Gerald. "Are there any disciples nearby?"

"They're all in the front. I'm the guard back here."

Ted walked quickly to the door and found it padlocked. "Do you know the combination?" he asked Gerald.

"We take the food to the children in pairs. Some of us know the first number, the rest of us know the last. We all know the middle number. I know the first two."

"Sounds complicated."

"Not really."

"What are the first two numbers?" Ted asked.

Gerald lit his flashlight to see the lock. "Six and six," he said, then worked them on the dial.

"Try six," Ted said.

Gerald supplied the final number and the lock opened. Gerald looked at Ted in disbelief.

"A lucky guess," Ted said. He pulled the heavy door wide and took the light from Gerald's hand, shined it into the cavern, swept it across the ceiling and the back wall.

The beam fell on the faces of three children. They were dirty, large-eyed, shivering. He moved the light to the other faces, saw them whimpering, crying. Their hair was matted, their lips chapped, cracked and bloody, their gazes both expectant and fearful. Some shrank away from the light, seeking the comfort of the darkness, others reached forward, squinting against the harshness, turning their faces away from the brightness, from Ted. The oldest among them might have been twelve, the youngest perhaps five.

"How many are there?" Ted asked.

"Twenty-seven," Gerald said.

"I thought there were more."

"Big Daddy lied."

"He lied?"

"He believes in Christ the Deceiver," Gerald said. Then, as if going into automatic pilot, he recited, " 'And the Lord said unto Moses, Make thee a fiery serpent, and set it upon a pole: and it shall come to pass, that every one that is bitten, when he looketh upon it, shall live. And Moses made a serpent of brass, and put it upon a pole, and it came to pass, that if a serpent had bitten any man, when he beheld the serpent of brass, he lived.' Numbers twenty-one: eight through nine."

"Are you okay?" Ted asked.

Gerald nodded, clearing his head by shaking it.

Ted shined the light around again. There was a stench of waste in the room and it felt wet and thick. He could imagine these faces on the bulletin boards of rest areas, on milk cartons, on the eleven-o'clock news. They had all come to look alike, desperate, misplaced, confused, faded, diminished. Several began to sob softly, then more loudly.

"I'm here to take you home," Ted said.

Even the oldest of the children couldn't speak.

"Come on." Ted reached a hand out to a girl, smiled gently to her, nodded. "I won't hurt you," he said quietly. "I'm going to take you to your mother."

The girl reached out. Ted felt her cold, soft, fragile skin and he thought of his own daughter, of how he had frightened her so badly and he wanted to cry, recalling how she had looked running from him across the backyard. He squeezed the child's hand and pulled her slightly, helping her find her legs and step toward him. He held her close, her face to his chest, and felt her melt, weeping, into his body and knew that he had done the right thing by coming back. The other children saw the girl find security in Ted's embrace and they moved to him, reaching for him, seeking his legs to hug, his hands, his skin, wanting to hear him make soothing adult sounds.

"It's okay," he said. "There, there. We're going home, my little ones. I'm taking you home."

CHAPTER THREE

THE SCENE OF THE children sniffing at the fresh, bracing air of the outside exhilarated Ted. He had to hold them back at the door to keep them from wandering into the dangerous, deadly light. He told Gerald to run across the final yards of the glow of the compound and wait in the darkness. Then he began to send the children running across the twenty yards in pairs, older with younger. The smallest ones were still crying, but not so loudly. They all, each and every one, hugged Ted as they passed, and with a gentle hand against their little backs he sent them to Gerald. He followed the last two, seeing the tiny eyes of the ones who had already crossed watching him. He heard the heavy shoes landing in the dust, heard the panting, whispers, then, halfway there, light fell on the young girl and boy in front of him. Ted turned to face the light as it found him.

Big Daddy's voice boomed, "The devil has returned! Behold the pernicious demon!" A covey of flashlight-wielding worshippers stood nervously at his heels.

"Run on," Ted said to the children caught in the middle with him, but they were paralyzed and they clung to him much like the sponges to the zealot.

More light appeared suddenly, this time from a helicopter over-
head. Ted looked up and was blinded. He shielded his eyes, but
could not see the machine in the sky. Dirt and dust swirled about
them and the light caught in the particles and made the world
jaundiced.

"I can't let you leave here with those children," the zealot shouted
through the din.

Ted said nothing in response.

Big Daddy began to scream into the sky, "Abraham begat Isaac;
and Isaac begat Jacob; and Jacob begat Judas and his brethren;

"And Judas begat Phares and Zara of Thamar; and Phares begat
Esrom; and Esrom begat Aram;

"And Aram begat Aminadab; and Aminadab begat Naasson;
and Naasson begat Salmon.

"And Salmon begat Booz of Rachab; and Booz begat Obed of
Ruth; and Obed begat Jesse;

"And Jesse begat David the king; and David the king begat
Solomon;

"And Solomon begat Roboam; and Roboam begat Abia; and
Abia begat Asa;

"And Asa begat Josaphat; and Josaphat begat Achaz; and Achaz
begat Ezekias;

"And Ezekias begat Manasses; and Manasses begat Amon; and
Amon begat Josias;

"And Josias begat Jechonias and his brethren;

"And Jechonias begat Salathiel; and Salathiel begat Zorobabel;

"And Zorobabel begat Abiud and Abiud begat Eliakum; and
Eliakum begat Azor;

"And Azor begat Sadoc; and Sadoc begat Achim; and Achim begat Eliud;

"And Eliud begat Eleazar; and Eleazer begat Matthan; and Matthan begat Jacob;

"And Jacob begat Joseph the husband of Mary, of who Jesus was born, who is called Christ!"

The disciples were in awe. Even Gerald leaned toward the man, saying softly, though Ted could hear him, "He recited all the begats. All of them."

"All the begats don't matter!" Ted shouted. "Joseph, and so Abraham and David, are only related to Jesus by marriage!" A devil's thing to say perhaps.

Ted saw the crazed look in Big Daddy's eyes, heard, amidst all the noise, the wet parting of the maniac's lips and then his eye as he slowly raised his rifle and tried to draw a bead on the smaller of the children standing beside him. Ted stepped in front of the children and accepted the three bullets into his chest. The reports of the rifle sent the helicopter twisting under its blades, coming down before rising quickly, making even more dust, its light dancing all over the ground, out into the dark desert and back to safety. The children screamed. Ted stood and faced Big Daddy. There was no blood pouring from him, no gaping wounds to speak of. As before, the evangelist began to quake, the weapon falling from his hands. Behind them, on the other side of the camp, the shots had caused mayhem. Scattered weapons fire split the air, soldiers shouted, disciples cried out for salvation.

Ted moved the children along and, with Gerald, got them into the darkness away from their captor. As he walked, he searched his chest with his fingers, finding one hole and pushing his finger into it. He pulled it out and smelled it, the putrid smell of death. When he reached for the hole again, it was gone. He touched the dirty hair of a little boy walking in front of him and felt a sadness, a cold stabbing deep in his middle that he could not explain.

* * *

A concussion, the doctor told her. A broken arm. Contusions. Hematomas. A possible detached retina. Three fractured ribs. But Perry was okay, they said. Gloria looked up at the dim ceiling from the cot and thought she was praying, also thought it was a little late, also thought it was a stupid thing to do. She heard the nurses' voices from outside and down the hall and wondered if they were talking about Perry.

Then there was a light tap at the ajar door. Gloria sat up to see Richard in the doorway.

"I didn't think you'd be asleep," he said.

"And you were right."

"I'm glad your son's all right."

Gloria nodded.

"I deposited Hannah and Emily at your house."

"I called Hannah," Gloria told him.

"Well, I just thought I'd come and check on you." He shuffled his feet. "I should let you get some rest."

"Okay."

As he turned away, she said, "Wait. Would you sit with me, please."

Richard sat on the chair beside the cot. Gloria lay back down and closed her eyes.

* * *

He could hear every whimper of every child, every settling of a foot in the loose sand of the wash, every echoing call into the air from the compound behind them. As they approached the bus, Ted could see that it was bathed in bright, ungiving light, just like everything else, washed in light, dirtied by light. He urged the children on, however, his voice steady, assuring and, he knew, soothing to them, calming. Gerald attempted to pause them, but Ted told him to walk on.

* * *

Sally saw the huddle of children in the darkness and had the soldier beside him shine his light on them. An officer said, "Well, I'll be damned." Then he and several men ran out to meet them. Sally saw Ted Street in the rear, carrying a fat boy wearing a striped shirt. Sally felt relieved as he considered Mrs. Street, but as he observed Ted Street's manner, the fixed eyes, the almost eerie quiet of him, he became afraid.

* * *

Ted was reassured to see the Guardsmen and the blue-jacketed ATF men ahead in the trail. He had worried that the crazy religious leader might follow and shoot at them and that he would be unable to catch all of the bullets. The soldiers came and took the children, leaving Ted to walk the remaining yards to the bus alone. A short man with a large mustache was clearly waiting for Ted.

"Mr. Street," the man greeted him.

Ted nodded.

"My name is Horatio Sally. I'm glad to find you. Your wife has been terribly concerned." He reached out to Ted.

Ted took his hand. "My wife is a kind woman," he said. "Are the children all okay?"

Sally looked around. "I believe they are. What about you?"

"Who knows?" Ted said. "Who knows."

* * *

While an excited Oswald Avery was attempting to regain entry into the base so that he could continue his research, he was shot and killed by a young soldier from Alliance, Nebraska. Mouthless Jesus 19 was still stashed away with Negatia Frashkart and her team of fervent believers. Dressed in white shirt and sweatpants as they all were, he was made to wash the clothes and handle the waste, septic and otherwise.

* * *

The all-too-familiar news crews came with cameras and yet more lights, turning the dim morning into the bright afternoon. Ted could not have been more lost in time. When had he died? When had he been a prisoner of the zealots? When had he last seen his family? His brain was so alive and his body was so dead, he knew it was dead, without pulse, without fluid. And deep inside him was the chilling stench of death. He had briefly experienced it and wondered why it did not seep out and tell everyone around him that the dead man was indeed dead.

The news people asked Ted how it felt to be a hero. He said he didn't know. They asked him how he knew about the children. He told them that how he knew about them was not important, what was important was that they were okay. They asked him if he knew yet whether he was dead or alive and he told them he did not. They called him a hero over and over, their voices shrill and grating. They called him a defender of children, a superstar, a champion of justice, a savior.

* * *

Sally was able to get Ted away from the vultures when the focus shifted to the children, as their stories and identities squirted free, their milk-carton faces finding names. The investigator got Ted into his Ford and drove him away.

"You're working for my wife?" Ted asked.

"I work for the insurance company."

"They should pay," Ted said.

Sally rolled his window halfway down and glanced at the sutures circling Ted's neck. "Why's that?"

"Because if anyone was ever dead, I am."

"So, I'm having a conversation with a dead man," Sally said.

Ted shook his head. "You're having a conversation with me and

I happen to be dead, out of life, without bodily function. I'm a ghost who still has his body. Is that so strange?"

Sally said nothing.

"I died, after a couple of days I woke up dead, and now I'm still dead, but that has nothing to do with my being here, with my talking to you, with my being able to touch your arm. What do you think about that?"

"I'm taking you home to your wife. Try to be alive for her. I think it will mean a lot to your family." They drove a few miles without speaking and Sally said, "Why'd you go back for those children?"

"I had to. They needed to be saved and I could save them."

Sally nodded.

"Are you afraid of me?" Ted asked.

"Should I be?" asked Sally.

"No, not at all." Ted watched the man's face, his eyes observing the road and glancing at his mirrors. "But you are. I wish you weren't, but you are."

* * *

When Gloria woke up at four in the morning and saw Richard asleep in the chair, she felt as if she had cheated. She felt unfaithful and that was just fine. Richard was kind and gentle and it was all just fine.

Perry was sleeping soundly and his signs were strong, the nurse said. Her tone was so relaxed that finally Gloria truly believed that Perry was going to be okay. Richard drove her home for a change of clothes.

"Hannah can drive me back," Gloria told him.

"If you're sure."

"I am," she said.

* * *

Gloria assured Emily that Perry was in good shape and went through the motions of preparing breakfast. The doorbell rang. She turned off the flame beneath the kettle and walked from the kitchen. She thought it might be Ted and she realized that her stride quickened, making her feel both excited and ashamed.

Emily followed her mother and stood by the stairs while she opened the door.

Gloria broke down when she saw Ted, falling to her knees. Emily ran to her mother and wrapped herself around her, cried just like her, burying her face as far into her mother as she could, muffling her own weeping with cotton and flesh.

Sally stood back.

Ted lowered himself and held them.

CHAPTER FOUR

THERE WAS SOMETHING IN the quality of their sobbing which was lost on Ted. He wanted to cry with them, but understood somehow that his homecoming was not the focus of their emotion. He looked to the stairs, to the living room, to the door of the kitchen.

"Where is Perry?" Ted asked.

Gloria and Emily cried harder.

"Where is Perry?"

Gloria paused, looked up at him, her eyes filled not only with grief and confusion, but with anger, with accusations, but also with pleading. Ted measured her face, her expression, and fathomed the unfathomable. He sank to his butt on the floor, but no tears came, no words came. He felt his skin growing cold the way his skin should have been all along, the way he was cold deep in his center.

Hannah came into the room and screamed when she saw Ted.

Ted looked at her. "Perry?"

"He's going to be okay," Hannah said.

Thoughts of Perry's reanimation flashed through Ted's mind, the pain of it, the sickness of it, and he was even sadder.

"Perry had an accident," Gloria said. But she didn't move closer to Ted. "He fell and he's hurt, but he's all right."

"He's—" Ted stopped. How could he ask what he was thinking? Did he die? Is Perry still alive?

"A concussion and a broken arm," Hannah said. "That's the worst of it."

Emily scooted farther away from her father. Not trembling, but on the verge of trembling.

* * *

Hannah took Emily out for a walk and so Ted sat with Gloria at the dining-room table in the dead-quiet house. They said nothing.

"I can't believe it," Gloria finally said.

"We should go see Perry," Ted said.

Gloria nodded.

Ted was feeling such loss, but he also felt, oddly, that the sadness was really Gloria's, that he was there to console her through his death, that somehow he was outside it all. Of course he was outside of it, he thought. He was dead to the world and so to the world of feeling. He touched Gloria's hand like a friend, with a strange detachment that fascinated but also sickened him. He understood now that the grief was not for himself, but for Perry, for nearly having lost him. He felt embarrassed that he was not feeling the same, but he was so removed from it, from them, from everything.

"Where were you?" Gloria asked. An accusation.

What could Ted say? Could he launch into his fantastic story of religious zealots, government scientists and having been sliced open and rearranged right then? How could he begin it all? *I was kidnapped by a man who held twenty-seven children hostage. In the middle of my journey I met twenty-seven Jesuses.* What could he say?

While they changed clothes in their bedroom, some television news stories called Ted a savior, but they capitalized it and so he was a *Savior* to the little children. On CNN, the parents of the fat boy in the striped shirt cried and said they had resigned themselves to the belief that they would never see their child again. They looked straight into the camera and thanked Theodore Street. "Thank you," the mother said, "thank you for saving my son. Bless you, you truly are an angel."

* * *

Ted tried to hug Gloria, but he felt her recoil, though only very slightly. He even experienced the icy coldness of his own being, the same coldness that Emily must have felt, that had caused her to run away. He was becoming more and more dead for Gloria.

"I'm so sorry," Gloria said.

"It's not your fault," Ted said. It was not perfunctory, his comment. "It's no one's fault."

"No one's fault," she repeated, as if searching for meaning in the words. "No one's fault." She leaned her head back and tried to stop her tears. "Why is this happening?"

"I don't know," Ted said.

"What *do* you know?" she snapped.

"I know *nothing*," Ted said.

"Well, that's just wonderful." Gloria wiped her eyes and stared at him. "What's happened?"

"I'm a screw-up," Ted said out of the blue. "I'm a freak and this thing, it simply, accidentally, for whatever reason, happened to me."

"I want to see Perry," Ted said. "Do you think he wants to see me?"

"I don't know."

* * *

According to the news, Theodore Street was a hero. His photograph was flashed again all over the world. DEAD MAN SAVES CHILDREN, headlines read. The parents of the found children, some of them missing for three and four years, called Mr. Street an angel. A group in New Mexico was fasting as a tribute to the saving angel.

Ted listened to the now meaningless words and watched the nonsensical images on television. The crews were again parked outside his house, but it felt less like a siege than before. He and Gloria walked out and to their car, the media giving Ted more room now. Perhaps because he was a hero. Perhaps it was fresh fear.

* * *

"You cannot be here," the nurse in charge of the desk on Perry's floor said.

Ted studied her frightened face and wondered if she knew just how right she was. "I have to see my son," he said.

"No." The woman shook her head. "They told me to tell you that you have to leave the hospital."

"I'm going to see my son."

"They said that you're not good for the patients, that you scare them."

"I haven't seen any patients," Ted said. "More important," he leaned in as if to confide in her, "they have not seen me."

"You're bad for morale," the nurse tried again.

"Then call security," Ted said and stepped past the woman.

Ted walked into Perry's room alone. Perry's throat was thankfully free of tubes, but he was obviously still weak. Ted thought he saw the consideration of a smile on the boy's face.

"Hey there, champ," Ted said, feeling stupid because he had never before called his son that. "Got banged up, eh?" He touched Perry's face and then the cast on his arm. "You gonna let me sign this thing?"

Perry said nothing, but he didn't look away.

"Okay, well, you get some more rest," Ted said. He left the room.

Ted and Gloria stood without speaking in the hallway outside Perry's room. Ted saw a man turn the corner, observe them, then walk back the way he'd come.

* * *

Security came and told Ted what the nurse had told him. The two men were shaking in their powder blue shirts. Ted looked at their eyes, at their patches, at their impressive belts weighted with hardware but no weapons.

"Don't be afraid of me," Ted said. "I'm leaving."

Ted stopped at the nurse's desk and looked at her. "Tell them not to fight it."

* * *

That night, after Gloria had put Emily to bed, Ted walked into the kitchen and said, "You should call your friend."

Gloria questioned him with a look.

"The man who was at the hospital. You should call him."

"What are you talking about?"

Ted cleared his throat.

"What are you saying?" Gloria was becoming mad, defensive. "What are you trying to say?"

"I'm not trying to say anything." He sat at the table and asked her to sit with him. She did. Ted reached over and touched her arm. "Gloria, I'm dead."

Gloria frowned.

"I know none of this makes sense."

Gloria pulled away, held her hands close to her chest, got up and left the room. Ted climbed the stairs minutes later, but did not enter their bedroom. He instead went into Emily's room and sat at the foot of her bed. He didn't want to wake her, to frighten her, but he needed to watch her sleeping. It was a fitful sleep, her face full of tension and small movements. Her pain saddened him. Outside and down their street, a small dog barked. A couple of guys in a news truck outside laughed. In his head, Ted could find no coherent thoughts, but knew he had something to think and say. He was fog.

* * *

Barbie Becker was again in the Street home, the living room alive with lengths and twists of cables, the buzz of lights, the cameras and the blank faces behind them. Barbie Becker had apparently had enough time either to forget about her first encounter with Ted or to realize the error of her earlier fear.

The red light told Ted that the world was watching him. Gloria and Emily watched from the stairs like strangers. Barbie Becker introduced him, much as she had before, and then he took the camera, took the world, looking at the lens, finding his own reflection in it, and talked to himself.

"I am dead. I died and I am dead and I can tell you no more about the meaning of life than I could when I was alive. But I know everything about the meaning of death. I saw no white light, attractive or otherwise. I felt no sweet feeling of relief or understanding or ease. I felt nothing. Happily, I can also report that I experienced no pain. However, now I am nothing but pain. To myself, my family and to you.

"I am no hero. I knew the children were there and so I did the decent thing, the right thing. I am no angel. There is no god for which I might serve as an emissary. I am no savior. I am no messiah. I am, *finally*, in this life, a decent man.

"I was dead, when my head was apart from me, I was dead. Death is not a bad thing and one ought to stay dead when death comes. If nothing else, I have learned this. I wish that I had no mouth, so that my silence would mean as much as my words. I wish that my words had no meaning. I wish that you could all feel my death, so that you would cease fearing it." Ted looked at his wife and daughter and offered a silent apology. He then reached to his neck, undid a knot of his sutures and began to remove them. He slowly pulled out each and every stitch. Gloria was standing now. Barbie Becker's fear had returned. The camera operators had stepped away from their machines. Ted grabbed his head between his two hands, removed it and set it in his lap, closed his eyes and stayed dead.